ANON PLS.

ANON PLS.

a novel

DEUXMOI.

WITH JESSICA GOODMAN

WILLIAM MORROW

An Imprint of HarperCollins*Publishers*

HarperCollins books may be purchased for educational, business, or sales
promotional use. For information, please email the Special Markets Department at
SPsales@harpercollins.com.

FIRST EDITION

DESIGNED BY BONNI LEON-BERMAN

Library of Congress Cataloging-in-Publication Data has been applied for.

ISBN 978-0-06-325780-1 (hardcover)
ISBN 978-0-06-328203-2 (international edition)

22 23 24 25 26   LSC   10 9 8 7 6 5 4 3 2 1

Guys, just a heads-up . . . While this book definitely draws inspo from events in my actual life, this story is obvi a work of fiction. Any mention of real people (celebs or normies), events, or establishments are intended only to give the book a sense of authenticity—and FUN. Everything else—characters, dialogue, incidents—I totally made up.

For the followers

CHAPTER 1

Today is the day my life must change. To everyone else on this cobblestone street in downtown Manhattan, it's just another Monday. But to me, it's the day I'm finally going to ask Sasha Sherman for a promotion.

I toss my paper coffee cup into the garbage on the corner and straighten my shoulders, commanding my post near the redbrick building where I've worked for the past eight years. I catch a glimpse of myself in the mirrored window: black Acne jeans, black Zara jacket, black Chanel boots snagged at a Nolita consignment shop. The uniform. At least that's what Sasha calls it. Wearing black keeps her employees invisible. And looking slim, which she reminds us of daily while also saying in the same breath that she's "so un-PC," not understanding that being "un-PC" isn't exactly a good thing.

But today Sasha's late, which can mean one of two things: Either she's having a lovely morning and stopped at Starbucks to pick up her specific English breakfast tea order or one of her kids was a little shit this morning and made her late, meaning the rest of us at her styling firm are about to pay the price.

I pull out my phone to see if she's already bombarded me with tasks. Nothing. No emails or voice notes or messages containing her usual long, disappointed diatribes. My phone is completely silent. No notifications from my boss—and no texts in the group chat. Probably because everyone else is doing *real* work, talking to *actual* clients, while I'm standing out here like an intern, waiting for Sasha fucking Sherman to show up in her big black SUV just because she likes to be greeted on Monday mornings like she's the Queen of England and not a former reality TV judge who became a fixture on morning shows by explaining how to pair flared jeans with a classic structured blazer.

I crane my neck to try to see farther down the street. No sign of her yet. I swipe over to Instagram and check my feed. Boring. Boring. Boring. But then someone—an oblivious tourist, probably—knocks into my shoulder and my thumb slides up to the upper-left-hand corner of the screen on my profile.

"Sorry," they call out, snapping photos of our block, which has become a stop on the SoHo must-see map for tourists, thanks to outdoor dining at Cipriani.

"All good," I say with a smile, straightening my jacket. When I look down at my phone, I see I've accidentally swiped over to my former account on Instagram. There's a pang in my chest when I catch a glimpse of the profile picture for deuxmoi, the old lifestyle account I created five years ago. That was back when I was naïve enough to think all I had to do to get a promotion was prove I could rack up two hundred thousand followers on Instagram, become an influencer, and be the kind of account that brands reach out to instead of vice versa. Sasha was always talking about how that number was the threshold. Build a brand out of nothing, and that will pique her interest.

But I lost steam after six months, when I topped out at thirty-five thousand. That was during a particularly rough period at this job. Back when Sasha was going through her divorce. She got crueler than she'd ever been, more demanding and critical, forcing all the assistants to work until midnight without overtime, throwing food containers and water bottles at her underlings daily, and screaming that I was an "incompetent half-wit who probably needed to get fucked a few hundred times before I ever felt joy again." She said *that* after I didn't laugh at one of her extremely inappropriate jokes about 9/11.

But it was also like she could tell that I was putting some of my creative energy elsewhere and she was interested in depleting it. She started giving me more work. *Garbage* work. *Pick up my tea* work. *Walk my dog* work. *Sit with me at my dentist appointment and read me my emails out loud while I have a cavity filled* work. I quit the anonymous account before I could even add my face to it, before anyone knew I was behind it. Now I'm glad I kept it anonymous. Less embarrassing when I threw in the towel.

Looking at it now, seeing all those posts, I feel a little rush of pride. It was good. *I* was good. Maybe if I ever got my shit together to actually apply for other styling jobs, I could use it as a portfolio. Maybe.

But I don't have time to think about that now. I swipe back over to my personal account and try to forget I ever started that other one. I sigh and tap my foot against the concrete. It's almost 11:00 a.m. now, and out-of-towners are streaming past, sticking out with their streaky highlights and ill-fitting T-shirts. As they walk by our office, with the massive gold *Styling by Sasha* logo emblazoned on the glass door, they swivel their heads, as if they can't believe they're seeing where *the* Sasha Sherman works.

Ever since Sasha appeared as a judge on *Collection*, the Emmy-winning design show from the early 2010s, it's been like this. People fell in love with her tell-it-like-it-is attitude and signature haircut, a pin-straight, shoulder-length asymmetrical bob. If only they saw how she treats me, her assistant. If only they knew that she refuses to get corporate credit cards for any of her employees so we always have to put massive charges on our personal cards and rack up interest until she finally decides we deserve to be reimbursed. Or that she once told me to hold her hair back while she stuck her fingers down her throat and made herself puke up a chicken Caesar salad wrap that had "a fucking obscene number of croutons" in it, as she told me mid-barf.

But that's changing today. It has to. I mean, I'm the only one from my assistant class still dashing out for coffee runs and getting screamed at in the hallways. All I have to do is present my case to Sasha—remind her of all the clients I've assisted her with over the years, all the hours I put in ordering lunches, coordinating with publicists, booking her hotel rooms . . .

Two middle-aged-mom types take a step closer to the door to snap a photo. I do my best busy-fashion-employee impression, keeping my eyes glued to my screen. But suddenly a black car pulls up and I'm greeted with that familiar sense of dread, the one that alerts me I have no idea what's coming, what kind of mood Sasha might be in or what she might want. Every day with her is an adventure. And not the good kind.

Edward, her longtime driver, steps out of the car and makes eye contact with me. He winks, giving me the indication that she might actually be happy. I spy a Starbucks cup in her hand from inside the window and feel a slight wave of relief.

Edward runs around the front of the car and opens the door for her, getting out of the way as Sasha steps out onto the street. She's wearing Prada straight-leg pants, a crisp white silk blouse from the Row's most recent collection, and a jacket hanging off her bony shoulders. Her platinum-blond bob is pulled back as always, behind the ears and sleek, and she's wearing her signature earrings—a long gold Vasiliki piece in the right ear and a two-carat-diamond stud in her left. It's this jewelry combo that made her stand out at the judges' table on *Collection* all those years ago. I used to watch that stupid-ass show and think, I wish I knew her. Now I wish I didn't.

"Here." Sasha thrusts her orange Birkin bag full of notes and fabric samples toward my chest, and it's all I can do not to drop the thing. It must weigh fifty pounds.

"Keep up," she says as she clip-clops past me in her Altuzarra strappy sandals. I rush to follow her through the lobby and into the elevator in the back. When I first started, she didn't let me come in with her. Said it was so she didn't have to hear me breathe. Bitch made me take the stairs.

Now I've earned a spot on her morning ride. Sure, I'm supposed to stand *behind* her, with my back pressed up against the wall, but hey, at least I'm not huffing and puffing up four flights in the drafty stairwell.

When the elevator opens on our floor, she walks to her office fast and I watch everyone in the room change their demeanors. Voices lower. Eyes dart across the room.

My best friend, Leon, who started with me on the very same day and was promoted to stylist three years and four months ago—not that I'm counting—raises his eyebrows. *Ask her yet?* he mouths.

I shake my head no and ignore Leon's judgmental face. *Later,* I mouth back.

He's wearing a boxy Comme des Garçons button-up that shifts when he shrugs his shoulders all the way to his ears. Leon spins on a platform heel, and his black Rick Owens slacks swish as he walks to the kitchenette.

Sasha arrives at her office and motions for me to follow her inside, like I always do. I take her coat and hang it up on the Lucite rack before starting to arrange the papers on her desk how she likes them, with the day's agenda on top. She takes a seat behind her desk and swivels around, looking out over SoHo, before exhaling deeply and loudly, an annoying tic I can never get used to.

Now's the time. It's perfect, just before the morning rush.

I clear my throat and take a chance.

"I was hoping you'd have a few seconds to chat before the meeting."

Sasha turns around, a somewhat amused look on her face that suggests I should go on. I take a deep breath and feel the words I practiced in the mirror bubble up in my throat, rest right on the tip of my tongue.

"I've been here for eight years now," I say, trying my hardest not to let my voice warble. "And I've done some excellent work for you—I assisted on Hannah Bronfman's wedding, forged excellent relationships with some of the smaller-scale designers, and have maintained an impeccable schedule for you. I've gone above and beyond my job description, and I've loved every single second of it."

I pause, hoping she can't tell I'm lying through my teeth about that one. I stand up straighter, lifting my chin. Confidence.

"I'm here to ask you for a promotion. I want to be one of your featured stylists. I'm ready for the challenge and the responsibility, and I hope you agree."

It's quiet now, the silence stretching between us. I try to read Sasha's face, but she's not giving me much. A smile, sort of. But not a happy one. Maybe she's . . . amused? For a split second, I think she's going to laugh, which wouldn't be the *worst*-case scenario, but definitely not the best.

Sasha nods slowly and takes a sip of her tea before making a terribly irritating lip-smacking sound. I try not to flinch. She spins around in her chair so she's facing the window, away from me. Bitch.

Then, still turned away from me, she speaks. "I'll consider it."

My heart leaps into my throat. "Really?"

"Don't act so *eager*." She spins around and rolls her eyes. "You've been my assistant for so long, I thought you actually *liked* this job. I thought you liked having me depend on you. Ha!"

I clench my fists by my side and try to stay calm. What kind of sadomasochist would actually fucking *like* that?

"You're not ready to style your own clients." Sasha looks at the Louis Vuitton planner open on her desk. "But . . ." she says, glancing back up at me. "We have that meeting with Ernesto this afternoon. Why don't you join?"

I try to hide my shock. I haven't been asked to join a label meeting since I got here. Certainly not one with Ernesto, one of the boldest, most storied brands in designer ready-to-wear. I've always been on the outside, waiting to get Sasha another drink or making up an excuse to help her escape boring style outs. Every time the reps from Ernesto come through the doors, Sasha shoos me away, as if I'm an ugly stepsister she needs to hide in the basement. But not today.

"Well?"

"Yes, of course," I say, nearly breathless.

"Come with some ideas," she says. "Good ones. For how we can pair their new collection with Madison Lee."

I nod and try to recall everything I know about Madison Lee, the massive TikTok pop star who just signed a mega-contract with Sasha, making her the eighteen-year-old's exclusive stylist through at least the summer.

Sasha taps her foot against her desk, making a knocking sound that irks my brain. "She's younger than their demo, but their new line is all about attracting the youth. Street style. Vibes. Or something like that. It was hard to tell at their pre-fall show." She waves her hand and sighs, as if it's all so boring. "Her reps told me she's trying to elevate her look." Sasha looks at me hard. "Prove yourself there and then we'll talk."

"I won't let you down," I say, though the words sound supremely idiotic as soon as they leave my mouth. Thankfully, Sasha, already turned back to her computer, isn't even listening. I hustle out of her office, shutting the glass door behind me, and dash over to my cubicle, where Leon is waiting.

"Well?" he asks, his eyes nearly bugging out of his head.

"I have to nail the Ernesto meeting." I fumble around for a pen and pad, my mind already spinning with ways to impress them. "Then she said . . . maybe."

"Maybe?" Leon asks, his eyes wide and shining. "Maybe is good. Maybe is *great*, even."

"How long did it take Alyssa's maybe to go to a yes?" I ask him, though I don't really want to know the answer. Alyssa Wilson's got a reputation for being a total sweetie, gifting her assistants with leftover handbags and shoes and telling them to take two weeks off around the holidays. She got her start in magazines, working her way up to become the first Black fashion director of a now-defunct Condé Nast shopping publication before Sasha poached her a decade ago. Since then, she's been beloved as an industry darling.

Leon's been on her team from the beginning, and she basically forced Sasha to give him the promotion. I'm pretty sure he goes to Pilates classes with her on Wednesday mornings, which kind of makes me want to gouge out both of their eyes.

But it's hard to have any bad feelings toward Leon, especially after we've been through so much together at this shithole. He's the one who gave me a pep talk over the weekend, telling me it was *finally* time to ask for the promotion—and he's also the one who convinced me to stay out at DUMBO House until 4:00 a.m. on Saturday, making him the absolute perfect friend.

Leon takes pity on me and doesn't answer. He squeezes my hand. "Who cares about me? Focus on your shit, because you're gonna kill it." But then Alyssa motions for him to head over to the freight elevator and Leon stands, pointing a manicured finger, painted in chrome silver, at me. "Kill it."

I repeat his words over in my head like a mantra until I convince myself that he's right.

CHAPTER 2

When I get to the conference room, I can already feel the warmth spreading under my armpits and I say a silent thank-you to 7:00 a.m. me for packing my sheer Veronica Beard Swiss-dot tulle blouse instead of the silk one, which would have already dampened under my arms, to barre class. Changing into it in the locker room, I knew it was a lucky top, one that screamed confidence and ease without being too try-hard.

Nothing can stop me today.

I stand at attention near the door and smile wide as the receptionist clip-clops down the hall, guiding Ernesto's CEO, Bill Baillon, and a few of their publicists to the room. "Welcome to Styling by Sasha," I say warmly. "Can I get you anything? Coffee? Tea? Espresso?"

But I know better. The Ernesto team members never want anything. They're known for popping in and out, eager to keep their meetings under thirty minutes. Sasha always says it's a miracle if they give us access to even a few pieces from their collection.

Bill and his cronies demure, like I knew they would, and then I step aside, sweeping out my arm so they can take their seats at the conference table.

Sasha waltzes in, her leather belted Jason Wu coat draped over her shoulders, and double-kisses Bill on both cheeks. She shakes hands with the reps while I keep a stupid smile plastered on my face, my spine rigid as a rod. Don't fuck this up.

"Let's get to it, shall we?" Sasha says. "Your time is precious, after all." She pats Bill's hand and his weathered, tan face contorts into a smile. Her charm factor is at a ten today, all *How're the kids?* and *Isn't Blackberry Farm lovely this time of year?* No wink at me to say thank you for the fact that I reminded her that Bill's kids' names are Joey and Jemma or that I was the one who told her Penny, the senior publicist, is renovating her place in Aspen. Sasha would fall flat on her face if I wasn't here, and we both know that.

But I try to remember that's not important today. Not now. Not when there's so much at stake.

For the first half of the meeting, I sit at the edge of the table and take notes, jotting down tidbits of conversation—pieces Sasha wants for our top clients, gowns that are already reserved for specific stars with other stylists, where Sasha can find recaps of their shows on our server—until finally, Bill tees up the conversation I've been waiting for.

"Who else do you have that we should be paying attention to?" he asks, playing with a button on his jacket. His dark hair is thick and full, styled into a slick coif that barely moves.

Sasha looks at me, her arms crossed over her chest, challenging me to speak. I seize it.

"Madison Lee," I say with my most confident voice. "She's just topped thirty million on Instagram and has a sponsorship with Glossier, the beauty—"

"I know what Glossier is," Bill says, not unkindly. He's looking at me with a mixture of confusion and surprise, like he didn't quite know that the mouse in the corner actually had a voice.

"Of course." I smile at him with the same smile I give to my well-meaning mom when she suggests I try to "work with Rihanna." I continue, looking intently at Bill. "She has a feature on Nicki Minaj's next album, and she's rumored to be starring in the new Hulu rom-com. She's about to blow up. Huge."

I pause. He's interested, leaning toward me, spinning his gold ballpoint pen in his hand. Hold off and he'll make the first move.

"You can get her?" he asks. "For us?"

I nod. "She's been wanting to level up, get into the luxury space with a storied brand that has your kind of reputation. Your legacy. She's going to be a major player in fashion. And luckily, she's Sasha's new client. You could be the first luxury designer she works with. She could introduce you to her demo. Fresh. Young."

Bill doesn't need to know that Madison Lee's originally from a small town in Canada but won over the whole TikTok scene after she got in early with her cheerleading-esque dance moves that she then parlayed into a not-totally-terrible singing career. Her whole family moved to L.A. right after she blew up, but since she relocated to New York, she's gained fifteen million followers as well as a rumored addiction to Adderall. Not to mention the fact that her dad's been known to hit up the Meatpacking club scene with illicit party favors and no wife in tow.

Bill's practically salivating, and he's leaning over the table like he's ready to leap across it, his arms outstretched, his cheeks rosy. Then, as if realizing what he's doing, he leans back, ducking his head toward Penny, whispering in her ear. She nods, jotting down a few notes on the pad in front of her.

"We're in." He drums his fingers on the table and snaps them together. "Send her the cerulean matching set. The jacquard one. And the pleated silk dress. Tell her to pair it with our chunky silver platforms. You have her sizes?"

"Yes," I say, excited.

He turns to Penny. "Messenger the clothes here now," he says before looking back at me. "Overnight them and ask her to post this week."

Penny jumps in. "We're launching the legacy collection, so it's the perfect time to introduce new blood, even in an unofficial capacity. Who knows, maybe there's collaboration potential?" She smiles, her eyes hopeful. "I'll work with—" She nods to me.

"Cricket," I say. "Cricket Lopez."

Penny's eyes crinkle as she smiles. "I'll work with Cricket on the details."

I glance at Sasha, trying to parse her expression, but all she does is press her lips together in a firm line.

"Well." Sasha stands, a signal the meeting is over, and snaps her notebook shut. "Very productive, I'd say." Bill gets up, too, and Sasha leans over, air-kissing both his cheeks before she ushers him toward the door.

They head out into the hallway, and I finally feel my stomach settle, the excitement of what just happened washing over me. I did it.

I half expect Sasha to turn around and pat me on the shoulder. To rush back and whisper something like *good job* in my ear, but I should know better. She's not Alyssa. She doesn't dole out compliments. Instead, she ushers the Ernesto team out the door, saying goodbye without even looking my way.

I make it back to my desk, clenching my fists with excitement, and slide into my seat before calling down to the mail room to ask for garment boxes.

"Rock star shit, huh?" Leon appears over my cubicle and shakes a small plastic bottle full of freshly squeezed orange juice from the deli downstairs.

"Aw, my favorite," I say, taking it from his outstretched hand.

"Glad this is a congratulations juice instead of a consolation one."

"Word travels fast, huh?" I can feel my cheeks blushing, but pride swells in my stomach. For once, people might see me as something other than Sasha's shit-eating assistant. Maybe, just maybe, they might see me as a player in this office, someone capable of having clients and relationships of her own.

"Oh yeah," Leon says, biting into a gluten-free, grain-free, dairy-free piece of banana bread. Leon grew up in Manhattan and went to LaGuardia for high school, where every student who gets in has to have an incredible artistic talent. His was fine art, and he's now an exceptional graphic designer. He puts those skills to good use as Sasha's go-to deck designer at work—though she never pays him extra. Since half of his classmates actually went on to become legit famous, à la Timothée Chalamet, he's never been one to hold celebs on a pedestal. Says it's too weird since he saw them as acne-prone teenagers trying like crazy to get fake IDs so they could hit up hookah bars on St. Mark's Place.

Leon's second-generation Chinese American, and back when he was in his party monster phase, he was known for throwing the most bonkers New Year's celebrations, which always ended with naked dancing on his roof even though it would be the middle of winter. But now that he's got a boyfriend, Giuseppe; sticks to a no-illicit-substances policy on nights out; adopted a mutt named Kylie; and has a pretty demanding role here at Styling by Sasha, he's calmed down. For the most part.

Leon swallows the last bite of his pastry and tosses the piece of parchment into the trash can under my desk. "Everyone's talking about it. Alyssa said, and I quote, *'That got Sasha's attention.'*"

"Shut the fuck up, babe."

"I will not. It's *true.*" Alyssa waves toward us, and Leon mouths something to her across the room before laughing. Then he turns back to me. "We're on for drinks Friday with Victoria, yeah?"

"Definitely," I say, making a mental note to confirm with my childhood best friend, who made the move to the Upper East Side when she married her insanely hot financier husband, Jake, and gave birth to their sweet albeit way-too-precocious sons, five-year-old Dax and three-year-old Chase.

Leon blows me a kiss and disappears while I dash off an email to

Madison Lee's manager, confirming the plan, before writing the pop star's Los Angeles address carefully on a delivery slip. I hang it on the metal clothing rack, ready for the outfits to arrive later today. Back in my inbox, Madison Lee's manager responds with a one-line note:

From: management@mmay.com

To: clopez@stylingbysasha.com

Date: May 10, 2022, 4 pm ET

Subject: Re: Madison Lee x Ernesto

FUCK YES!!!!! SHE'S IN FOR IT ALL BABY!

I lean back in my desk chair, rocking back and forth, relieved. If all goes well, Madison Lee will get the looks tomorrow, and according to this little email, she'll post photos of them by the end of the week. And I, god willing, will be on a sweet, sweet ride out of assistant hell.

My phone buzzes, and I slip it out of my pocket, checking the screen. The words "Fuckboy Orthodontist" pop up, and even though I hesitate to give Doug the time of day after he booty-called me at 2:00 a.m. last Thursday, I swipe to see what he's said.

It's just a tongue-wagging emoji and little spurts of water. I should be disgusted, but after the on-again, off-again bullshit he's put me through, it's nothing out of the ordinary. I consider deleting the message or telling him to fuck off. But then I remember that little tongue thing he does when he's on his knees in front of me and . . . well, a little celebratory hang sesh couldn't hurt.

My place at 10.

It's a good fucking day.

CHAPTER 3

Leon perches on the corner of my desk and plunks down a cup from the fancy coffee shop we like but is two blocks too far for us to go to on a regular basis. "Bone-dry cappuccino with four pumps of sugar-free vanilla. Just the way you like it, freak."

"My hero." I take a sip and press my hand to my heart.

Leon furrows his brow before leaning over my cubicle, resting his chin on his hands. "Any word from Madison Lee's team?"

I clear my throat and shuffle some papers on my desk. "Not yet."

"It's only been a few days. Celebs are like this, babe, you know that." He gives my shoulder a soft squeeze.

Leon's always been the best at pep talks, even when we were assistants. One afternoon, only a few weeks after he started here, Leon found me freaking out in the back stairwell, mustard splattered across the brand-new Theory blouse I had found in the discount section of Nordstrom Rack. When I told him Sasha went ballistic because I gave her a ten-minute break in between meetings instead of a twenty-minute one and tossed a bunch of open condiment packets at me in the kitchenette, he didn't tell me to laugh it off or suck it up. Instead, he hugged me, careful to avoid getting mustard on his own chic outfit, and told me Sasha was a fucked-up asshole and that it was okay to feel devastated.

"She's a bully," he said. "And the best way to fuck with bullies is to not let them see you hurt. So, cry all you want in here, just don't let her see you as anything less than perfect out there."

Leon didn't say it then, but over the years of our friendship, I learned it was the same tactic he used to deal with all the hypercompetitive artists in high school and later NYU, where he went to study graphic design. Over martinis, he once told me that so many of his peers would sabotage one another by hogging all the lab space before they were due to present their portfolios. He found that whole world revolting, so he ditched his dream of being a creative director at an ad agency and started pursuing fashion his junior year. Unfortunately, he found that this industry's just as cutthroat. But often with more perks.

Sitting at my desk, Leon smiles down at me with optimism. But we both know that if Madison Lee doesn't post the photos by the deadline Bill and his team demanded—and even though her manager promised me via text, email, *and* voice memo that she definitely, 100 percent would—the odds that she'll post anything at all are not in our favor.

I squint down at my phone, which is open to Madison Lee's Instagram feed. "Maybe Gia Denim had an exclusive on her for twenty-four hours or something," I say, though I know they don't have the kind of money for that. "She posted about their high-waisted skinnies yesterday."

"Totally," Leon says, not convincingly. He glances toward Sasha's office, where my boss is currently pacing back and forth, screaming at someone over the phone through her AirPods. "It's only Friday. Maybe she'll do it over the weekend or something. Big engagement on Sunday mornings, blah blah blah."

We're both quiet for a beat.

"Has *she* said anything?" Leon asks in a lower tone, while his eyes stay on Sasha.

As if on cue, Sasha bursts out of her office. "Did she do it yet?" she barks.

"Not yet!" I'm using my most hopeful voice, but Sasha just grunts.

"Bill called again," she says, loud enough for every employee in our vicinity to hear. "This better happen by the end of the day, because I am *not* running interference on your mistake during *my* weekend."

Her door slams, and I try not to jump.

"Kill me now," I mumble, and Leon throws me a sympathetic look before standing to go back to the comforting cocoon of Alyssa's office.

"At least we have drinks later," he says.

I down half my coffee and turn back to my phone, refreshing Madison Lee's feed, as if that might will the post into existence. That's the trouble with this noncontractual, relaxed, not-so-sponsored content. All you have is the celeb's team's insistence that *of course* they'll share pics of gifted clothes. But when they don't . . . the brands get mad. And *we* get stuck in the middle. I've seen it happen before with less important clients—D-list reality stars and mommy bloggers.

Once, everyone blew their fucking lids when they found out that a former *Bachelor* star resold a bunch of comped clothes on an online luxury consignment shop the literal day after receiving them. Would it hurt to wait one season before trying to cash in on freebies?

All of a sudden, my stomach sinks. Could Madison Lee have done something like that? There's no way. She's not *that* desperate. She just got that Nicki Minaj collab. But that would explain why her assistant has been ghosting me since Wednesday and why her publicist stopped insisting the post was only minutes away from going up this morning.

I might as well *check* that consignment site the *Bachelor* star used just to put my mind at ease. No harm in looking, right?

I pull up the site with shaking fingers and hold my breath as I type *Ernesto* into the search bar. It takes a few seconds, thanks to the shitty internet Sasha refuses to spend money to upgrade, even though she takes a black car to and from work every day *and* expenses every single aspect of her life.

But when the page finally loads, my heart drops. The most recently acquired items are listed first, and right there in the top five spots are all the items we sent Madison Lee, in her exact sizes, proclaiming that they're new. With tags!

I clench my fists and feel my cheeks flush. What the fuck do I do? Sasha is going to kill me.

I grab my phone and dial Madison Lee's assistant with shaking fingers. No answer. Obviously. As I listen to this woman's voicemail, suggesting I leave a message, I try to decide what to do. Ream her out and leave evidence? Text her and tell her to call ASAP?

There's no time to decide because the beep goes off and I go with my gut.

"Heeeey, it's Cricket over at Styling by Sasha. Just wanted to check in because I saw something a little surprising online—can you give me a call back?"

My voice sounds a little bit desperate, but I hang up thinking I did the right thing. Definitely. Obviously. This is just a simple misunderstanding. It will all work itself out. I'm a fool for even thinking—

"What the fuck is this?"

Everything in my body freezes, and I'm scared to even let out a breath. I know that voice, that tone. It's the one Sasha uses when she chucks her wrong lunch order at my face, when she tells me I look too tan, too pale. Or that I should get a manicure or my brows done. Or that I'm a *fucking* idiot loser who has no business being in fashion.

I try to compose myself, making sure my face is still and unreadable, before I force myself to spin around in my chair. Sasha is staring at my computer, hands on hips, scowling so hard her brows form a deep V above her eyes despite all the Botox in her forehead.

"Um . . ." I start.

"Are those the clothes Ernesto sent Madison Lee? On a goddamn consignment site?" Her voice is loud, so loud that it seems like everyone else in the office has turned to listen to Sasha Sherman berate her assistant. Again. I want to melt into the floor.

"I—"

"Don't you fucking speak," she yells, lunging toward me. For a second, I think she's going to slap me, but Sasha learned to stop doing that after her first assistant threatened a lawsuit. Heard about that one *after* I accepted my offer. Instead, she pushes me to the side so I roll away in my chair and leans over my computer, scrolling and clicking on every single piece we sent Madison Lee. "That ungrateful little bitch."

I let out a sigh of relief. She knows who the bad guy is here, and it's not me. At least she can recognize that.

"I know, right?" I say, smoothing my hair down as I roll back toward her in my chair. "It's so unprofessional."

But then Sasha turns her head so slow it scares me. Her eyes are full of fire, and she opens her mouth, ready to spit venom.

I spoke too soon.

"Unprofessional?" she yells. "You know what's unprofessional? Having this happen at all. You should have gotten this deal in writing. A contract. With a lawyer. None of this handshake bullshit you and your dumbass generation are so fond of. What, you thought she was just going to give away free press? Idiot. You're a goddamn idiot."

I blink twice, forcing myself not to cry. Do not cry.

"Aren't you going to say something?" she snarls. "This is my fucking reputation on the line. Bill is going to throw a fit."

"I—"

"You what?" Sasha is standing now, her arms crossed over her chest, making the same disgusted face she made when I booked her a middle-of-the-room table at Pastis instead of a back corner booth, or the time I couldn't get her in first class for a flight to Los Angeles during my second week on the job. Now, she's looking at me like she wants to rip off her Alaïa stiletto and jam it right into my carotid.

I have to say something. I have to stand up for myself. Give a reason. Especially if I want her to still entertain the idea of giving me the promotion that I know I deserve. I rise to my feet, preparing for battle.

But instead, I say the worst thing possible.

"This isn't my fault."

Sasha throws back her head and laughs, an uproarious one that makes the three people who weren't watching crane their necks to see what's happening.

"Oh, fuck off," she says, waving her hand at me. "You think you're becoming a stylist now?"

My face reddens, and I try not to catch Leon's eye even though he's standing right behind Sasha, secondhand embarrassment written all over his face.

"You just set yourself back *years*," she says. "Years."

Sasha turns on her heel and storms off, back into her office. The rest of the room is quiet and frozen, until finally I sink down into my seat, dropping my head in my hands. Rage thumps all over my body, and I just want to break something, to scream. At Madison Lee and Sasha, sure, but also at myself, for having no idea how to clean up this horrible mess.

CHAPTER 4

"She said *what*?" Victoria looks at me in horror, her perfectly symmetrical features all out of whack when Leon recounts what exactly happened to make me need three vodka sodas with splashes of pineapple before even ordering appetizers.

We're at The Standard Grill, where we've spent *many* raucous evenings, though in our early twenties we'd put all the drinks on Victoria's tab, since she worked at a massive PR firm and could technically expense our orders and claim they were business meetings. Now that she's traded her corporate card for one her husband pays for, she just charges *him* and never lets us pay. It gets harder and harder to pretend to try, but Leon still puts up a valiant effort.

I take a sip from my tumbler. "You heard him," I say, resigned to the fact that I may have just had the worst day of my professional life. But at least I can close it out in this cozy leather booth with the people I love most.

Victoria covers my hand with hers, and her eternity wedding band sparkles, each quarter-carat emerald-cut diamond winking back at me like a secret. She's been my best friend since middle school, when we were paired together in a social studies class to do a project about the Berlin Wall. We've been through hell and back together—like when her parents got divorced, making her split her time between Bedford and where we grew up in the suburbs of Philadelphia, or like when I walked in on my college boyfriend fucking my freshman-year roommate and Victoria maxed out her emergencies-only credit card so I could take a last-minute train ride to visit her at Georgetown, where I had a dance floor make-out with a random dude at her sorority mixer.

Weirdly, that was also the night when she met Jake, who became her college sweetheart. They married two years to the day after graduation and had the most beautiful wedding at the Pierre. I was a bridesmaid, of course, and got to wear a Vera Wang dress she picked out for me specifically so I didn't have to match the rest of the wedding party.

She's heard the worst of Sasha over the years and has always been supportive, even when Sasha made me late to Victoria's bachelorette party in East Hampton because she wouldn't let me leave the office before 9:00 p.m. since she—and I quote—"needed a warm body in the empty office in case Angelina Jolie called." The phone never rang.

Our lives couldn't be more different now, especially since Jake landed the high-level partner gig at some tech security firm whose name I can never remember and they bought a place on the Upper East Side. Her sons are now firmly planted in the Manhattan private-school-to-Ivy-League pipeline, but she's always made time for me, even though my problems probably seem paltry to hers. Plus, she most often offers to come downtown, since she knows we despise the wine bars she and her mommy friends go to after playdates.

"She's such a see-you-next-Tuesday," Victoria says, motioning to the waitress that we need a round of shots. Aaaaand that's why I love her.

"Sasha or Madison Lee?" Leon asks as a cone of French fries and a silver cup full of plump jumbo shrimp cocktail are set down in front of us.

Victoria throws up her hands, and the sleeves of her Alexander McQueen puff-shoulder top barely miss the cocktail sauce. "Both!" She swipes a French fry through a puddle of ketchup and wags it around. "Entitled a-holes. I mean, we expect this from Sasha. After all you've been through, babe." She pets my head like I'm a stray puppy. "But tweenager celebs who think they can do whatever they want?" Victoria bites her fry with rage in her eyes. "I can't stand that shit. I see it all the time at SoulCycle."

Leon nudges me under the table and raises one eyebrow. Victoria's always trying to pretend like we live on the same planet. But since she left her job at the PR firm, she barely remembers what it's like to deal with people who snub you on a daily basis.

We must do a terrible job of hiding our amusement, because Victoria shakes her head and leans in for emphasis. "Seriously!" she says. "I see that woman who got cut from last season of *Real Housewives* there all the time being a D to people who work at the front desk."

"You can say *dick*, you know," I say, twirling my straw around in my drink. Victoria thinks swearing is as tacky as bandage dresses, even though they're kind of back in style.

Victoria ignores me and keeps going. "She's always asking for free leggings if she posts about her workouts. It's so desperate. Like, honey, you can obviously afford those."

"People are the worst," I say.

Leon rolls his eyes. "I've been telling you guys for *years*. All those kids I went to school with who are now famous? Their fans would die if they knew what they were like when no one was watching. Like, who resells clothes, who demands free crap, who tips well." Leon keeps talking as the waitress sets down a few shot glasses in front of us. "The extremely small pieces of gossip are what people actually care about because *that's* what no one's discussing."

I've never had a real inside look at celebrity culture like Leon, who was getting into red-carpet parties when he was seventeen, or an encyclopedic knowledge of stars like Victoria, whose husband gets them invites to the *Vanity Fair* Oscar party through an old college buddy. Every. Year. But I *have* always been intrigued by the way people treat celebrities like they're untouchable. Beyond human. Working for

Sasha, I've realized they're just people, flesh and blood and bags of bones like the rest of us.

Leon's on a roll, though. "Take Cam Dunne, for example. She's one of Alyssa's clients, and she's a total sweetheart. Sent me a gift card for five hundred bucks on my birthday even though I've only worked with her for six months. So sweet."

"Duke Dudley does the same thing, you know," I say. "He's one of the biggest stars on the planet and always remembers my name when he comes in for meetings. Last time, he brought me some fancy chocolate truffles from Paris because I once told him I liked them."

Leon throws his head back and slams his hand on the table. "Duke Dudley! What a gem!"

"Not to mention Sasha's biggest client," I point out.

"Ooh, you know Teddy Treadwell? That late-night talk show host?" Victoria asks.

Leon raises an eyebrow. "Isn't *Page Six* always talking about him going on benders and blacking out?"

Victoria seems to ignore him as she continues. "Well, his kids go to school with the boys and he's a gem at pick-up," she says, popping an olive from her martini in her mouth. "He even baked peanut butter blossoms for his son's birthday. Like *he* did. Not his nanny."

Leon snorts. "How the hell do you know that?"

Victoria winks. "I have my ways." But then she leans in. "Dax said he bakes whenever they're over there for playdates. Like warm brownies and muffins. That kind of thing. I can barely make oatmeal."

I slump back against the booth. "I wish more people knew how Sasha Sherman treats her staff. The golden girl of reality fashion competitions calls her assistants 'talentless fatties' while denying them raises for years? Good look. Real good."

I drop my head in my hand, deflated and powerless, and down my drink.

Leon wraps an arm around my shoulder and pulls me to him. "Our poor Cricket. A caterpillar just tryna be a butterfly."

I pout and lean into the crook of his arm. "At least I have you guys."

Leon motions for the waitress to bring yet another round of drinks and when she does, we hold them up, clinking them together.

"To . . ." I start.

"Dismantling elitist celebrity star-fucker culture?" Leon tries.

"Teddy Treadwell's delicious brownies?" Victoria offers.

I shake my head. "New beginnings," I say. "You *know* I need one."

We throw our drinks back and clink the glasses together above the table. Victoria checks her phone and smiles, her lips curving up devilishly. "Jake's put the kids to bed, so Mama's off duty. Should we head to Mike's?!"

●●●

I fumble to get my keys in the lock, but when my front door finally clicks open, it's sweet, sweet relief. I'm not just tipsy, like most Friday nights spent with Leon and Victoria. Tonight, I am officially drunk, especially after Victoria dragged us to Mike's, that new West Village bar owned by a bunch of celebrities, including the downtown playboy Nate Clyburn, who everyone says is a minor investor. She wanted to see if he would hit on her, just for fun. He did not. But Leon did end up knowing the bartender from his circuit-party days, and the guy gave us a few free rounds of shots, which sent me on my ass and Victoria in search of a slice from Prince Street Pizza.

I throw my bag down on the side table and kick off my boots. All I can think about is diving headfirst into the leftover artichoke quesadilla from the Butcher's Daughter that I know is in the fridge, and within a few minutes, I'm satiated, crumbs strewn all over my top, a tall glass of cold water beside me.

I'm so exhausted from the day I could pass out right here, at my little kitchen island. The one that's seen me through so much shit, so many times I've cried on the phone with my mom, wondering why the hell I put up with Sasha's bullying, or all the moments Doug went down on me, my bare ass pressed into the counter as I willed myself to forget about the nights he left me on read.

But tonight, it's just me, this quesadilla, and the memory of Sasha screaming at me in front of *everyone*.

I dump the empty box into the recycling and pad down the hall. My bedroom is pristine as usual, an oasis of cozy neutral blankets and throw pillows. The calming smell of Kai linen fragrance wafts through the air. I wish I was the kind of girl who could pull back the covers and get in, fully clothed and covered in crumbs. But I'm not that person, the one who says *fuck it*. Maybe *that* woman would have stood up to Sasha instead of making excuses.

So, I drag myself into the bathroom and do my skincare routine, washing away the trash day. I pull my hair into a braid and throw my clothes into the hamper, stepping into a marble-colored Skims pajama set. Then, finally, with every last ounce of energy in my body, I pull back the covers and slide into bed.

The sheets are cool against my skin, and my pillow is exactly the right density. I close my eyes and wait for sleep to come. But almost immediately, I know it's no use. Not right now. My head is spinning from all the vodka, and I can't get Sasha's words—her fucking face— out of my head. The whole day is morphing into one of those core memories I know will haunt me when I least expect it, years from now, way after I've entered a new chapter where working for Sasha Sherman feels like a bad dream. I hope it will be, anyway.

I reach for my phone and swipe over to Instagram. The feed is boring, and the stories are even more basic, full of posed photos at no-name restaurants and babies who look like carbon copies of the people Victoria and I went to high school with, the people we lost touch with on purpose.

I swipe to exit the app, but then I remember my old style account, the one I saw earlier in the week. Curiosity gets the best of me, and I tap over to deuxmoi. The name had no real meaning, just a silly bit of French nothingness that sounded fake-fancy in my head.

Now that I'm scrolling through the posts, I see they're cuter than I remember, with trendy outfits and funny captions.

I should have tried harder to make deuxmoi a *thing*. I should have put more effort into it. But somehow, it still has nearly thirty thousand followers, even though I haven't posted in years. I tap over to the followers tab and take a look at who's still there. Various influencers, a few C-list celebs, some reality TV stars, and a whole slew of fashion people who probably forgot it existed. Actually, it's kind of a gold mine of the industry.

What if . . .

I prop myself up against my headboard, my heart beating fast, and try to make sense of the potentially ridiculous idea brewing in my brain.

Eh, fuck it. What's the worst that can happen?

I make a quick story, just white text on an old photo of Britney Spears stepping out of a car from the early 2000s. My fingers fly over my screen, typing the words that come to mind.

> Better than any tabloid out there . . . DM me any celeb stories (first or secondhand) that you're willing to share. And I will, too. Unedited.

I post it fast and immediately make another one.

> I'll start . . . Madison Lee resells designer clothes on The Original gifted to her from brands.

I twirl a strand of hair around my finger, then keep typing.

> Another one: Late night legend Teddy Treadwell is a gem at kindergarten pick-up. He bakes homemade cookies for kids' birthdays.

I lean back and close my eyes, a sense of calm spreading through my body. When I open them, I look at my screen and nearly gasp. There in the top right-hand corner are notifications. Forty-three of them in less than ten minutes.

What the hell have I done?

Celebsy.com

Anonymous IG Account Accuses Pop Star Madison Lee of Reselling Gifted Clothes

Ruh-roh. A new anonymous IG account dishing out celeb gossip in the middle of the night just accused "So You Wanna" singer Madison Lee of accepting designer clothes as gifts from brands and then reselling the pieces on consignment e-tailers. Not a good look.

We have no clue who runs the account, called deuxmoi, but it also shared a few other pieces of harmless goss (CBS's Teddy Treadwell bakes cookies for his kids' school . . . aww!!). Deuxmoi didn't link to any of Madison Lee's consigned pieces, but some eagle-eyed sleuthers found resale accounts linked to her assistant's email address. The clothes in question? To-be-released matching sets, gowns, and party shoes from storied Italian designer Ernesto that you can find on The Original.

Madison Lee, wyd?????

CHAPTER 5

Scooped-out everything bagel with vegan veggie cream cheese.

That's all I can think about when I open my eyes in the morning. My head is pounding, and my mouth is dry and sandy. A hangover pulses through my body, which is currently all aches and pains. How many drinks did we have last night? Did we end up at . . . Mike's? The image of Victoria lobbing tiny cocktail onions at a group of bros dripping in Supreme trying to talk to Nate Clyburn and his *One Percent* co-stars comes to mind.

I groan and throw my forearm over my eyes to shield them from the sun streaming in through my window. I fumble around for my phone and see that it's only 8:30. On a Saturday.

Water. I need water. I push myself to stand and hobble into the kitchen, pouring myself a glass from the Brita in the fridge. I chug it all in a few hearty glugs.

The couch calls, and I flop down, burrowing under a faux fur blanket. My phone blinks back at me, and I see I have a few texts from Fuckboy Orthodontist, aka Doug.

One from 3:30 in the morning. *Where you at?*

Another at 4:00. *Come on, don't you wanna see me???*

And a final one at 4:35, a little more sober-seeming. *Miss you, hon. Hit me up in the morning. I wanna take you out tomorrow.*

I try to ignore the pleased feeling settling into my stomach. He's never said anything like this before—that he wants to go on a real date. Maybe one night of not texting him back immediately finally made him realize I'm worth taking out, like *really* out.

I start typing.

> So where are you taking me?

Then I see a selfie from Victoria in our group chat, sent an hour ago. In it, she looks god-awful, hungover as shit, snuggled up with her kids and a white paper bag, which undoubtedly contains a croissant from Ladurée.

Never have kids, she wrote.

Finally, I tap over to Instagram, but when I see what's on the screen, I nearly choke on my water. There are *so* many notifications. Dozens. No . . . hundreds.

I barely have two thousand followers.

What the hell is going on?

But then I see the user icon. Deuxmoi. And all of the final moments of last night come roaring back. Me posting about Madison Lee. The stories that flooded my inbox, how I stayed up for another hour, sharing all of them, even the one about the A-list actor Mike Yen, who likes to have sex while wearing big-ass headphones that blast music he never shares with his partners.

I chew on my bottom lip as I scroll through the messages.

Then my eye catches the follower count. It's gone up by three thousand. In one night.

I drop my phone like it's on fire. What the hell?

My phone erupts from the floor, and I peek down at it, almost scared to see who's calling. Thank god it's just Leon trying to Face-Time. I swipe to answer, and his face fills the screen.

"Babe, what the actual *fuck* is going on?" He's in bed, bare-chested, propped up against a bunch of pillows. His dark hair is wild, standing on end, and based on the circles under his eyes, he's got a hangover that rivals mine.

I bury my head in my hands. "You saw it?"

Leon's eyes go wide, and I sense his frustration brewing on the other side of the screen. "Obviously I saw it. The whole fucking world has seen it."

"Shit."

"Ah, there's Victoria. She must have finally checked Insta. Hold, please."

It takes a second, but then Victoria appears, too, now wearing a bright cropped top from Carolina Herrera, her hair pulled back into a smoothed-out Upper East Side Mom ponytail.

"Where are you going, Sarabeth's?" Leon asks.

"Paisley Parker is having a birthday party, you dumbass." Her eyes flick offscreen. "Ten minutes, boys! Ten! T-E-N!" Then she turns her attention back to us and hisses into the microphone. "Um, Cricket, what the hell did you do when you got home?"

Leon's boyfriend, Giuseppe, pops his head into the frame and hands over a coffee mug. "Morning, lovely humans who turned Leon into a drunken wreck last night," he says, waving at us. "I hear Cricket was busy. Good thing that account's still anonymous, huh?"

Leon shakes his head. "I cannot believe you posted about Madison Lee. Sasha's going to freak the fuck out."

"Oh my god," I say, the reality of what I've done starting to crash down on me. "Who else knows this is me?"

"No one," Leon says. "Remember, you made us promise to keep it a secret until you hit fifty thousand? Looks like you're kinda close now."

"Jesus Christ." I cover my face with my hand.

"You posted about Teddy!" Victoria says. "I told you that in confidence. What if someone at school finds out *I* blabbed?"

Leon nods. "And what if someone at work finds out that *I'm* friends with whoever runs this account?" He shakes his head, "Vic, we need to unfollow right now. Immediately."

Victoria purses her lips. "Good call." She taps a few times. "Done."

I groan. "Guys, can you please not be so selfish right now?"

Leon gives me that *oh really?* look and cocks his head. "Babe, you can do whatever you want, but please do not rope us into whatever insanity you're up to. You posted about *Madison Lee*."

"I know, I know. It was a moment of drunken weakness. No one knows it's me, though. Right?"

Victoria shakes her head, but then she peers down at her computer. "Was that all of the responses? I feel like you got a lot."

"Lemme check." I pull up Instagram on my computer and see that the inbox is full of unread messages, all of them threatening to share so much information. I lean my head back against the couch, trying to ignore the pounding in my brain. "There's more. Much more."

"Damn," Leon says. "The people want to spill."

"Oh my god!" Victoria sits upright, and her eyes go wide. "You reposted photos of Nate Clyburn at Mike's last night. I better not be in them."

Leon snorts. "You're definitely not."

"What should I do?" I ask. "Like . . . do I keep sharing?"

"I mean, you should definitely stop this shit if you want to keep your job," Leon says. "But . . . it's kind of fun. As long as you don't post anything else about Sasha's clients."

"Or people whose kids go to my kids' school," Victoria chimes in. "We're still trying to get into the East Side Racquet Club."

"As if this would stop you from getting into a country club, Vic."

She pouts but doesn't say anything.

"Can I get in trouble for this?" I ask, mostly to Leon.

Leon cranes his neck. "Giuseppe," he calls. "Can Cricket get in trouble for doing this? If it's anonymous?"

I can't hear what Giuseppe says, but Leon looks back at the camera. "The entertainment lawyer in the room says no." Then Giuseppe appears wearing a form-fitting tee and workout shorts, a picture of health mocking our current state.

"A free piece of legal advice," he says. "Add a disclaimer."

"What?" I ask.

"A disclaimer. Something that says you're not liable for defamation, that you have no idea if the tips are fake or not."

I must look confused as fuck, because Giuseppe breaks it down.

"No one wants to see you get sued. Here. I'll text you some language. Just add it to the bio and make sure nothing on the account is attached to you—email, phone number, old posts that might link to your real account. Do that. Then post away."

Victoria's mouth drops open a bit, and Leon looks on in awe.

"Maybe I should deactivate my personal account," I say. "What if there's something on there that can tie me to this?"

Leon nods emphatically. "One hundred percent. Shut that shit down. At least Sasha doesn't follow you on Insta. She'd rip your throat out." Then Leon's face changes. "Not to mention what she'd do to *me*. She knows we're best friends."

Victoria's eyebrows arch. "Ohmigod, there are dozens of photos of us on your personal account. Delete that thing right now."

I give them both a death stare. "I cannot believe you're both worried about *your* asses right now. I'm the one who got wasted and did this."

Leon leans into the camera. "Yeah, and *we're* your friends! We're collateral damage here."

"Fine," I say. "It's not like anyone follows my personal account anyway."

"Truth," Leon says, and I pretend to swat at him through the phone. But I know they're right. Sasha would probably decapitate me if she knew I blabbed about Madison Lee. I need to delete all evidence that might tie me to the account immediately.

My phone buzzes with a text from Giuseppe: *Copy and paste this and you're golden: "Statements made on this account have not been independently confirmed. This account does not claim any information published is based in fact."*

I read it once, then twice, then toggle back to FaceTime, where my friends are looking at me, curious. "Should I . . ." I ask, my voice somewhat stunned. "Keep this going?" I inhale sharply and hold my breath, waiting for their responses.

They pause, but then Victoria smiles just a bit and leans into the phone. "Just keep us out of it."

Leon looks upward like he's thinking it over. "Only if you can make sure you're totally anonymous."

Victoria nods emphatically, the curled ends of her hair swinging back and forth. She looks off-camera, her eyes narrowed. "Put that down, Chase!" Then back to us. "I gotta go. Paisley time. Bye, babes."

She blows a kiss into the screen, and Leon starts waving. "Gotta go, too. If I don't leave with Giuseppe now, I won't make it to Barry's Bootcamp. Let me know if you get anything *really* juicy."

The screen goes dark, and for a second, I feel a sense of unease but also urgency, like I'm at the top of a roller coaster, about to descend into the unknown. I sink back into the couch and open Instagram, curious to see what the hell is waiting for me. The messages extend all the way back to the night before, just after I fell asleep.

There are dozens from randos and strangers, people with ten followers or two hundred. But there are also a bunch of industry names I recognize, influencers and assistants, producers and photographers. People like me who have orbited celebrity for far too long and are ready to dish. I spy a handful of blue check marks—reality TV stars and D-list actors, jewelry designers and restaurateurs, entertainment reporters and athletes.

I open one at random and skim it. Something about a comedian who's known for hitting on college students when he's on tour. It ends with a phrase that makes me pause. *Anon pls.* I read another one.

> Server at Buvette here. Hate to say it but a certain hip-hop star came in with a whole entourage the other day and I can confirm the crew SUCKED. Ordered a shit-ton of bottles of wine and cocktails, stayed for a while and DIDN'T PAY OR LEAVE A TIP FOR ME! It was super disappointing. If you post, just keep me anonymous.

> Local Scarsdale barista chiming in: Gossip Girl filming in Westchester today. The actors are 10x more gorgeous in real life. Anon pls!

Suddenly it dawns on me. A lot of this stuff is . . . real. The gossip is hot as hell, and the sources are legit. All these people want is to get the word out, to share their sightings, their random pieces of information. They're willing to do so as long as they stay anonymous.

A sense of excitement sweeps over me. I tuck my bare feet under the blanket and readjust a throw pillow behind my back. Then I prepare to do what everyone in my DMs wants me to.

I post.

@AdamMathers: rainy day in ny spent reading every single deuxmoi story. Who is this and when can I buy her a drink?
10:00 AM May 15, 2022 Twitter for iPhone

@ConnieCohen: what the fuck is deuxmoi and why is everyone on twitter talking about her?
11:15 AM May 15, 2022 Twitter for Android

@retroredux: Messy bitches, take note! There's an anon IG account called deuxmoi spilling so much tea I'm scared to leave the app
12:34 PM May 15, 2022 Twitter for iPhone

@politicalpete: at this rate, deuxmoi's gonna announce the next SCOTUS nominee
2:35 PM May 15, 2022 Twitter for Android

CHAPTER 6

I wiggle my toes, and it's only then do I realize the whole left side of my body fell asleep. When exactly that happened is anyone's guess, but my fingers are curled around my phone, and as I glance up toward the window, I see the sun is starting to set, casting a warm glow across my living room.

Crap.

The clock on my phone says it's just past seven in the evening, which means I've been on Instagram, posting and reading DMs, for more hours than I'd like to admit. But holy shit, since this morning it's been like a tsunami. I've posted so many stories that the little advance bar at the top of the screen is now just a line of teensy dots, and there's no way I can keep track of the inbox in an organized way. The insights say that thousands of people are reading each slide and the drop-off rate is low as people click through the whole damn thing. *Very* low. Meaning people are watching all of them.

The follower count has been ticking up all day, too, another five thousand in total. I can see that many of the people who are new to the party are actual celebrities, reporters, or entertainment-adjacent hangers-on. The blue-check users keep on coming, sending me messages with even more gossip and sightings. A few celebs, like the hip-hop star who was rumored to be a bad tipper, have even responded to the rumors in tweets or Instagram posts. The guy in question posted a statement saying he thought the meal was comped and apologized.

Others have been sliding into my DMs with clarification on what's been posted, like this one from a British actress who is pissed that I posted a message that she hooked up with an A-list action star:

> That message about me hooking up with George Bellamy is completely wrong and I would really appreciate you taking it down given the fact that it's defamatory. I can't even say I know the guy, so the fact that you post just anything without fact checking is crazy. Are you aware that anyone can write a lie and you are reposting things as they were facts and defaming people left and right? If I wanted to ruin someone it's that simple to make up a lie. It's literally crazy!!!

I cringe as I read her words, so right then and there I make a decision that if any celeb reaches out with clarifying info or requests for stories to be taken down, I'll acquiesce. I'm not trying to ruin lives here, just have a little fun—bring some much-needed joy to pop-culture-hungry people. So even though her claim that this post is "defamatory" is wild as hell, I tap out a response before deleting the story:

> No prob. I'll take it down!

But why was she *so* upset to be associated with George in the first place to the point she would consider any association with him defamatory? Maybe because he's known as the threesome king of Los Angeles or that he has a reputation for hooking up with literally *anyone*, according to multiple people who responded to the post in my DMs. I even received a message about him being into a certain kink that involves your sexual partner's fist being inserted into a body part that sounds slightly painful. No shame in his game—whatever gets you to relax. Even so, being linked to someone like that does *not* constitute defamation.

She hearts my response immediately and sends a smooching emoji. At least I made a frenemy out of this one.

Even Madison Lee followed the account, making a statement in her stories about how someone on her team sold all of Ernesto's clothing without her knowing. Sure.

My phone pings with a text from Doug, the orthodontist. Shit. I totally forgot we were maybe going out tonight. That's a first.

> Weather Up at eight?

I check the clock again. I'm still in my pajamas, unshowered, with my hair tied in a messy topknot from the night before. But fuck it.

> See you there.

...

I can't take my eyes off Instagram in the hallway of my building, but as soon as the elevator comes and I see it's full of neighbors, I make the decision that I can't open the account—can't even look at it—in public. What if someone follows it and sees me posting? My whole anonymous cover would be blown. So, even though it pains me, I don't look at deuxmoi while walking to the bar. But I can feel my phone buzzing through my coat pocket, the DMs coming in at a rapid clip. I make a mental note to turn off notifications. This is *not* sustainable.

As I approach the bar, I realize it's the first time I've gone out with Doug that I don't find myself full of nerves, anxious butterflies flitting around in my stomach. I'm not worried about how the night will go or if he'll treat me like an actual partner this time. For once, I have other things on my mind, things like, Is that disclaimer enough to keep me free from legal troubles? And, As soon as I get home, I should really set up an email account where people can send tips. And, Does this account need a website? It's like my brain is on problem-solving overdrive in a way that it hasn't been in years.

I arrive at Weather Up and grab a small table by the wall, so I can sit with my back up against it. That way I can check deuxmoi while I wait for Doug to come and know that no one else will be able to see my screen.

While I wait for the server to come around, I post a few more tips—the stars of *Outer Banks* partying at an L.A. club the night before with bottle service, J. Lo's standing order at Carbone (which is veal Parmesan, spicy rigatoni, and *all* the desserts on the menu), Steven Tyler's recipe for muffins that actually sounds pretty good.

"What can I get for you?" a perky waitress asks.

Flustered, I shove my phone in my bag and order my usual, a vodka soda with a splash of pineapple. When she disappears, I check my phone again and see a few messages from readers, ones that tug at my heart in the most unexpected way.

> I'm working an overnight shift in the ICU wing and I'm sharing all of these celeb stories with the other nurses. These totally make our day.

> I'm sick at home with the nasty flu going around DC and these are giving me LIFE.

> I thought I was the only one obsessed with this shit! Loving this!!!!

> E! News, GTFO. Obsessed with you!

Damn. People are . . . into this, though I guess I shouldn't be surprised. There's a reason why mags like *Us Weekly* and *People* are still in business, why blind-item gossip has been around since the dawn of journalism. Maybe people are glomming on to this because I'm presenting it in a different way, primed for this specific moment in time, when most celebs have total control over their own images thanks to the power they glean from their own social accounts. I shake my head, unable to really wrap my head around all of this, but then I check the time and see Doug is twenty minutes late. Just like last time.

I sip my drink and scroll through a few more messages, new ones that have come in with more tips since I sat down.

Finally, five minutes later, I spot Doug outside puffing on a Marlboro Light as he finishes a phone call, laughing like he's got all the time in the world. He's wearing khakis and boat shoes, a simple tee under a Patagonia fleece that looks like it should be emblazoned with an investment bank's logo. Even from here I can see his hazel eyes bright in the night, his boyish smile, and if I look really closely, I can probably make out the tiny scar on his chin, the consequence of a high school hockey injury that his socialite mother begged him to get fixed. He said he liked the way it looked.

Doug runs a hand through his thick dark hair and finally hangs up the call. Then, he opens the door casually, no rush about him at all.

"Hey, Crick," he says when he gets close. "Sorry, the traffic was crazy." He leans over the table and kisses me on the cheek, demure. Almost platonic.

"All good," I say, sipping through my straw.

"You already ordered."

I shrug. "What was I supposed to do?"

He looks miffed but flags down the waitress and asks for a beer before glancing around the room, looking at everyone but me. It's familiar, this dumb game we play, the one that suggests we mean nothing to each other. But Doug has been this way since we met in high school, when he was a junior on the hockey team and I was a senior, only in his orbit because I made varsity tennis that year. He felt me up at a beach party once but didn't speak to me again until we met at a mutual friend's birthday dinner on the Lower East Side a few years ago. He had just graduated from orthodontal school and was working as a resident uptown.

Once we made the connection and I jogged his memory about the whole grab-a-tit thing, he invited me straight to his place, where we fooled around until four in the morning. After, he sent me home in an Uber, saying he had an early shift. We've been off and on like this forever, always meeting one-on-one, never with friends or for dinner, really.

Victoria thinks he's using me. But maybe I'm using him, too. Maybe I don't really *want* a relationship like she or Leon have. Maybe I like being free to fuck who I want when I want and to say yes to a date with the fuckboy orthodontist every now and then. Doesn't hurt that every time we hook up it makes me feel like I'm seventeen again, hungry and waiting for the world to open up.

But . . . even I know that's all bullshit.

I paste a smile on and shake out my hair. "How was your week?" I ask.

He shrugs his shoulders up around his ears. "Fine. Lots of braces. A few retainers. Our secretary's a total dumbass." He takes a big swig and swallows so hard, his Adam's apple bobs up and down. "Think I'm going to have to fire her."

"How come?"

"She fucked up my lunch order," he says. "Twice. And my coffee order. She's a moron."

My skin prickles and I straighten my spine, fighting off flashbacks of Sasha throwing her stiletto at me the one time the French café messed up her Niçoise salad. Or the time she called me a "no-taste ignoramus" when I asked her to confirm her country home's zip code for a flower delivery.

"Maybe she had a lot going on," I say. "Maybe the patients were laying into her and she made a mistake."

Doug looks at me like I've got six heads and smirks. "Just because you're still an assistant doesn't mean you need to stand up for every single crappy employee." He laughs at his non-joke, and I clench my fists under the table. Time to change the subject.

"So, did you wanna go around the corner to Bubby's for dinner?" Everyone always talks about their pies, but I know Doug loves the homemade biscuits.

Doug shakes his head. "Nah. Can't do dinner. I gotta go to my buddy's birthday after this in Williamsburg."

I set my drink down on the table. "Excuse me?"

He looks at me funny, cocking his head. "What? I thought we'd just meet for a drink now and then . . ." He rests his hand on my bare knee under the table. "Maybe meet up later?"

Fury builds in my chest as I knock his hand away. "Let me get this straight," I say, not even trying to keep my cool. "Your version of taking me out is meeting up for a drink where you're almost a half hour late, then ditching me to go to a party with your boys, then hitting me up for a fuck later? At like two a.m., after you've already been out all night and reek of Bud Heavy and cigarettes?"

I've never spoken to him like this. The color drains from his face, and he turns his cheek away from me ever so slightly, like he's not sure if I'm going to reach across the table and scratch out his eyes, which I very well might. He toys with loose collar of his shirt, which I can now see has what might possibly be a dark-red lipstick stain on the inside of his fleece. He says nothing.

"Did I get that right?" I ask.

"I— I just—" he stammers. But all of a sudden, I'm so over him and this bullshit that's been going on way too long. Looking at his face, I can't even see what I ever found attractive about him, especially since last time we fucked he couldn't even stay hard.

"You what?" I continue. "Thought I would be your fuck buddy forever? Just keep hanging around, hoping you'll want something more? Being grateful when you throw me anything more than a late-night text? Fuck this."

I push my chair out and stand, grabbing my purse.

"Wait," he says, but he makes such a halfhearted attempt to get up that I can't help but sneer at him in disgust.

"I'm done with whatever the hell this is."

"Aw, come on, we've been having so much fun."

"It was *fun* three years ago. Now, it's just pathetic."

I shake my head, anger swirling in my stomach. I push past the hostess stand and break out of the bar into the cold night. I wrap my coat around my stomach and set off back toward my apartment, where I know I'll probably just order takeout and pop an edible. But as I cross the street, I feel my phone buzz inside my bag over and over and over again.

Wait.

There's something else I can do, too.

I lean up against a building, making sure no one can see what's on my screen, and pull up Instagram. There, I find a hundred new followers since I sat down and dozens of new messages. A small smile spreads on my face.

Who needs the orthodontist when you have all of *this* waiting for you?

Reddit
r/CelebNews

bigfan: anyone else get a load of a new account that's been posting AMAZING goss on IG? deuxmoi? I'm in love.

    hickory458: oh yeah she's legit

    pieceapizza: who is she????

    jiggalojelly: feel like she works in fashion . . . maybe PR or something . . . def in the know

    oopsiedaisy789342: friend of a friend said she's an A-lister's assistant. Once they find out who she is, she's never gonna get work again

    lollipopkid: who said she's a she? Sexist much?????

    kiddo_iconic: idc who runs it, I just want more

CHAPTER 7

By Monday morning, my neck aches from leaning over my phone the whole day before, and my fingers are cramping from swiping and typing more than I ever have. As I brush my teeth, my eyes never leave my screen. It's the first time in years that I've deviated from my morning weekday routine, which, before today, included a 6:30 a.m. alarm and a 7:15 a.m. barre class before getting to work around 9:00.

Now, I'm bleary-eyed in my bathroom at 8:30, ditching my blow-dryer so I can have a few extra minutes of posting time before rushing off to meet Sasha outside the office.

The account has gained another few thousand followers overnight, thanks to the fact that I spent all of Sunday on the couch, sharing more tips and stories as they came through my inbox.

After a few hours, it became obvious what the people wanted: small pieces of info that feel intimate and real, like how someone treated waitstaff or where stars were dining over the weekend. Like, when I posted that a bunch of the *Euphoria* cast members were spotted having drinks at the Bowery Hotel, followers wanted to know how much PDA two newly-in-love cast members were putting on. Or when I shared that Nate Clyburn popped by the Smile for breakfast, everyone was curious about his order and if he was with a certain petite brunette he's rumored to be dating. Based on the number of tongues and water droplets in my DMs, it seems like the people are *fiending* for him. I'll have to remember to post anything about him that comes through. He even slid into my DMs with a bunch of laughing emojis, so at least I know he's down to play along.

I spit out my toothpaste just as a message comes through from someone verified. *Kelsey Holleran.* I don't recognize the name at first, but when I pull up her profile, I remember she's an influencer and actress with her own line of graphic tees, married to the star of some old action movie that was popular when I was in high school.

I rack my brain trying to think why she might be popping up in my inbox, but then I remember I posted a tip about her last night. It said something like:

> Kelsey Holleran is known in the beauty world to be the biggest mooch, which to me is similar to starfucking. She sucks up to brands via Insta/DM to get free products in exchange for posting. Does it SO much. It's gross.

And now she's hitting me up.

I open the message and see text fill the screen. It takes three full scrolls to get to the top. My heart beats fast, and I'm almost scared to see what she has to say. But as I start reading, my fear turns to amusement.

> Saw your post about me and would love to know who said this! I've never asked for any products so it's a blatant lie.

I take a look at her feed and see that every other post is a close-up of a new bottle of face serum. I gnaw on my toothbrush as I type out a response.

> Babe, you know I can't reveal my sources. I'd lose all credibility! But I asked which brand she was talking about and she named a pretty popular one. Happy to take the post down if it's false.

She reads it immediately and writes back.

> Weird. I would NEVER do that!! Can you please take it down??

Oddly, I feel a burst of boldness, knowing she has no idea who she's speaking with. I could say anything, including how I *really* feel for once, but I choose to try to squash that urge because I can tell she's obviously upset. Part of me feels for her—I wouldn't want to be in her position and read something about myself that isn't true, but it's hard for me to believe that since she's legitimately an influencer that she's *never* asked for anything for free.

It's gone, I write. *People are going to think I'm weak for taking it down, though.*

> I don't want that.

> Haha I know

> Do u want to call me?

I shake my head. She wants to talk . . . on the phone? I contemplate it for a minute but quickly decide that would be a horrible idea. I'd be one step closer to giving up my anonymity.

> Girl, this account is just a hobby. I don't think anyone takes it seriously. Can I just post that we DMed and cleared up the situation?

> I can give you every beauty person I've worked w for reference.

I shake my head and gargle some mouthwash before rushing back into the bedroom to finish getting ready.

> It's fine.

I pour myself into another all-black outfit and grab my bag, heading for the door. But then I see she's posted a bunch of stories to her own account and—oh god—when I watch them, I see they're about this whole debacle. And that my DMs are blowing up.

This is ridiculous.

I believe u, I write to her in a DM. *Feel free to send me something on the record to repost.*

I hold back a laugh. On the record? Who the fuck do I think I am?

The clock is ticking down, and I know I need to keep dealing with this on my way to work. I'll never make it if I walk like I usually do. I bite my lip and try to figure out my next move. But then I decide to take a page out of Victoria's old PR job playbook and—fuck it—order an Uber that I'll add to my expense list at the end of the month. I do have a box of costume jewelry that was delivered to my apartment instead of the office by mistake, so if I bring it with me, the ride *is* kind of legit. Plus, that way, I'll be able to check deuxmoi in the privacy of the back seat.

I call a car and stuff my phone in my pocket as I head out into the world and down to the street. When I'm safely inside the nondescript sedan, I decide to respond to Kelsey.

But then I see an enormous block of text from her, giving me a whole diatribe about how it's probably this one company that was going to give her a discount but then didn't and that made her upset.

Then I see she's sent a few voice notes, one that spans nearly a minute. I pop in my headphones and listen to her speak in a hurried voice about how this whole story is ridiculous and she can't imagine who would say such a thing. "I get paid to post things on Insta. I don't ask for things for *free*."

Another message comes in. *You must think I'm nuts to care so deeply about this*, she writes.

If you get paid to do things on IG I don't think ur nuts, I reply. *But maybe people are sensitive to all your spon con, ya know sometimes it rubs people the wrong way if that's all you're posting.*

> I get paid by juvederm! Not this small stuff!

A selfie appears of her sitting in an all-mirrored bathroom, the camera close on her face. If she has had fillers, she must have a great doctor, because I can't tell.

I'm almost at Sasha's office, so I really need to nip this in the bud. I check my DMs and see that so many people have written in about what I perceive to be an extremely silly, very small moment. It's truly beyond me why people seem to care, but I start to wonder if I'm underreacting to these situations. Either way, I decide to be real with her.

Just be honest, I write. *I don't think that someone saying you ask for free makeup or whatever is that big of a deal based on what you have going on.*

She starts typing but then the bubble goes away. It reappears once more, then disappears, before finally, she writes, *I'm just sad about the comment. I had to unfollow u not out of disrespect but just to protect my feelings. Hope u understand.*

I look up and see I'm right outside Styling by Sasha, with only a minute left to spare.

Do what you need to do! I write before stashing my phone in my bag, my head spinning, wondering if every single tip will lead to mind-boggling interactions with celebs like this.

...

I wait outside for ten minutes before Sasha sends me a text telling me she's coming in late and that I should be waiting with her tea at 11:30. Then she sends another message.

> You better have gotten your nails done over the weekend. They were chipped af on Friday. You looked lazy and cheap.

I guess I should be grateful she's not mentioning the Madison Lee shit show, but I can't help but feel resentment beat deep within my chest. I look down at my nails, a haphazard mix of bare nail and old red polish, and remind myself to borrow some remover Leon keeps at his desk. But when I get out of the elevator, I sense something in the office is . . . off. There's a tension on the floor that I can't quite place.

I head into our sad excuse for a kitchenette and begin to make myself a coffee with creamer when I see a pair of midlevel stylists huddled around the window, looking down at something. I walk over to them, and as soon as I get there, I feel a sense of unease.

"Everything okay?" I ask.

Nelly, a perky midwestern transplant with a penchant for faux fur, looks up, terror in her eyes. "Did you see this?" She thrusts her phone toward me, and when I see what's on the screen, my heart rate picks up. It's deuxmoi.

My throat is dry and scratchy, and I can't find any words.

Orion, a muscle daddy who only dates ballerinas and has worked on Alyssa's team for nearly a decade, stretches his eyes wide and starts nodding vigorously. "It's some anonymous gossip blogger. They've been posting tips and blind items all weekend."

"Really?" I ask, feigning shock. "Like what?"

Nelly starts listing off familiar stories, each one banal and funny, but then she leans in closer. "They posted about Madison Lee. How she resold those clothes."

My stomach flips, and my shoulders go rigid. "No!"

She nods solemnly. "Sasha's going to throw a fucking fit."

"Does she know?"

Orion looks at me, confused. "Shouldn't we be asking *you* that?"

"Why?" I ask, trying to keep my voice still, trying not to panic.

"Because you're her assistant, duh." Nelly rolls her eyes. "Has she mentioned anything?"

It's getting close to Sasha's arrival time, and I have to get back to my desk. "Not yet."

Orion glances back down at the phone. "I wonder who this bitch is. She's got intel, that's for sure."

"Who does?" A sharp, clipped voice sounds off behind me.

My spine stiffens, and I clench my fist by my side. I spin around and paste a smile on my face. "Sasha," I say. "You're early. Let me get your tea—" She holds up her hand, cutting me off, and sets her gaze on Orion.

"Who has intel?" she asks. Her voice is low and impatient. "Give me that." She swipes the phone out of Orion's hand. "What is this?"

We're all quiet, and I swear everyone can hear my heart beating right out of my chest. Nelly elbows me in the stomach, but I refuse to speak.

Orion takes one for the team. "Just some stupid account that started over the weekend. Celebrity gossip and stuff."

"Huh," Sasha says, thumbing through the stories. *My* stories. The ones *I* posted yesterday and this morning. I think I'm gonna barf. "Any of our clients on here? Nothing about Duke Dudley, right?"

Orion shakes his head. "Definitely no Duke."

Sasha nods, pleased. "Anyone else?"

"Um . . ." Nelly starts. I want to punch her in the gut. Can she be any more obvious?

Sasha looks up, her eyebrows in a deep V, and shoves the phone back to Orion. "Who?" She sounds the word so loud that I jump.

Leon walks by and catches my eyes, giving me a terrified look before lingering by the fridge.

"Who?" Sasha yells again. "Who the fuck from our roster has been on this bullshit?"

Nelly sighs and pulls something up on her phone before turning it back to Sasha. My knees nearly give out. She screenshot the Madison Lee post from Friday.

Traitor.

Though I don't know if she can be a traitor if she didn't know it was me. She *doesn't* know it's me, right? Nelly bites her lip. She looks scared, too. No one wants to be the messenger when we all know Sasha likes to bite messengers' heads right off and play with their insides.

Sasha's eyes scan the screen, and her mouth forms a thin line, her lips almost disappearing.

"What. The. Fuck. Is. This?" she asks in a quiet voice that makes the hair on the back of my neck stand up. "How did anyone find out about this?"

No one speaks, and my mouth drops open.

"Well?" Sasha bellows. "Who was it?"

Orion and Nelly compose themselves and shake their heads. Leon gives me a death stare, and I finally force myself to calm, my heart rate to slow. Get your shit together.

But before I can get out a word, Sasha turns to me. "Was it you? Is this you?"

The lie comes out easy, smooth like butter.

"Of course not," I scoff. "You think I'd jeopardize my job for this?" I wave my hand, and Sasha frowns, clutching the phone in her hand.

"Who could it have been then, huh?" She's beating her black leather Saint Laurent boot in a maniacal way, *tap-tap-tapp*ing against the concrete floor, echoing through the drafty loft. She spins around then and turns to the rest of the office. "Who the fuck is deuxmoi?" she yells out.

I clear my throat and shrug my shoulders up to my ears. "Everyone in Ernesto's camp knows about this," I say. "Maybe someone over there wanted to get back at her—blackball her from luxury, you know?"

Nelly starts nodding, emphatic, with wide eyes. "Or maybe Madison Lee's assistant." She leans in. "I heard she's a terrible boss to everyone on her staff. Maybe someone got fed up and started the account to dish."

I resist the urge to hug her out of gratitude.

"Totally." I cross my arms over my chest and nod, twisting my face in agreement. "I have a friend who works at a different consignment site, and she says this is super common. Loads of stars do this, like Beyoncé and Bieber. Maybe Madison Lee's done it with other designers, too."

Orion drums his fingers against his chin. "Hundred percent."

I can't tell if Sasha's buying it, but she shoves the phone back at Orion, right into his chest. "Fine." She flips her hair over her shoulder so fast her Oscar de la Renta statement earring almost flies out of her ear and takes a few big strides back to her office.

I glance back at Orion and Nelly and shrug before following Sasha close at her heels. "Do you want me to prep—"

Sasha spins back around, causing me to stop short. It's a miracle I don't spill my coffee all over her Dolce & Gabbana pussy-bow blouse.

"You're right, you know." She's literally never said that before, and I find myself a bit shocked. "It probably isn't anyone here, is it? It's not like you all have much free time, with how many clients we have. You probably have no social life, no dating life at all."

My face reddens with embarrassment. But this is a good out. "Running that thing looks like a shit ton of work. I'd never have time for that. Whoever does must not even have a job."

Sasha nods, pleased, and spins back around, taking off toward her office. "And if I *do* find out that someone in this place is running that account, I'd fire them on the spot."

"Yep," I say, but the word comes out garbled because I know if I want to have a future here, to have everything I worked so hard for over the past few years be *worth* something, then I can't keep posting on this account. I have to end it.

Because if I don't, I could lose just about everything.

@liveforgossip 3h
it's been 4 days and I need my @deuxmoi fix . . . wya boo?

@bananarama 16h
where's @deuxmoi ☹

@hunnymoney 5h
I need a version of @deuxmoi strictly for Nate Clyburn updates. Why am I obsessed with him? And where are youuuuu DM?!

@lostthewar 35m
No, you spent the better part of your workday refreshing @deuxmoi, hoping for more tea

CHAPTER 8

"Killed it today, Cricket!"

I stretch out my arms and smile at Joanna, my regular barre instructor, who I've been going to for the past three years. After skipping Monday to work on deuxmoi, I vowed to go most every day this week and followed through, including this beautiful Friday morning. It's actually helped me forget about the account. Well, sort of. Not completely.

I give Joanna a high five and leave the studio, feeling weak in my calves. In truth, I haven't been able to stop thinking about deuxmoi all week, and even though I haven't been looking at it, Leon and Victoria have been begrudgingly sending me updates when I bug them to.

It's got a thousand more followers despite my silence and a newly launched Facebook group dedicated to figuring out the blind items. Leon chocks up all the buzz to the fact that a ton of screenshots made their way to Twitter, and then to *Page Six* and the *Daily Mail*, both of which rereported my information as news, naming me as the place where the stories originated.

I shower and change into a black blazer from the Frankie Shop and a pair of my favorite Frame jeans. I take the time to spray a bunch of dry shampoo in my hair and go through my skincare routine, another thing that went by the wayside last weekend when I was all about deuxmoi.

Feeling fresh and glowy, I walk the few blocks to the office and prepare for what we all call D-Day, aka whenever Duke Dudley comes into the office. Duke's one of Sasha's biggest clients and has been with her since the beginning, when Sasha was just getting her footing and Duke was in his early twenties, starring in network teen dramas. Sasha hadn't yet gotten the reality TV gig, and Duke was a decade away from winning an Oscar for playing a World War II spy.

When he married Celine, a hairy-armpitted model-turned-folk-singer he met at the Grammys, a few years back, Sasha planned every single outfit for every single member of *both* their families. It was the biggest contract the firm ever had, and it helped Sasha land dozens of clients she'd been chasing for years who adored her pairings and sensibility for the four-day extravaganza in San Miguel de Allende. Duke has the power to make or break Styling by Sasha, and everyone knows it.

The first thing on my agenda is to make sure the arrangements from Emily Thompson Flowers have arrived and that they're set up in the entryway—check—and then I poke around in the mini fridge below my desk to check that we have Duke's favorite coffee, cans of La Colombe draft oat lattes, to offer him as soon as he walks through the door.

I do a final run-through of the floor, stashing away stray pieces of paper and hiding loose garment bags in the hall closet, before I decide that the office is 100 percent Duke appropriate.

"It looks lovely in here, Cricket." I spin around on my heel and see Alyssa walking down the hall, her manicured hand wrapped around the handle of her lime-green Goyard tote. "Those flowers are re-markable."

"It's D-Day," I say, giving her a wide smile.

"Oh," she says, as if surprised—and not in a pleasant way—which is kind of weird, considering Alyssa *loves* Duke. Leon told me they used to party together back in the early-aughts in the Hollywood club scene with Paris Hilton and Nicole Richie, and that *she* convinced him to give Sasha a tryout to style him. Once, while on *The Tonight Show*, Duke even gave her a shout-out, saying he wanted to give a thanks to "his dear friend Alyssa" for getting him to give up skinny ties.

"You didn't know?" I ask Alyssa.

The exposed skin on her neck turns blotchy. "Just forgot."

"I'm sure you'll see him. He should be here soon. Want me to find you before he leaves so you can say hi?"

Alyssa shakes her head. "All good. My schedule's packed." She reaches for my arm, placing her finger pads against my skin gently. For a second it looks like she wants to say something. Her brow is furrowed, and her lips open slightly.

But then she shuts her mouth, and before I can ask another question, she hustles off down the hall and turns into her office, closing the door behind her. On another day, I'd wonder what was up, but today is D-Day and I can't waste any more time.

As the rest of the employees file into the office, I make sure we have all his decks printed and prepped in leather-bound folders, like he prefers. There are lookbooks for his next press junket, a weeklong yacht vacation in Croatia, and a slew of corporate speaking engagements.

Just as I'm putting the finishing touches on the floral arrangement in the conference room, I hear Sasha's laugh coming from down the hall. I rush to the door and stand up straight, smoothing down my black Rag & Bone blouse.

"—and then I told Marvin to just buy the goddamn estate instead of renting it!" A bunch of other people erupt in laughter, and I peek my head outside the frame only to see she's walking with Duke and his publicist, Allison.

Shit. They're early.

I don't have enough time to rush back to my desk to grab his latte, but at least the lookbooks are already projected onto the flat-screen TV and the hard copies are sitting in a nice little stack in front of Sasha's regular seat.

They're getting closer to me now, and when I catch a good glimpse of Duke, my stomach flips. He's a lot taller in person, which is rare for a star, and his chiseled jaw only looks sharper when you see him up close, when you can take in his Greek god–like body in three dimensions. Right now, he's pressing a thick, tanned palm against his chest, which is covered by a nearly see-through white cotton T-shirt from Acne we picked out last spring. He's wearing those old-school Levi's he refuses to throw out, and his gold wedding band, a family heirloom from his great-grandfather, catches the sun streaming in from the picture window. His normally thick hair is cropped into a buzzcut, which compliments the dark stubble coating his face.

Duke's gaze flits around the office and lands on Nelly sitting at her desk. She smiles coyly at him, and Duke's megawatt smile grows larger. But then, out of the corner of my eye, I see Alyssa approach Nelly and whisper something into her ear. Nelly's face changes, and she stands, following Alyssa back to her office. Weird, especially since she declined to see Duke when he was here. But he doesn't seem to notice.

Sasha's face tightens when she sees me standing there, and I step to the side, motioning for them to come in.

"Hi, Cricket." Duke says my name like it's the most beautiful word in the world, and I have to fight hard to not break eye contact when he looks at me straight on. So many other stars we work with have reps who instruct us to never look their clients directly in the eyes. But Duke's always been the opposite, eager for connection, to *know* us. "Love the hair," he says, extending a finger toward me. "New?"

I know I'm blushing, but I can't help it. "Cut it a few weeks ago."

"So chic," he says, smiling like he means it. "Right, Sasha?"

Sasha's eyebrows go up half a centimeter.

"You always get the cutest assistants," Duke says, elbowing Sasha in the ribs.

My stomach twists itself into knots, but a ball of discomfort forms inside my stomach. I try to ignore it as Duke's publicist shoves him softly in the shoulder.

"Who was that one I always liked? The girl from the South?"

Sasha's mouth fits into a firm line, probably out of jealousy. "Eleanor."

Duke snaps his fingers. "That's right. She made a mean latte."

Crap. "Speaking of," I say. "I'll be right back with your La Colombe."

"You're a saint." Duke puts his hands into a little prayer position.

"Sparkling for you, Allison?" I ask.

She nods as Sasha leads them to their seats, shutting the door without looking at me.

My stomach finally settles as I hustle back to my desk, grabbing drinks for them. I'm juggling the glasses in my hands as I pass Leon, looking impeccable in a Rick Owens bomber jacket.

"I got you, girl." He takes the latte I'm about to drop and follows my lead back to Duke. "The assistants on my side of the floor are finding *any* excuse to walk by this room," he says.

"I mean, the guy has that effect on people."

"Too bad he doesn't swing both ways." Leon snorts a laugh.

"Too bad he's married."

"Did he remember your name today?"

"You know it."

"One of the good ones." We get to the little kitchenette outside the room, and I grab a wooden tray to place the drinks on.

Leon peeks through the door and shakes his head. "The only perk of being Sasha's assistant is getting some face time with that guy."

"Seriously," I mumble, pouring San Pellegrino into a tall glass and adding a lemon wedge. Glancing up, I see Alyssa rushing off to the elevator, her face hidden behind a curtain of hair. I nod in her direction. "Alyssa was kinda weird this morning. Said she didn't want to see Duke. I thought they were tight?"

Leon shrugs. "Her cal's packed today. She's heading to Tribeca to meet Gabrielle Union and Dwyane Wade. Trying to land the contract for their next yacht trip."

"Ah shit," I say. "That's a big one."

"Huge."

"The bikinis alone . . ." I shake my head and make my eyes wide, feigning stress.

Leon's eyes go wide in earnest. "Shit, let me make sure she has the sample cover-ups." He trots to catch up with Alyssa while I grab the tray and head on inside the conference room. When I open the door, I'm greeted by a chorus of uproarious laughter. Even Sasha, who *never* laughs, is bowled over, wiping tears away from her eyes.

"—and then I swear, he jumped right off the roof right into the pool!"

The room continues laughing, and I set down the drinks, trying to make as little noise as possible.

I pop the top off Duke's can and place it on a small white cocktail napkin in front of him and he looks up, his eyes still full of laughter. "Thanks so much. You're the best." He taps the back of my palm with a few fingers, letting them sit for a moment.

I press my lips together and take a seat at the back of the room, listening to them finish up the meeting as Duke approves all the outfits we selected for him to wear over the next few months.

At the end of the session, he stands up and stretches his arms above his head, revealing a sliver of abs and a small trail of hair leading down to his waistband. He catches me staring and just smiles, holding my gaze.

But all I want to do is post about this whole situation immediately. Something like . . .

> A certain A-list male actor is one of the nicest guys in Hollywood—and a total flirt. Always remembers assistants' names.

I trail behind the group as Sasha walks them back to the elevator, where she double-kisses both Allison and Duke on the cheeks.

"Get back to L.A. safe," she calls. Duke waves and pulls out his cell phone, pressing it to his ear.

But before they leave, Allison turns back to Sasha and ducks her head, low enough for just us to hear.

"I almost forgot," she asks. "Have you heard about this new Instagram account? Deuxmoi? Posting celebrity gossip anonymously?"

"Ugh." Sasha wrinkles her nose like she's smelled something awful. "What now?"

"Nothing," Allison says. "They've been quiet all week, but we're keeping tabs. Just to see who's talked about, you know? Do you know who runs it? I heard it's someone in fashion."

My ears perk up, and I bite the inside of my cheek.

"They don't work *here*, do they?" Allison asks, her voice firm.

Sasha scoffs. "Of course not," she says. "And if I found out they worked anywhere *near* here, they'd be fired in a heartbeat. Destroyed. Run out of New York and fashion altogether."

Allison shakes her head and gives Sasha a knowing look. "Well, we all know Duke's in good hands. I'm not worried."

The elevator arrives just then, and she and Duke, who's still on the phone and totally oblivious, depart, leaving Sasha standing there in front of me, fuming.

She spins on her heel and looks right at me.

"Cancel all my meetings for the rest of the day and call the Shibui Spa." She pushes past me, stomping down the hall. "I need a ninety-minute session. ASAP."

"You got it," I say, trying to stop my voice from quavering, from giving away any indication that I'm the one they're all secretly afraid of.

CHAPTER 9

Ever since Duke came by the office, I can't stop thinking about getting back to deuxmoi and seeing what's waiting for me in the DMs. I try to busy myself on this Saturday morning, heading to barre and then to the RealReal's brick-and-mortar shop. I walk through Dimes Square and nearly bump into Julia Fox, wearing a full latex getup at eleven in the morning and still managing to look fabulous.

But all that does is make me want to post spotteds.

Closer to home, I stop into Sweetgreen for a chopped salad and head back to my apartment. My headphones are on, some Nicki Minaj blaring in my ears. But that doesn't fully distract me either. It was easier during the week, when Sasha put the fear of god in me, when we were so worked up over D-Day and making sure every single thing was perfect.

Sasha still doesn't seem to suspect that I'm behind the account, though. Leon agrees, assuring me that I'm in the clear. Apparently, Sasha told Alyssa she thinks it's someone on Madison Lee's publicity team, which made Leon come down from his whole *you're going to get me fired* moment. Sasha's now convinced everyone hates that TikTok queen as much as she does. But at least my boss has turned her ire away from me, even though she's pretending that I didn't ask for a promotion just before that whole shit show went down.

It's starting to rain, and I pull my hoodie up tight over my hair, racing the few blocks back home. When I throw open the door, I shake off in the vestibule. There's no one in the elevator, and without thinking I pull up my phone and tap over to Instagram. But then I remember I deleted my personal account right when I started posting on deuxmoi.

I find willpower all the way into my apartment, while I shower and towel off, blow-drying my hair even though I have nowhere else to be.

But when I plop down on the couch with my lunch and an empty, rainy weekend day in front of me, I know it's only a matter of time before I break. Especially since Victoria and her husband, Jake, are off looking at country houses in the North Fork and Leon is at a Broadway matinee with Giuseppe. I could call some other friends, people from college or Nelly and Orion from work, or Doug the orthodontist, though that would be a *terrible* idea. I could get my nails done, but that would please Sasha too much for it to actually be an enjoyable experience.

I could . . .

Oh, fuck it.

My fingers fly over my screen and I log back in to deuxmoi, my brain working on autopilot. When I see what's there, I feel a jolt of dopamine and then another of adrenaline. There are more DMs than I can count.

> Can confirm two A-listers who started dating while filming a new superhero movie split—press is going to be a nightmare! anon pls

> NYC media sorta-mogul who thinks he's hot shit has been dating that one socialite turned reality star. They were spotted at The Nines over the weekend. He's a big tipper and she's a scene queen. Could work! (PS: It's Kyle Johns)

100% fact that a well-known Hollywood couple broke up over the holidays. Divorce will happen soon—within the next 2 weeks—and they're tryna keep it amicable for the kids, even though one mom (hint!!!!) prefers the poly life.

I have it on very good authority that the darling male lead of a much-anticipated movie was hanging with his older female director/co-star this weekend in Miami. Wonder why they were there together hmmm. Pap pics may come soon

I matched with John Mayer on Raya and scared him away by quoting "Your Body Is a Wonderland." Still stand by that one.

Psst: A certain a-list musician likes to make it rain on the people he sleeps with. YELLOW rain. Won't say more than that. ANON.

I post them all. Then, as more people start to engage with the account, I share updates to the posts, addendums, postscripts. The tea keeps coming, some juicy and some banal. More messages flood my inbox, and strangers lay it on thick.

Omg this is the hungover shit I need rn.

I was hoping you'd be back this week.

The blind item queen of my dreams.

A bubble of pride swells in my stomach, and for a second, I wonder what all this means. Sure, it's just celebrity gossip. At its base level, it's frothy, superficial bullshit. Chatter about people we don't know. People we *pretend* we know. But based on these messages and the dozens of people who are chiming in, there's something going on here. An untapped well. It's almost like this has become a space for people to vent about something they didn't know they needed to vent about, that I've become a faceless confidante to these strangers. For whatever reason, there are so many people out there who want to spill, to be part of the conversation.

I stretch out on the couch and twirl the ends of my hair around a finger, knowing that I'm not moving for another few hours, not until I get to the end of the messages, until I hear what everyone has to say. Who knew they needed someone to say it all to?

■■■

> Nate Clyburn and the whole cast of One Percent are at the Bowery Hotel Bar taking over the whole back area . . . Right fucking now!

> One Percent cast partying like literal rockstars rn at the Bowery Hotel Bar. Honestly, looks so fun.

These are the messages that give me the idea that maybe, just maybe, I should take this whole deuxmoi thing into the real world. Perhaps it's a sign that some of the account's most beloved celebs are hanging out together at one of *my* favorite bars. It's too perfect to pass up.

It'd be sketchy to show up alone, though, especially at 10:00 p.m. on a Saturday, and then have any real gossip appear on the account. An eagle-eyed stranger might pin it back to the random solo girl. Thankfully Leon answers on the first ring.

"You want to *what*?" he asks when I share my plan.

"I told you. Go down to the Bowery and do a little firsthand spotted situation. Some party reporting." I dab Dior eyeshadow on my lids and pat my cheeks with a Milk Makeup blush stick, wondering if I should go full incognito with that old blond wig I bought for Halloween a few years ago. But then I figure it might make me even more conspicuous. "So?" I ask. "In?"

For a moment, I wonder if Leon might actually say no. He has only ever turned down an opportunity to hang out once, when he had kidney stones during Pride six years ago, and even then, he promised he'd be at Victoria's bridal shower tea at the Plaza the next day. He was.

But going out in the name of deuxmoi? I don't know . . .

Leon sighs. "I cannot believe you are back on this bullshit," he says.

"I promise there is no way this will trace back to me. Or you." I know I'm pleading, but I need my best friend in on this with me. "Please?"

"You are asking for trouble," he says, tsk-tsking, "but fuck yeah, I'm in."

"My hero. See you there in twenty."

■■■

Leon meets me out front, wearing a fitted tuxedo shirt and black leather pants with Chelsea boots, and I adore him for understanding the assignment of trying to fit in at a *One Percent* party while also being an undercover sleuther.

He loops his arm in mine and gives my elbow a little squeeze. "Okay, fine. I admit Cindy Adams–ing with you is already extremely fun," he says, directing me inside the hotel.

I follow him back toward the bar, through the lobby with over-

stuffed leather couches and dim lighting. Hotel guests sit close together, coupe glasses set out on coffee tables in front of them on little
square cocktail napkins. A woman wearing a strapless corset sits at a
piano, playing something soulful as we walk by.

Leon throws his head back to give me a wink. When we get to the
bar, he makes chitchat with the hostess, who ushers us into the dark
back room, where it's easy to see that, yes, the *One Percent* cast has
taken over the whole back half of the bar. Their tables are piled high
with bottles of Veuve and Belvedere, silver platters full of crudités
and oysters, and, randomly, a massive tower of chocolate éclairs.

I sidle up to the bar and order us drinks, while Leon leans back and
looks around. "So, what's our game plan?" he asks.

I hand him his tequila and turn back around, taking in the scene
with him. Nate Clyburn is dancing on a leather booth, and because
he's as tall as an NBA player, his head almost touches the chande-
lier above him. He's all toned muscles and scruffy beard, and in this
light, I guess I see why the followers are so obsessed with him.

A dozen or so nonfamous people—you can tell, you can *always*
tell—gather around him, raising their arms as if bowing down, mag-
netized by him. Nate's co-stars laugh and down shots, acting like they
actually like one another, which checks out with what's been going
down in my DMs. None of them seem to care about being spotted
or keeping a low profile. They're not paying attention to the dozens
of normies also hanging out here, taking not-so-clandestine pictures.
They're just posing for their own Polaroids, their own selfies.

But then I watch Nate climb down off the booth and take a few
long strides over to the other end of the room, where his co-star Iris
Leonard is sitting. On *One Percent*, he's always trying to seduce her,
but, ever the bumbling idiot, he never succeeds. Tonight, he reaches
for her hand and she stands, beaming up at him, before pressing herself into his body. He wraps his arms around her and pulls her up, so
her legs are wrapped around his middle.

"Uh, I had no idea they were an item," Leon says. "They're practically fucking on the dance floor."

"Me neither," I say, totally mystified.

And suddenly, I have an idea.

If I post this kind of jaw-dropping information just as a story in my own text, then everyone will know that I was actually here. And if someone photographs the evening at the wrong angle, I might appear in some errant picture, a suspect in the whole deuxmoi mystery. But if I get *Leon* to send deuxmoi a photo of this whole situation, and repost *that* screenshot with his name blocked out . . . then everyone will think I just got a tip, that I'm not an on-the-ground source.

I turn to Leon and lay it out, plain. "I'm going to the bathroom," I say.

"You're leaving *now*?"

I shake my head. "While I'm gone, I want you to take a photo of them dry humping. Then DM it to me from your account."

I can practically see the wheels turning in his head as he figures out what I'm trying to do.

"Then you'll post it."

"On-the-ground reporting."

Leon lets out an exasperated sigh. "This is the opposite of not getting tangled up in your deuxmoi mess."

"Shh!" I hiss when he says the account's name. "Come on," I say. "No one will know it's you. I'll obviously block out your name. I just need something to screenshot."

Leon takes a sip from his drink and frowns in my direction. But then he says the magic word: "Fine."

I wrap my arms around his neck and plant a kiss on his cheek before dashing off to the nearest restroom.

"You owe me!" he calls after me.

I squeeze past a crew of young women in wide-leg pants and bucket hats, reapplying lipstick at the mirror, and lock myself inside a stall, where I wait for Leon's message.

It only takes a minute before he comes through.

> Nate Clyburn and the One Percent cast are getting ROWDY at the Bowery Hotel bar rn. Rumors are true: they all seem to be obsessed with each other! But PSA, I literally saw with my own two eyes Nate and Iris making out and being flirty with each other on the dance floor. They are def together in some capacity, and honestly, they are soooooo cute. Really hope it's legit.

Then the pic comes in. I clasp my hand over my mouth to hold back a laugh. Leon was right. They're practically fucking. She's got him pinned against one of the dark padded walls, one knee wrapped around his hip. You can see Iris's tongue halfway into Nate's mouth and his shirt is all the way unbuttoned, completely open, while she grabs at his waist. His hand is burrowed between her legs, disappearing under her skirt.

Leon messages again.

> Anon pls.

Perfect. I share it, followed by screenshots of the other DMs I received earlier about the whole *One Percent* cast throwdown.

Leon shoots me a text, clearly having just seen my posts. *Happy? Let's get the fuck out of here before anyone spots us.*

Back over on IG, the DMs are already coming in, full of shock and elation. A few people say they're rushing down here as we speak, which kind of makes me uneasy. I make a mental note to tell the bouncer they're about to get flooded with fans and to tighten up security. I scan the messages until I see a recent one from a blue-check account. Their bio says they work in the hair and makeup department at *One Percent* and have a slew of other production credits.

> Damn! Glad to see they went public with it. Honestly, they're cute as hell on set. Everyone at One Percent knows they're an item. Anon pls.

> Good for Iris!!! Word out here is that Nate loves taking trips downtown (ahem ahem). He made my BFF a frittata the morning after they met at Mike's. Swoon.

I share that one, too, and send the artist a thank-you DM before stuffing my phone in my pocket and heading back to meet Leon out front, where I'll treat him to one last drink before calling it a night.

Mark Cronen, co-host: Good morning, daily dirties! It's your host Mark Cronen here to fill you in on the most delectable pieces of goss you may have missed over the weekend. Let's start with one of the hottest stories setting Hollywood ablaze right now: the rumors that *One Percent* co-stars Nate Clyburn and Iris Leonard are actually a thing. The two were spotted together at the Bowery Hotel bar this weekend with the rest of the cast, and they were photographed making out all over the place.

Penelope Richtor, co-host: No one in either camp will comment directly, but they were spotted looking super cozy . . . and low-key hot! And! Heavy!

Mark: Let's be blunt. They were sucking face!

Penelope: Excuse me? They were basically making babies!

Mark: The sightings were first reported on deuxmoi, an anonymous Instagram account that shares blind items and tips to the account.

Penelope: Mark, are you as obsessed with deuxmoi as I am? I can't stop refreshing it. I'm living for Sunday spotteds, where they post everything insane that happened over the weekend.

Mark: Yes. I am obsessed. Deuxmoi, whoever you are, I need more of you in my life.

Penelope: Should we go to Via Carota so we can be spotted? Or so we can send in some tips? We need her to be our friend.

Mark: Deuxmoi, get at us!!!!!

Penelope: We'll give you comped tickets to our comedy show next Tuesday at the Bell House!

Mark: Wait. Is this the new sign that you've *made it*—if you appear on deuxmoi?

Penelope: Oh, definitely. You're no one until you've been featured.

Mark: Note to all the dirties out there: Pen and I need to be on deuxmoi. If you see us out, please, for the love of god, snap a pic and send it in.

Penelope: Mark, you make us sound so desperate.

Mark: We *are* desperate!

CHAPTER 10

It only takes a few weeks before deuxmoi takes over my life completely. Whereas my weekly routine used to consist of a leisurely morning of exercise, coffee, and getting to work on time, I'm now spending every waking moment looking at the account, responding to DMs, and trying to suss out which sources are actually credible. But I've also tried to make the whole endeavor a bit more professional, a bit more . . . legit.

Even with all his whining, Leon offered up his high-level design skills and made me a simple but smart logo, which now adorns the site and the Insta account as its profile picture. I also set up an email address and a very low-budget website that has an email form so people can send tips to me that way, too, without giving their real information. After I add it to the profile and share info about the tip links in stories, my inbox is flooded with more blinds than I can count. But reading through ones sent from "fuckitup@gmail.com" and "biebergetsmewet@yourmom.edu" makes me realize there's no way to verify any of these when so many are sent from obviously fake email addresses.

Before posting any of them, I try to weigh the pros and cons of sharing that kind of information—sure, it can be really entertaining and kind of hilarious, but there's literally no way to know if they're real. At least when people DM me from their real IG accounts, I can message them back and ask for details that help me confirm what they're saying, which I often do.

After hemming and hawing for over twenty-four hours, I decide that I won't post any of the super-fucked-up stories, like the ones about a certain pop star snorting lines on a table at Swan in Miami. But for the other ones, anecdotes about who sold a stolen screenplay and casting news and which beloved country star secretly loves to hit the strip clubs in Nashville . . . those are harmless, especially if I block out names. Instead of throwing up the emails on the account with no context, I decide to write out a disclaimer template that I'll share every time I post screenshots of emails.

After getting stoned and watching an old Meg Ryan movie, I'm inspired to call the series "You've Got Fucking Mail!" Then I type out a slide that explains how I have no way of verifying the tips and everyone should take them with a grain of salt—*or* write in to share if they know any additional details. The followers are so fired up about this that they start turning the emails into a sleuthing game, DMing me with additional pieces of info that confirm or deny the rumors. When I post their responses, it starts to feel like a conversation, like we're all on the hunt for the truth together. A few people thank me for my transparency, and I know I made the right call even though that whole situation absolutely destroys my sleeping schedule and keeps me up until 1:00 a.m.

And yet, I can't seem to stay asleep past 6:00 a.m., when I jolt awake, desperate to figure out what I missed overnight. At work, I feel like a spy, hunching over my phone, which is nestled in between my knees under my desk. I'm desperate for Sasha not to see and find any excuse to rush off to the bathroom or pop out around the corner to get her lunch. And on the weekends, it's a bit easier, since I spend most of the days at home, learning and relearning who and what the followers care about. Which stars are hungry to share gossip of their own.

Sundays are the best, though, when I unleash an explosion of sightings. Hundreds of them that followers have come to love, waiting patiently all throughout the week. I've already broken a few pieces of actual news, too—a late-night star who has been known to have a wandering eye marrying a legit A-lister in a small ceremony outside of New York City; a few fresh collab lines from reality TV stars and talk show hosts; a former boy bander turned legitimate heartthrob is now dating his older, maybe-still-married film producer; and that one of the most famous rappers in the world and his reality-star-slash-business-mogul wife are divorcing.

Each piece of news, like actual real news, gives me a little jolt of satisfaction. I've never had a desire to be a journalist, but I can see how breaking stories like this can become addicting. Knowing things first. Confirming what's right. The rush of the chase. But there's a certain sense of responsibility that comes with sharing this kind of information, one I'm just starting to understand.

What's been most surprising to me is that so many tipsters write in about non-A-listers. Sure, there have been blind items about Duke Dudley and other Oscar winners, as well as requests for information about beloved pop stars with nostalgic factors like Kayla Cole. But most of the truly vile, most egregious stories are about the celebrity-adjacent folks, the people who are desperate for fame, hungry to stay in the spotlight.

People like celebrity chefs who sexually harass waitresses in their own restaurants but claim to support pay equity when called to address Congress, all-star agents who still send their clients into meetings with directors who are known abusers, and, of course, a certain former reality TV show judge who treats her staff like trash cans.

Yep. Someone wrote in about Sasha. Fucking. Sherman.

I was shocked when I received the first tip about her two weeks ago. It was short and sweet, claiming that "the woman who used to judge *Collection* was known for being the worst stylist to work with . . . pushy and abrasive and lazy." I didn't post it because it wasn't that interesting or specific. But this morning, while I'm chugging a cup of coffee in my kitchen, still in my pajamas with unbrushed teeth, I receive a message from someone with a super familiar name: Eleanor Cauley Rhodes. It only takes me a little scrolling through her profile to realize I recognize her from my job interview with Sasha eight full years ago. Back then, she was just Eleanor Cauley.

I remember her being so thin I could see her collarbones peeking out of her black cotton tee. She was disheveled and dejected, with dark circles under her eyes and hands that shook when she handed me a plastic water bottle. When I had my closed-door meeting with Sasha, she spent a good fifteen minutes complaining about Eleanor and how "clumsy, dumb, idiotic, brain-dead, and anorexic" she was. All that trash talk should have been an immediate red flag.

It wasn't clear if Eleanor had been fired or quit, but when she walked me out, back toward the elevator, she grabbed my wrist for just a second and opened her mouth. She didn't say anything, just stared at me with her lips parted like a dead fish. No words came out, but her eyes gave me a look that said *run*. Sometimes I wish I had listened.

Peering at her account now, I see she looks good. Healthy and strong and totally different, with long blond hair set in mermaid waves. In most of her photos, she wears loose-fitting, no-name work-out clothes in neutral colors, and her bio says she works as a Pilates instructor in Savannah, Georgia. Her account is littered with yoga phrases that mean nothing, information about her teaching schedule, smoothie bowl recipes, and pictures of her husband, a rugged man who looks like he goes camping and wears a lot of cargo shorts. She has a few hundred followers and a rescue mutt named Charlie. She looks happy.

The message, though, nearly makes me choke on my coffee.

BLOCK MY NAME OUT PLEASE!!!!! But the people have to know: That stylist everyone loves from her reality TV show days is a fucking nightmare. She treats her employees like garbage. One time, she had her assistant walk her dog and screamed at them because her dog "didn't seem tired" after the walk. She never returns the clothes she borrows from designers and even charges clients for her own personal items. Everyone thinks she still has a chokehold on the industry but people HATE working with her. If you're not an A-lister she doesn't GAF about you. If she didn't have that one big client, she'd be out of business. Too bad she also has a habit of pimping out her underlings to that same big client. SUPER ANON!

Good for you, Eleanor, I think as I press reply and thank her for writing in.

Sounds like a nightmare, I say. But when I read her message again, the *pimping out* language makes me pause, and I feel a ball of nerves form in my stomach. What exactly does she mean? What did Sasha *do*?

Eleanor responds immediately. *She is. Leaving her and New York was the best thing I ever did.*

Her message gives my stomach another little jolt, a confused feeling about what I'm doing, still here in Sasha's clutches, when people like Eleanor got out. Found new lives.

But I know I'd never be happy being a workout instructor in Savannah. Her future is not mine, I remind myself.

Okay to share?

She gives me a thumbs-up and writes, *People have to put two and two together. She's a monster enabler. Worst I ever encountered.*

I share the screenshot and set my phone down as I slather moisturizer on my face and try to finish the rest of my getting-ready routine as quickly as I can. But when I check the account, I see there are dozens of replies to Eleanor's comments, chiming in with similar Sasha stories. They know *exactly* who Eleanor is talking about. I recognize a few as former interns, people who endured her wrath just so they could have Styling by Sasha on their résumé.

I share one about how Sasha screamed at an intern for leaving a shoot to go to her grandmother's funeral, and quickly call an Uber so I can head to work, vowing to expense it yet again. As I rush downstairs and hop into the car, my phone pings with a text from Leon.

> You've gone way too far . . . she's gonna know it's someone in her orbit. You're flying too close to the fucking sun here and I don't like it!!! Are you trying to get us both fired as fuck?

I shake my head even though he can't see me. *I'll ask for more stylist stories*, I say, the idea coming to me as I type. *Bury the tips. Plus, it's not like these ones SAY "Sasha."*

Leon responds immediately. *I guess she's not the only rage-aholic in the industry. But that funeral one . . . we all know it's her.*

Then he sends another text: *This shit better not come back to me, babe.*

I grip my phone and try not to be annoyed, but I can't help it. There are only so many ways I can say "this is not about you," so instead I just write, *It's going to be fine. No one has any idea.*

Leon sends me some side-eye emojis, and I head back over to Instagram to refresh the feed and see that I have a few dozen new followers. One of them makes me pause.

Alyssa.

My stomach flips, and I wonder if she'll alert Sasha to what I've just posted. I don't know whose side she might be on. Leon's right. I should probably spread the wealth and post about Sasha's peers, too.

Sourcing more stylist content works, and pretty soon I've got enough messages about Sasha's asshole contemporaries to run a twenty-slide story, which I try to post as fast as possible before I arrive at the office.

> One stylist to the stars used to not pay her interns but would make them work from 8 am to 1 am. She wouldn't let them eat craft services at shoots, either!

> My old boss used to style HUGE actors for the Oscars, etc. She would make us lay out money and say she'd reimburse us but would take months to get us our money back for things like gas and parking. If she forgot about a charge, she'd DECLINE the Venmo request and we'd be shit outta luck.

> Stylist stories yessss. When I worked in fashion, I had hangers thrown at my head on the reg. Once my boss asked me to create fake invoices to charge a client more.

> I went to a few Met Gala fittings this week. Celebrity stylists are going under the table and making money off their celebrity clients. Sooo handbag/jewelry/accessory companies are paying these SHADY stylists to have their celebs wear these smaller brands without the knowledge of the designer and talent. LOTS OF MONEY. And they are being extremely shady about it, handing things off like a fucking drug deal. I work in PR and this is not PR. this is GREED. There is one stylist that is particularly horrible. I will spill in a week or two.

DEUXMOI.

> This particular stylist talks so much shit behind her clients' backs and then acts all BFF with them on IG. She wants ALL the credit for her clients' coveted street style looks and gets soooo pissed when the clients don't name her in interviews. Oh, she also calls the paps every time her client steps out the front door to make sure her looks get photographed.

There. That should do it.

I exhale a puff of air as I charge through the office, making a beeline for my seat so I can start getting Sasha's schedule ready for the day. But as soon as she arrives, it's clear she knows what's been on the account, even though I *know* she's not following it. She stomps through the floor, wearing a floral Ulla Johnson dress with puff sleeves and metallic Dior platforms, her face beet red. I wonder if Alyssa told her. Or if Nelly let it slip in the kitchenette again. It's a Friday, thank god, so I'm staring at the clock, just waiting for it to tick down. It's around 5:00 when I hear Sasha finally mention deuxmoi to Alyssa from inside her office, the door wide open.

"Whoever runs that account *must* work in fashion," she says with a snarl. "I wish it weren't illegal to torture people. I'd get everyone in this office to talk like that." She snaps her fingers in front of her face.

"It's not that bad," Alyssa says, exasperated. "We don't even know they're about you."

Leon walks by and purses his lips at me in an exaggerated manner. But I just keep my head down, hoping Sasha won't pay me much attention.

The saving grace is that Sasha would never own up to her behavior in public. Even though we all know how awful she can be—can spot those stories from a mile away—she'd never admit that they were about her. That would mean acknowledging what she was doing was *bad*.

"No," Sasha continues, wagging her index finger at Alyssa. "I'd sue them. There must be some legal action to take, right? That little bitch would have to lawyer up *real* fucking fast."

My insides go icy when my phone erupts with a text from Victoria in the group chat. *Drinks tonight? Jake is taking the kids to his parents' house in Westchester. Said I should go out tomorrow and have the night to myself!!!!!!!*

Hundo percent yes, Leon says. *Can Giuseppe come? Pleassseeee?*

I pick up my phone and start typing. *Sounds good.* I look up to see Alyssa stomping back to her office, her fists clenched by her side. *And yes to Giuseppe. I think I need some legal advice . . .*

CHAPTER 11

By the time Leon and I get to the bar at the Crosby Street Hotel, Giuseppe and Victoria have already grabbed a table in the back. They're facing each other, their heads almost touching over the table. Martinis sit in front of them both, and Victoria's laughing at something Giuseppe just said.

Leon always likes to say we are a perfect foursome, that when we go out together, there are no bad seats. But the truth is that Giuseppe and I have rarely, if ever, spent time alone together. The two of them double-date with Victoria and Jake regularly. They've traveled together to go skiing in Aspen or to a villa in Mustique. I was supposed to join them for that last one, but I had to bail after I caught the flu from Sasha, who sneezed in my face and didn't cover her mouth.

I was devastated to miss the trip, especially when they all came back, chatting about how Giuseppe and Victoria bonded over their shared love of stand-up paddleboarding. I just said a silent prayer that Jake had no interest in being part of our little crew as a regular member, meaning I didn't have to play fifth wheel *that* often.

But I try not to care. Especially because ever since Giuseppe came into the picture two years ago, Leon's been so freaking happy. Victoria's desperate for them to get married, but Leon thinks the whole concept is so "boring and hetero."

Leon rushes over to the table and slides in next to Giuseppe, giving him a tender kiss on his clean-shaven cheek. I do the same to Victoria, who throws an arm around my shoulder. I lean back and see she's wearing a silk turtleneck from Victoria Beckham tucked into matching slacks. Her hair's pulled back behind her ears, showing off diamond hoops.

"TGIF, am I right?" Victoria says, cheersing her glass into the air.

Leon looks at her, deadpan. "You've been spending too much time uptown if you actually just said those words out loud."

Victoria waves him off and drains her martini. She motions to the waitress, who's walking by. "Casamigos on the rocks for this one," she says, pointing to Leon. "Tito's and soda with a splash of pineapple," she says, thumbing over to me, "and another round for us."

The waitress looks bored but returns in a few minutes with our drinks, perfectly made.

Giuseppe picks his up. "Okay," he says. "*Now* we can cheers." We thrust our glasses into the center of the table, and he clears his throat. "Actually, I'd like to make a little toast." He holds his glass a bit higher, sloshing martini onto the cuff of his crisp white collared Mr P. shirt. "To Cricket."

"For what?" I ask. "Continuing to be Sasha's *bitch*?"

Giuseppe's eyebrows shoot up, and his mouth turns into a bit of a frown. "Hey, come on. Even though these two over here are fearing for their lives, it's pretty amazing that you've turned your little side project into a legit *thing*." My face flushes, and I try to wave him off, but Giuseppe insists. "*E! News* did a whole feature on the tip you posted last night, and I saw the *Daily Mail* did a whole story on one of your posts about Kanye."

"Which tip?" I ask.

"'Which tip'?" Victoria says a little too loudly. "Look at this honey! Too many hot tips to keep track of them all."

"Oh yes, the one about who's going to be the new Marvel superhero." I remember now. A casting assistant slid into my DMs, 100 percent confirming the rumor that the kid from all those Netflix rom-coms was taking over the role. Once all those fandom blogs got wind of the news, the fallout was wide and I gained a ton of new followers who are obsessed with superheroes.

Giuseppe slams his hand down on the table. "You're like Woodward and Bernstein if they had Instagram and cared about beautiful people. And nobody knows but us."

Leon takes a swig of tequila and sets the glass down on the table hard. "Let's just keep it that way," he says, giving me a knowing glance.

"Let it go, babe," I tell him. "No one at work knows. No one else on the entire planet knows."

"You can't blame me for being nervous," Leon says. "I busted my ass to get promoted. You of all people know how hard it is to succeed in this shitty industry." He nods to Victoria, to Giuseppe. "We don't have Jake money or law degrees. I just don't want you to fuck up your life. Or mine."

Something stings inside my chest, but I know where he's coming from. He's put everything he has into his job, just like I have. And let's be real, he has more to lose than I do since he's an actual stylist. But all I want is for him to realize that my actions aren't going to affect him. Even if I am found out, it won't come back to bite him.

But I know Leon well enough to know that there's no use bringing all that up now. Instead, I let myself enjoy the praise from Giuseppe and the fact that at least here I can talk freely about what I've been up to the past two months. It's our secret, and man, it feels juicy.

"So, cheers to you," Giuseppe says. "We ordered a little something extra to celebrate." The waitress comes over with a big tray of oysters, served on the half shell over ice.

"Thank you, G," I say, really meaning it, and under the table, even Leon squeezes my hand in a truce, at least for the time being. Soon, Victoria changes the subject and we spend the next few hours talking about everything and nothing before Victoria starts yawning and excuses herself to get an Uber XL back uptown.

Giuseppe and Leon are about to peel off back to their place in the Village when I suddenly remember why I wanted Giuseppe here in the first place. I rest my hand on his shoulder.

"Legal advice," I say, turning to him.

"Come again, darling?" he says, a little drunk.

"I overheard Sasha talking about how she was going to sue deuxmoi for defamation. Is that a thing I need to be worried about? Can she like . . . subpoena whoever runs it?"

Giuseppe shrugs his shoulders into his leather jacket from Ralph Lauren and twists his mouth up like he's thinking. Then he shakes his head. "Well, you have that language in your bio, right? The one I suggested when you first started?"

I nod.

Leon pulls on Giuseppe's hand. "Come on, babe. We gotta take Kylie out for a walk." He starts walking to the door and Giuseppe looks back at me, concerned.

"What are you worried about, really?" he asks.

"That I could be in a huge amount of legal trouble," I say. "That she could find out it's me and I'd be fucked, personally."

He nods, thinking it over. "Did you start an LLC or an S-Corp or something?"

I shake my head. "What?"

"Like a business entity. Did you start one? Pay the website server fees through it? That kind of thing?"

"Uh, no."

Giuseppe nods. "Do that. If you run all the business through a company, you don't have personal liability. Plus, no one will know it's you."

"Shit," I say. "How long does that take?"

Leon tugs on Giuseppe's jacket. "The pup's waiting!"

Giuseppe leans in to kiss me on the cheek. "Only a few days to get one sorted. Call me Monday, I'll find someone who can set it up for you. We'll just need your address, Social Security, and a few things like that."

"But that's, like, all my identifying information."

He waves his hand. "Don't worry, only your address becomes public. Besides, who the fuck is going to look up the business account's *address* to find you? Psycho behavior."

He kind of has a point.

"Don't worry. You're safe."

I throw my arms around him and press my face into his chest. "I fucking love you," I say. When I pull back, I wave at them as they walk hand in hand west, up toward the Hudson River.

The air is warm but finally cooling off, exactly how a perfect summer night in New York *should* feel. I spy a gaggle of underage girls huddled on the corner, swaying back and forth on their high heels, laughing at some secret inside joke. The air smells like greasy pizza and crisp leaves, of all the New York possibilities.

By the time I get back to the safety of my home and open Instagram, I find about seventy-five new unread messages in my inbox that have appeared since I left for drinks. I scan the list for familiar names—people who have become regular sources, waiters at celeb-friendly restaurants, trainers at Barry's Bootcamp, C-list actors looking to control their narratives.

No one really stands out except for one verified user I don't think I've seen before. Some guy named Ollie Snyder. I tap it open and read. The message is bland, one I'd scroll past and delete if there wasn't a blue checkmark next to his name.

> Love what you've been doing. We should work together. I've got ideas.

But when I click on his profile, I'm intrigued. Based on his picture, he's hot. Like fucked-up Los Angeles–level hot. Promising. I scan his bio.

> British born. LA made.

Okay, barf.

But then I see the next line.

> Former rugby star, current Elaborate editor in chief.

Huh. *Elaborate* is one of the oldest entertainment magazines in existence, known for breaking news and getting exclusives on casting and first-looks. Even if it's not as popular as it was in its heyday during the nineties, it's still got a vise grip on the industry. If they confirm one of my rumors, everyone knows it's legit.

But . . . if this dude works in entertainment media, he might actually be useful to me. And if he wants to work together, I wonder what that might mean. I tap back to his message and start typing.

> Oh yeah? How?

He reads it almost immediately, and my heart rate spikes. Jesus. I gotta get my shit together if I'm starting to think that DMing with a seemingly hot guy as an anonymous gossip blogger counts as flirting. I haven't wanted to fuck a guy I chatted with on Instagram since I hooked up with Harvey Weinstein's assistant a zillion years ago in the bathroom at some rooftop party in Tribeca. His phone was blowing up with demands from Harvey during foreplay.

You've got a valuable thing going here, Ollie says. *I'm totally intrigued. Elaborate could maybe even learn a thing or two from you. We should talk sometime. Call me.* He leaves his phone number, with a Los Angeles area code, and I wonder if I should just pick up my phone and give him a ring. I start to dial the numbers, but something stops me.

I can't lose all sense of security because a random hot dude slides into my DMs. If this is what's happening right now, I need to get laid. Immediately.

Plus, he probably really just does want to talk about working together. Maybe he has some sources he wants to connect me with. Maybe he wants *me* to be a source for him. After all, *Elaborate* was once the most popular entertainment magazine in the world back when weeklies dominated the industry. But now, even I know that *Elaborate* is kind of floundering, losing out to digital-first outlets and Instagram accounts, who post faster, with more frequency and a stronger voice. Obviously, there will always be people who trust mags like *Elaborate*, and the editors behind them, more than secret accounts like mine, but . . . social media is very obviously forcing them to level up their game.

I read his message again, this time with a bit more skepticism. What if he's working on a story about me? What if he's just trying to expose me? Get me to slip? If that's the case, there's no way in hell I'm going to call this guy—at least not from my personal phone number.

I need a burner phone or a Google Voice number—something that can't be traced back to me, especially since my number is out there, tied to things like my barely used Facebook or my PayPal.

In the time it takes to register for a Google line, I craft a response to Ollie. Something casual that keeps the door open. Easy, breezy, but kind of professional. Simple. I draft it in the Google Voice app and read the words over, feeling ridiculous that I'm caring this much. Then I bite my lip, feeling the vodka rush to my head, and paste in his number.

Hey. It's deuxmoi. Let's talk here.

Elaborate.com

At *One Percent* Premiere, Anonymous Instagram Account Is All Anyone Can Talk About

As your devoted party reporter, I often spend my days flitting from one fete to another, on the prowl for little nuggets of gold, overheard in line for the bathroom. But at the recent premiere of *One Percent*'s new season, hosted by HBO at the Chateau Marmont, there was only one word on everyone's lips: deuxmoi.

The anonymous Instagram account has been posting sometimes mild, sometimes wild pieces of celebrity gossip for about three months now and nearly every conversation I inserted myself into began with the question "Do you follow deuxmoi?"

For now, no one seems to know who's behind the account—and no one seems to care. When asked why it was so fun to watch her stories, *One Percent* star Iris Leonard told *Elaborate*, "Who doesn't love a little gossip here and there? I'm not above it. And clearly neither are you."

Though she *does* make regular appearances on the account, often in a favorable light. We have to ask . . . Iris, are you deux?!

CHAPTER 12

I wake up bleary-eyed and immediately check to see if there are any additional texts from Ollie. The last thing I remember is curling up with my phone, with an old sitcom on my TV, watching our chat grow longer and longer as we texted about nothing—movies we like, celebs who interest us, what kind of books he likes to read. Within a few hours, it felt like I was texting with an old friend, someone who was down to teach me a few things without the whole condescending-mansplainer vibes. His last message must have come in right after I went to bed.

> You're fucking smart, you know that?

I roll over as a warm feeling spreads throughout my chest. No guy has ever told me I was smart before, and in all honesty that's a bigger compliment than being called hot. Plus, it sure beats waking up wondering if Doug, the fuckboy orthodontist, hit me up the night before.

Before I dive in to looking at deuxmoi, I tap over to my email to see what kind of shit-show tips came in overnight. But the first email in my inbox makes me sit up in bed.

From: kjohns@johnsglobalmedia.com

To: Deuxmoi@gmail.com

Date: August 5, 2022, 4:05 a.m. ET

Subject: Let's talk

> Hey,
> I love what you've built here and think we could work really
> well together. Are you monetizing at all? Feel like there's a
> big opportunity here . . . Hit me up anytime.
>
> Kyle Johns
> CEO Johns Global Media

I read the message again, pausing on the word "monetize." This guy sounds familiar, but I can't quite place him yet. Probably some sort of big talker trying to get a piece of whatever the hell it is I'm doing with deuxmoi.

I do a quick Google search of his name and realize why I recognized it. Kyle Johns. He's that guy who launched the women's media company a few years ago, even though he's a middle-aged white guy known for being a playboy in the uptown Manhattan scene. His bread-and-butter site is a lifestyle website, with classic clickbait stories about celebrities and fashion, but in recent years it's been making a move into investigative journalism, with hard-hitting features about politics, policy, and business—and really excellent profiles. They often write up *my* stories as news, and I have a soft spot for them since they always link back to deuxmoi and aren't shy about naming me as the original source. A rarity, I've learned.

According to one *New York Times* article, he's hoping to take Johns Global Media public and is looking to acquire more assets before doing so. No wonder he sees something in deuxmoi. He's probably looking for ways for it to complement his other properties—a mommy blogger site, a home cooking channel, a beauty brand.

But what does this mean for *me*?

I dash off a quick response, deciding to keep it short and sweet. I don't want to give up the fact that I haven't really even started thinking about making money off the account—especially if he views me as someone who might be easily swayed into signing some deal I barely understand. Best to pretend I've thought this through as much as he seems to have.

> Happy to speak with you. What do you have in mind?

I send it off and then refresh my phone, surprised to see a response so fast.

> CC'ing my assistant to schedule us on a call. In the meantime, curious: Is this your full-time job?

I respond back, *Nope.*
He replies.

> Feels like you could make a killing if you did this 100% of the time. Based on what I've read about you, you could get some serious cash via investors. Unless you have an incredible day job, which if so, great! But I quit my day job in consulting to go full-time building Johns Global Media. Sometimes you gotta take a risk to join the big boys . . . More soon.

I read the message again and wonder, for the first time, if I've been viewing the account all wrong. Maybe it's not just a distraction—something to fill the time and help me gain a sense of confidence, of purpose. Maybe, just maybe . . . it's a way out.

...

On Monday, I'm standing in line at the French café down the block from the office, reciting Sasha's lunch order over and over in my head. Niçoise salad, no egg, no dressing, no potatoes. No fun. Every time I order it, the guy behind the counter winces a little and says in perfect French, "*Quel dommage.*"

Once they left the dressing inside the takeout container in a little plastic cup and I didn't notice until I set it down in front of Sasha. She chucked the whole box at my head and screamed, "I said *no* dressing! Not *dressing on the side!*" But thankfully I ducked so the viscous liquid got on the concrete floor and not my dry-clean-only Ganni sweater. I had worn it that day for a meeting I thought she might let me attend. It was only mildly humiliating when I had to get on my hands and knees and scrub away the Dijon mustard vinaigrette while she stepped over my hunched back to escort the reps from Gucci down the hallway to the conference room.

When I approach the counter and recite my order, the cashier and I do our little dance—"*Quel dommage*"—before he wiggles his fingers toward the pickup area, where I can wait.

I pick at my nails and my mind wanders back to the email I received over the weekend from Kyle Johns. We have a call set up for later this week to discuss whatever it is he's plotting, and I can't help but feel a buzzing in my stomach whenever I think of doing something bigger with deuxmoi. Maybe he's right. Maybe I do need a partner, or someone with business experience, to help me figure out how to use the account in the right way. But right now, I don't even know if I *want* that.

The bell jingles on the door, and I glance up just in time to see a former member of the *Real Housewives of New York* step inside. She's wearing a leather baseball hat over her stick-straight hair and an Aviator Nation sweatsuit under a leather jacket. I think about taking out my phone and trying to snap a pic to post on deuxmoi, but before I can do that, she pulls her hat down low over her head and pops open the door on the drink fridge near the entrance. She pulls out a Juice Press bottle of Ginger Fireball and I wait for her to get in line to pay. But instead of hopping behind the line of UPPAbaby strollers, she tucks the juice into her oversized Celine tote and walks right out the door.

My jaw drops open as I realize I just watched a washed-up reality star shoplift a ten-dollar juice for seemingly no reason. I shake my head and try not to laugh as I type out an email to deuxmoi on my phone, so I can post it later.

> Former fan fave on RHONYC spotted stealing a freaking juice at Bonjour Café in SoHo. Bitch, WHY?????

Just as I hit send, my phone erupts and Sasha's name appears on my screen. *Shit.* According to her schedule, she should still be in a meeting with Alyssa and the other senior stylists, so if she's calling now, that can't be a good thing. I clench my phone in my hand, the sides digging into my palm, and pick up, bracing myself for her angry tone to fill my earbuds.

"Where the fuck are you?" she says hurriedly.

"Getting your lunch. It should be ready in—"

"Lunch? You idiot, I'm intermittent fasting."

I want to say, *Well, you specifically texted me this morning asking me to pick up your lunch so it would be sitting on your desk at 12:15 p.m. on the dot,* but she hates excuses. The best thing to do when this shit happens is to pretend like it's my fault. Minimal fallout.

"Oh crap, Sasha, I'm *soooo* sorry." They call my name and I grab the paper bag, rushing out the door. "I'll be back in five," I say through huffs and puffs, trying not to dwell on the twenty-five bucks I just spent on this salad, thinking I'd be reimbursed.

She grunts. "Run your ass off this time. We need to get the deck together to send to Duke's team for award season."

I bite my tongue and don't mention the fact that I sent her this exact deck to approve three weeks ago. I'll simply print it out and give it to her as soon as I get back.

"You got it?" she practically screams.

"Got it." She hangs up without a goodbye, and I sprint the final few blocks, the joyless salad jostling up and down in its bag.

But I know I have to keep running. Duke's someone we drop everything for.

Including this salad, apparently, which has now spilled out onto the street. Green beans bounce in traffic and I give up, cursing the disappointed Frenchman who definitely didn't seal the lid properly just to spite this sad salad order. I don't even blame him, but I *do* want to scream over my shoulder, *I like dressing! I like potatoes! I even like eggs! It's for my shitty boss!*

I toss the now-empty bag in the trash in front of our office and pull the door open as hard as I can. There's a line for the elevator, so I bolt for the stairs in the back of the lobby and take them two at a time.

When I get up to our floor and sink into my office chair, I can't help but glance at my phone, hidden under my desk. There are a ton of Instagram notifications, but there are also two messages from Ollie, who must be starting his day on the West Coast.

Can't stop thinking about what you said, he writes. *That there was a void in the market in terms of celeb content. You're filling it obviously.*

Warmth spreads throughout my chest.

I want you to feel free to hit me up if you need help on the "is this legit?" front, he writes.

What do you mean? I respond.

He wastes no time answering. *Like if you need to figure out if a tip is bogus or not. I've been in this swamp for twenty years. I have sources and contacts people would kill for.*

I smirk. *Honestly, I do, too.*

Touché, he says. But then another message appears.

> But it's hard to suss out who's giving you real talk and who's blowing smoke up your ass. Trust me. If you ever need a second opinion I'm here.

> How do I know YOU'RE not blowing smoke up my ass?

> Guess you'll have to trust me on that one . . .

I send him a thinking-face emoji and lift my gaze for a second to glance at my email, only to see a note from Sasha saying she'll be back in the office in ten. Shit.

I stuff my phone away, deep in my bag, before getting back to the reason I sprinted to the office in the first place. It only takes me a few minutes to print out the deck for Duke and place it on Sasha's desk in a black leather folder. Alyssa walks by just as I'm leaving Sasha's office, my heart rate finally slowing down to a normal pace.

"That the Duke deck?" she asks, the usual warmth gone from her voice.

"Yep," I say. "Resort season, then all those for-your-consideration press events. I think he's got Oscar odds again." I look down at his file, open on my laptop. "Oh yeah, he's also in that Regency TV show, *The Viscounts*. Sounds like it's going to be big."

Alyssa nods curtly and heads back toward her office. Weird.

I plop down at my desk and refresh my email. Sasha *should* be here according to her last message, but based on her location, which I begged her to share with me after I tried to find her for four hours for a last-minute meeting with Ernesto, only to find out she was at the spa down on Wall Street getting a lymphatic drainage treatment, it looks like she's stuck in traffic, definitely not ten minutes away. Liar.

I pull out my phone and prop it up on my knees, under my desk and out of sight, and open the deuxmoi email account.

There are a lot of the usual sightings and casting news, but then there's one that makes me pause.

I tap it open and start reading.

8/8/22

Sent via form submission from <u>Deuxmoi</u>

Pseudonyms, Please: Dutchess Fudley
Subject: Not looking good for this A-lister

I have it on good authority that a beloved Oscar winner will probably be recast in the highly anticipated Regency romance series. It's supposed to start filming this summer. No idea why but people close to the studio think he's seen better days. No one wants to announce before award season kicks off, since he's got the supporting actor statue in the bag (another WWII role! Shocker!) and the film's from the same studio that's financing the show. But they'll prob break the news in the spring. Prove me right, DM!

My heart tugs a bit for Duke. He's always been one of Sasha's better-behaved clients and has sent me a two-thousand-dollar gift card every single holiday season, along with a handwritten note thanking me for helping to make him look good. His team is kind, too, a major rarity in this industry. Whenever his publicist Allison calls, she makes sweet small talk and asks me if I'm "hanging in there," like she knows what a major asshole Sasha is. She once caught me crying on the street outside a photoshoot in Meatpacking. Sasha had promised I could attend and help out with steaming clothes, but then she decided I didn't look presentable enough when I showed up wearing high-top Vans. "You don't work for Brad Goreski, for Christ's sake!" she'd said.

Allison witnessed the whole thing and bought me an iced coffee and a cookie, squeezed my hand, and gave me the number of another stylist she likes who she heard was kinder to assistants. I never got up the courage to make the call, thinking Sasha would sabotage me if I ever tried to leave her tight grasp. But I haven't forgotten Allison's kindness, especially when so many people in this business pretend you're invisible unless you have your name on a building or a mile-long IMDb credit list.

Bet they'd all fall over in shock if they realized some longtime assistant had the power to share this kind of gossip with a few hundred thousand people in an instant.

But I know posting this kind of story about Duke, one that's basically innocuous, is probably a good idea if I want Sasha to keep thinking that it's run by someone outside her office. Sasha would never think that an in-house employee would post about Duke, since harming his reputation could harm our own—or even our bottom line. So, I do what has become so natural, my fingers leading the way with muscle memory: I take a screenshot and share with the followers.

PopNews

Duke Dudley Recast in Regency Romance?
So Says Deuxmoi

Academy Award winner Duke Dudley likely to be recast in Eliana Gilbert's forthcoming Regency romance series, *The Viscounts*, according to everyone's favorite gossip Insta account, deuxmoi. "No idea why but people close to the studio think he's seen better days," said the tipster who sent deuxmoi the blind item that was obviously about Dudley.

No doubt we can't believe everything we hear on the almighty anonymous IG, especially when they come in via email, as longtime followers will know, but the account has been right about a bajillion other casting decisions this season: Fox's choice to pick a no-name to be the next Wonder Woman, CBS's call to hire *Friends* star Matt LeBlanc to host their next big game show, and ABC's plan to tap an NBA point guard as its next Bachelor. So . . . we're gonna believe her on this one. (We reached out to the studio for comment and they did not respond. Dudley's publicist Allison Brent didn't respond either.)

Dudley got his start on network TV dramas like *Lincoln High*, where he played a high school quarterback, but he hit it big five years ago when he starred in *Spy Games*, which earned him his first Oscar. He's only done films since then, and *The Viscounts* was supposed to be his return to the small screen. (Netflix is rumored to have paid him eight figures!!!)

But Dudley's nonplussed, according to his Instagram account. Just yesterday he posted a shirtless selfie at a beach in Costa Rica, where he's filming a *Lincoln High* reunion special. He wrote, "Sunny days, can't complain."

Comments:

Dukehead456: Omg, Duke Dudley out of The Viscounts? I was counting down the days until I could whack off to this shit!

Lottie_iseeu: Boycotting Netflix until they recast him in The Viscounts!!!!

Spygamesfan101: Duke Dudley hive rise up!!!!!

Opalicon: Dude's got the best publicist in town to have everyone in the world thinking he's the boy next door. Smh when they find out who he really is

underthegun5nes: Unpopular opinion, but Duke Dudley should be canceled. Man's got a loooooot of skeletons in his closet that are just waiting to come out.

Kelleran1092: JUSTICE FOR DUKE DUDLEY!

ploppyesnw: Where's the studio on this? They should have made a statement by now 👀

starfuker59: idk why everyone's so in love with DD. He's . . . not a good guy

CHAPTER 13

I pick up my phone, preparing to dial, but hold my breath before pressing the numbers. I'm sitting cross-legged on my bed in my comfiest Free City sweats, after a day of running a lint roller over fifteen racks of clothing at the office. All I could think about was this call with Kyle Johns and what he might say—what it might mean. But thankfully, Sasha jetted out of the office around 2:00 p.m. and I lied to everyone else, saying I had a doctor's appointment so I could leave and take the call at home.

In between spurts of steam cleaning clothes, I spent most of my phone time googling Kyle and his previous ventures. There's a ton out there about him—interviews in financial magazines and media columns where he talks about how to turn fledgling blogs into actual, viable businesses. Last month, he apparently bought the rights to some URL that used to be a hipster blog and has plans to revitalize it as a new culture website.

He seems kind of corny, but maybe . . . maybe in a way that might be beneficial to me. In one interview he told a reporter that the one property he *didn't* have was a solid celebrity site, one that could *actually* make money. And based on our email exchange, he thinks mine might be able to.

But doing all this research also makes me think about what I might do if I did have all the resources to work on deuxmoi full-time. The account is still so new that there are a million directions I could take it, in a business sense.

Sure, I could build a website like all those other gossip brands out there. There could be blog posts and breaking news articles, social media posts that send readers to the site for clicks that generate ad revenue. But all of that seems . . . unappealing. I'm not sure it's the best use of my skills—or that I would even want to be beholden to metrics like that. What if it failed? What if *I* failed? I'm not a journalist. I'm not even a writer.

My brain is buzzing as I tap his number into my phone, taking extra care to call from my Google Voice line so he won't see my caller ID. He picks up on the first ring, eager and excited.

"I don't even know what to call you," he says. "Deux? Deuxmoi? Mystery media maven?" He laughs at his own non-joke and doesn't leave room for me to answer. "So glad we can finally connect."

"Likewise," I say, but before I can get anything else out, he starts again.

"I don't like small talk. Not a chitchat guy. I want to be blunt." Something hard sends a thwacking sound through the speaker and I wonder if he's bouncing a ball against the wall. "I don't just want to invest in deuxmoi. I want to buy deuxmoi. I want to turn your account into the most popular website on the internet, and I'm convinced we can do it in only a few months. Six, tops. I'm going to make you rich as fuck."

The line is so cornball I can't help but roll my eyes. I wait for him to continue, but he pauses and I wonder if he expects me to accept this vague non-offer right here on the spot.

"How?" I ask, leaning back against my headboard. "How are you going to make me rich as fuck?"

I hear him inhale on the other end. Was he not expecting me to ask a follow-up question?

"How?" he echoes.

"Yeah, how? It's not like digital media is making money off advertising like it used to," I say. "Plus, I have no interest in becoming the next TMZ. How would this be different? What are you *actually* offering?"

Kyle stutters on the other end. "Well . . ." he starts. "I've turned around dozens of media brands."

"But I'm not a media brand."

"In a sense—"

"And I don't need to be turned around."

"Yes," he says, with a little more confidence than before. "But you don't have a team. No legal, no finance, no adults in the room. We can offer you business development, advising, and tech support." He's a bit breathless now as he gets into it, ticking off the items like they're a grocery list. "Editorial advice, management consultation, access to new tech products—all the things you need to make you legit. That can make you bigger than you ever dreamed."

I'm quiet, letting him continue.

"I'm having my finance and investments team draw up a proposal for you," he says. "But we're offering you three hundred thousand dollars. Up front."

My eyes widen, picturing the numbers in my head. The enormous numbers. Life-changing numbers. That's the kind of money that would allow me to walk right into Sasha's office and rage quit—that would allow me to divert the entire trajectory of my life.

But . . . what would I be giving up?

"Interesting," I say, hiding my excitement. "What are the terms?"

"Well, we'd be buying you," he says. "So, we'd own the name, the logo, the website, everything associated with the account."

Control. That's what I'd be giving up.

"And you'd work for us."

Nerves flare in my stomach.

"How do you envision I work for you?" I ask.

"Well, you could run the site as editorial director under a salary," he says. "With help from a real journalist, of course. Some former editor in chief looking for a new challenge. Or we could work something else out if you don't want to actually *work*. You could be an advisor or whatever bullshit title suits you."

"But you would be in charge," I say. "*You* would run deuxmoi. You and some former editor in chief."

"Only nominally."

The silence extends between us, and I bite down on a nail, nerves shooting down my spine.

"I have to consult my team," I say, thinking about Leon and Victoria. Maybe even Ollie. He did say I should lean on him for advice. "After you send over the terms and all."

That gets a laugh out of him. "You do that. We'll be here," he says. "Waiting. Until then . . . don't post any shit about me, you hear?"

I laugh. "I already posted about you supposedly dating that one socialite. See that one?"

"Yeah, when we went to the Nines. You called me a big tipper."

"Are you?"

"If we were in person right now, I give you a middle finger for suggesting I wasn't," he says. "But I guess I'll never find out who you are, even if we work together, huh?"

"Nope."

"Hm," he says. "Fascinating. Think it over, deux. Could be fun . . ."

He hangs up with little fanfare, and I lean back against the pillows, closing my eyes as I try to picture what my life might be like if I say yes—if I allow someone else, some other company, into my little world. It could be a mess, but it could also be . . . fun. Smart, even. I blink my eyes open and head over to Instagram to check the most recent DMs as a bubble of hope forms in my chest.

Excerpt from Solution.com

Deuxmoi Is Curing My Existential Dread

Right now, my only real hobbies consist of staring at my phone and holding my puppy close as I contemplate how depressing the world is right now.

Some people (aka my therapist) might call this depression, but I call it extremely normal behavior. Especially now that my scrolling antics are largely taken up by the anonymous Instagram account deuxmoi. You cannot venture around Dimes Square without hearing someone utter the name like a dove cooing into the night.

Deuxmoi.

Deuxmoi.

She's everywhere.

Unlike other celebrity gossip sites or blind item blogs, deuxmoi focuses mostly on the mundane. Sweet little stories about how Zendaya and Tom Holland acted on the set of *Spider-Man*, and how nice Kristen Stewart is to the hair and makeup teams. Sure, there are tales of sex parties, adultery, addiction, divorces, and literal bad actors (Nate Clyburn, stay golden plz!), but it's these tiny moments that make me realize we're all just li'l humans, trying to get through the day. Like, yes, I obviously want to know that Adam Driver walks his dog in Brooklyn Heights almost every day and that The Weeknd probably-definitely hooked up with Angelina Jolie.

Plus, deuxmoi speaks directly with the people she writes about, who now head to her account to share their own gossip or to right wrong rumors out there. She corrects her mistakes and lets us in on the fun by asking for what sorts of stories we want to hear. She sources them for us, providing tiny bits of gossip I didn't know I was missing in my life.

For whatever reason, reading the endless Instagram stories has given me a warm sort of cozy feeling deep within my chest that I can usually only get from my anxiety-reducing weighted blanket. It's like she's holding my hand and whispering into my ear, "Don't worry, sweetie. We'll all get through this together."

And by "this" I like to think she means the existential dread we're all living in at this exact moment. Because even if the world is about to burst into flames, even if all our politicians will fail us, and even if a deadly disease is about to spread throughout the earth—at least we can all laugh about the fact that if you fuck Mike Yen, he'll probably be listening to Christina Aguilera ("Genie in a Bottle," for sure) on headphones while he goes down on you.

CHAPTER 14

"Sorry, sorry!" Victoria slides into the banquette next to me, her face flushed like she just walked all the way downtown even though I know she took an Uber XL. We're tucked into a cozy leather booth in a corner of Pastis, and she smooths out her high-waisted, wide-legged Frame jeans, leaning her body into mine to kiss me on the cheek. "Jake wanted to *you know what*," she says, lowering her voice to a whisper, "before I headed out."

I roll my eyes. "He wanted to fuck?"

She swats me on the arm, her face growing even more pink, and I try not to picture the very demure sex I know they must be having, not that she's shared the gory details with me at all since they got engaged a million years ago. That's the thing about friends who get married—no one tells you they also stop sharing their sex lives with you, even though they still want all the dirt on who you, the single friend, are fucking. You can bet your ass she wanted to hear all the dirty details about Doug, though she was quick to remind me that I deserved to be treated better.

"Anyway, I'm here," she says, slapping her hand on the table. "Girls' night! Let's do it. Martinis?"

I hold up my drink and shake it a bit so the ice clinks against the glass. "I'll take another."

She smiles wide and flags down the waiter, and soon we're on our second round with a plate of steak frites between us. I'm filling her in on the whole Kyle Johns conversation and the maybe-sort-of-flirty texts from Ollie, which segues into us laughing our asses off over how I told Doug to fuck off, a story that causes Victoria to stomp her feet in glee. "Finally!"

But I still can't help but look at my phone, wondering what's going down in my DMs and what I might be missing by not spending every waking moment checking the inbox.

Victoria notices my twitchiness and nods toward the bathroom. "Why don't you go check on everything? See if there's anything good in there." When I hesitate, she furrows her brows. "Come on. I know you're dying to see what's new."

Relief fills my stomach, and I wrap my hand around my phone, feeling the weight and warmth in my palm. "You don't mind? It'll only take a minute."

She waves me off. "Go, go. I'll get us another round . . . and some more fries."

"Perf," I call, even though I'm already halfway toward the restroom.

Once I'm inside, I pull up Instagram and do a quick check-in, searching for notes and tips from any verified accounts or regular sources.

I scroll fast, my thumb pressing hard over the screen, until I see one from the pop star Tori Cee. There's a blue check mark next to her name, and I tap over to her account, kind of shocked that it's *actually* her. We've never corresponded before, but I have posted a few stories about her hanging out at Tower Bar and hitting up Machine Gun Kelly's birthday party. Tori had her heyday in the early 2010s, when she was the surprise guest on Kayla Cole's Super Bowl halftime show. It was around the time that the two dominated the charts and swept the Grammys with their beloved collab, "Put 'Er on Him." Some outlets even called them the next Britney and Christina.

But Kayla retreated from the spotlight for a while after a super public lip-sync debacle followed by a major wardrobe malfunction during the Grammys. She backed away from the public eye, making a statement about "rest and relaxation" through her team. But fans were skeptical, since it was rumored that those same spokespeople were emotionally abusive and supplying her with pharmaceuticals she doesn't need.

Kayla hasn't done an interview in a decade, even though she's been holding down a massive world tour since her comeback a few years ago. Apparently, she's been in a wildly oppressive contract, and the record label doesn't allow her to control any of her career. The followers are always asking about her, hoping for news that she'll finally speak out about what she's been up to, but no one ever writes in about her.

I tap open Tori's message and read it, my eyes widening as I get toward the end.

> Someone's gotta say it: Everyone's got the whole Kayla Cole story wrong. What people don't understand is that Kayla's breakdown came about after years of abuse from the people around her. Her family isn't really in the picture, which has not helped the whole situation so she's totally alone and isolated. Yeah, her record label sucks but those of us who used to know her are worried about what might happen if she ends up in control of her life again.
>
> We're concerned that she * does * need help and guidance but that she refuses to get it. I'm totally terrified that every time people claim she needs freedom they don't actually know the real story.

I read the message once, then twice. What the hell am I supposed to do with this? I press my lips together and then try to formulate a response.

Whoa, babe, I type back. *Is this well-known?*

Tori responds immediately. *Those who really know her know the truth. I don't want this getting out but I just want YOU to know so when you get tips about her you actually have an idea of what's going on.*

Thanks, I reply. *Appreciate it.*

You can see for yourself if you want, she types. *She's performing at a corporate event in Meatpacking tonight. There's going to be an exclusive after party at Le Bain. She'll be there. Just tell them you're part of the Tori Cee's Brigade. That'll get you in.*

I twirl a strand of hair around my finger and press my lips together, wondering if Victoria would be down to wing woman this with me. I gotta at least try, I decide, and head back to the bar.

Victoria's eyes go wide as I lower my voice and explain what just happened. Before I can even ask her if she wants to come with me, her jaw drops open and she tilts her head toward mine.

"We have to go," she says, her face stoic. "Like, we have to go *now.*"

"Are you sure? What about the whole getting into the Racquet Club thing?"

She waves me off. "I may not *love* that you're doing this but how often do we get to crash a Kayla Cole party? Plus, you said we don't have to use our real names." She shrugs. "Eff it."

I throw my arms around her. "I've never loved you more."

"Oh please," she says, her voice muffled in my hair. "You know I've been a Kayla fan since I was twelve years old. I'm calling a car—now."

■■■

"Name." The bouncer manning the VIP line at Le Bain is puny in a tight black T-shirt, a diamond stud adorning his ear. His cheekbones are high, and he's wearing bright pink lipstick on his mouth, which is currently curled into a snarl, as if he's already determined we're not getting into this party.

But as soon as I say "Tori Cee Brigade," his demeanor changes and he straightens his back before waving us forward. "Right this way."

He stamps our wrists with pink ink and ushers us through a velvet rope and down a hallway, and when we're out of sight, Victoria grabs my palm, squeezing it in hers.

"That was effing hilarious," she squeals, and skips ahead. But then she stops and I run right into her back. When I look up, I realize why.

Ahead, there's a dark room lit only by pink neon signage, all of which says "Kayla Cole" in different fonts. They're hanging from every wall, even the ceiling, and in the middle of the space is a massive pink disco ball, suspended by a string of pink crystals that catch the light when they hit the right angles.

"Did Barbie design this place?" Victoria grabs two cocktails—also neon pink—from a tray sailing by us. The room is packed, mostly with music industry types: well-manicured men wearing thick, shiny jewelry and head-to-toe Supreme; tall, gazelle-like backup dancers in neon-colored dresses; a handful of old-school label execs in Zegna suits and boxy Rachel Comey dresses. Over by the plant wall, accented in pink, of course, I spot Tori Cee tucked into a leather booth, flanked by her publicist, rumored girlfriend, and a few of her longtime friends who make appearances in her music videos. There are open bottles of Grey Goose and Dom on the table in front of her, even though there's a rumor that she's sober now, but she's glued to her phone, her fingers flying fast. She looks up, glances around the room, and I wonder if she's trying to figure out which of the random people here is *me*—deuxmoi.

I avert my eyes, letting my hair fall over my face. "Come on." I motion to Victoria that we should do a lap around the room. "Let's try to spot Kayla."

Victoria nods and takes a slurp from her straw. She adjusts her chest so her cleavage is a little more prominent. "Now I'm ready."

Together we check out the party, first scoping out the freebie table, full of Kayla Cole–branded perfumes and lipsticks, Diptyque candles from Kayla's latest collab, and a new line of lace panties she put out with Fenty last year. Then we make our way to the barely touched grazing boards, piled high with bite-size snacks made by Momofuku's David Chang, who's schmoozing in the corner with Rich Torrisi, the chef who helped start Carbone.

I pop a mini pork bun in my mouth and take a look around the room, wondering where the hell Kayla might be. Victoria must read my mind, because suddenly she gasps next to me.

"Trent Cole," she says, close to my ear.

"Where?" I whip my head around looking for Kayla's older brother, Trent. He's kind of a nobody, someone you'd only spot if you spent years obsessing over Kayla like Victoria has. I haven't seen pap photos of him in years, but as soon as Victoria puts her hands on my shoulders and directs me toward him, I recognize him immediately.

Sure, his hair is thinning and he's wearing an Adidas tracksuit that should really only be seen on fifteen-year-old hype beasts, but he's still sorta cute, with boyish charm and high cheekbones.

"Follow me," Victoria says.

She throws her shoulders back and juts her chest out, walking right over to Trent, who seems to be in the middle of telling a not-so-compelling story to a bunch of bored-looking wannabes. Their eyes flit around the room, telling me they're looking for a better conversation. But Victoria seizes the moment.

"Which one of you boys knows where the real fun is at this party?" she says in a fake, exaggerated Southern drawl. I take a swig of my drink to keep myself from laughing.

Trent's mouth turns into an amused smile. "I think you came to the right place."

A breeze whips through the room, and Victoria's nipples harden beneath her shirt. Trent notices, and I try not to roll my eyes.

"There's gotta be a VIP room or something, right?" she asks, touching his forearm softly and batting her eyelashes like a cartoon.

"Totally," he says as he eye fucks Victoria. "I'm just out here to say hi to some of the money people." He nods toward a slim door I didn't notice before. "The finance bros throwing this thing built out a separate room in here," he says, opening it so we can walk through the narrow entryway into a dark hallway. "Right this way, ladies."

Without hesitation, Victoria steps through and I follow. But behind us the door we came through closes and suddenly I'm very aware of the fact that it's just the three of us in this quiet, creepy space. I squeeze Victoria's hand and remind myself that if it came down to it, we could totally take this loser, two-on-one, no problem. But just as quickly as my nerves come, we're spit out into a small room with low ceilings, draped in velvet and low lights.

The pink gaudiness of the main room is nowhere to be seen, and it's obvious that Trent was right—this *is* where the real party is: A few serious A-list actors are lounging on the couches, their limbs relaxed and sloppy while a bunch of rappers from the Atlanta scene help themselves to a few bottles of vintage wine by the bar. Trent heads their way to stock up, and then, finally, I spot Kayla, sitting on a velvet couch toward the back of the room with that record label exec Tori was alluding to. Her legs are tucked up under her, and there's a silver tray sitting in front of them on a coffee table, covered in neat little rows of white powder, ready to be snorted. She leans forward, a thin gold straw in her hand, and does one line, then another, before throwing her head back and murmuring something. Her eyes are closed, and she extends an arm out, reaching for something.

The exec sticks a hand in his pocket and pulls out a glass pipe, handing it to her out in the open, and all of a sudden I don't want to see anymore. Victoria must agree, because I can feel her tense beside me.

Trent spots Kayla and then looks back at us, his eyes narrowed, and I know he's probably regretting letting some random hotties into the back room.

"Shit," Victoria says. "Maybe we should . . ."

"Get the fuck out of here?"

"Yup."

We both spin around and rush back to the door that Trent ushered us through, and when we get back to the main room, I feel an overwhelming sense of sadness, having seen that what Tori Cee was trying to warn me about was true.

Victoria grabs our coats from the check, and when we're in the elevator alone, she turns to me, her face serious. "You're not going to post about that, are you?"

I look at her, dumbstruck. "Are you fucking kidding? Who do you think I am, a monster?"

"That's a no, right?"

"Of course I'm not going to post about that." I shake my head. "Some things aren't meant to be blasted all over the world. Some people just need help."

Deuxmoi Facebook Group

Rachel Shepsfield

Rumor has it Kayla Cole was in NYC partying after a big corporate event. Has DM posted anything about her recently that I missed? I feel like I never hear about her.

Like   Reply   9h

Lori Poole

Nah, not that I've seen. We NEVER see Kayla out n about, except when her manager wants her to be photographed.

Like   Reply   8h

Orion Greene

Who cares???? She's a whatever wannabe-hot-but-old-as-fuck-star. Give me Madison Lee any day of the week.

Like   Reply   5h

Yelena Marks

Did Madison Lee write this???? Where are my Tori Cee stans?

Like   Reply   3h

CHAPTER 15

"I cannot believe we are going to a kiddie *squash* game," Leon says in the back seat of a car. We're heading uptown to watch Victoria's son Chase *crush* some classmate named Tree at an interschool tournament and we are both, rightfully, salty about the whole thing. Though I definitely owe Vic for coming to that Kayla Cole shit show with me.

"I believe it's called a match," I say, to which Leon waves his hand around.

"It's a Thursday, for Christ's sake. Giuseppe had a primetime reservation at Carbone tonight."

"Please tell me he could reschedule."

Leon winces. "Only for a Monday at nine four weeks from now."

"Did you take it?"

"Fuck no."

I laugh. "Hey, come on. Bieber had a ten p.m. reservation last Tuesday."

Leon frowns. "I'm not going for a celeb sighting, Cricket. I'm going to eat spicy rigatoni at the time I want to eat spicy rigatoni."

I wave at him. "Whatever, no one can get a reservation there anyway."

"Hm, wonder whose fault that is." He widens his eyes and taps his finger against his bottom lip.

"It's not like I *planted* celebrities there. I don't have that kind of power."

"Mmm, you kind of do, though. You can't go there *or* Via Carota without running into forty-five Instagram models trying to get noticed."

I roll my eyes and turn back to my phone just as our Uber driver stops short in front of a midsize redbrick building with a neat black metal gate and a manicured garden out front. "This you?"

I look around at the very obviously Upper East Side parents standing outside with children wearing white polo shirts and shorts and realize, unfortunately, it is us.

We get out of the car and head inside, following signs for the juniors' tournament. Victoria's sitting in the bleachers next to what looks like a glass cage holding a few children with plastic goggles and rackets. They look like mini investment bankers, but I have to admit the whole thing is kind of adorable.

Victoria stands and waves us over to her, motioning to the saved seats next to her. I scooch past a woman with a pastel-pink Birkin that's the same shade as her Gucci loafers and smile politely as I try not to step on them. Off to one side, I see Teddy Treadwell, that late-night host Victoria raved about months ago, holding three massive Tupperware containers full of brownies. Just like Victoria said.

"Thank god you came." Victoria wraps her arms around us both. "Jake's in London and all the other parents here are truly *insane*."

Leon gives Victoria a once-over. "You're literally wearing a 'Charles Day School Squash Mom' T-shirt."

Victoria glares at him but then reaches into her purse and retrieves a mini bottle of Casamigos. "I brought you presents."

Leon throws his head back. "Okay, fine, I love you." He takes a swig and shouts toward the glass box, "Go, Dax!"

"You know Chase is the one playing, right?" Victoria says.

I hold back a laugh and look around the room, where parents and teachers are cheering, coddling children who lost, or scarfing down some of those brownies from Teddy while trying not to stare at him so obviously. Then I remember he was rumored to be newly separated from his wife. According to one of his neighbors, there were one too many household "accidents" that were a direct result of his being overserved.

I elbow Leon in his side and nod over to where the talk show host is chatting with a few squash moms with stars in their eyes. "Can you send in a tip about Teddy and the brownies?" I whisper.

Leon follows my gaze and pauses. "Here? I don't know." Before he can say anything else, Victoria swats at his phone.

"Absolutely not," she hisses. "What if it's traced back to me?" Her voice is low and a little nervous. "I'm not interested in having parents here think I'm sending tips to my *best friend's celebrity gossip account.*"

Her tone stings, and I recoil. "Geez, it's not like I'm running a drug cartel."

She rolls her eyes. "Come on. This is way too close to home. My kids' *squash tournament?* This isn't a random bar. It would be extremely easy to deduce who sent it."

Leon looks at me, waiting for my response, and I guess she kind of has a point, though I don't think that anyone could figure out that I ran the account—or that Victoria had any connections to me—based on one photo from a goddamn squash tournament, but I let it slide.

"Fine," I say, and Victoria settles back into her seat, relaxed again.

"I *am* going to get one of those brownies, though," she says.

"Bring us back some!" Leon calls.

It hasn't even been an hour since I last checked the account, but I'm acutely aware of my phone pressing up against my thigh as it sits in my pocket. I can't wait any longer, and while Vic is chatting up Teddy, I excuse myself to go find the bathroom and see what's new.

When I get inside the restroom, I see it's one of those bathrooms for kids, with tiny toilets and short stalls. It's cramped, but with my knees pressed up against the door, I start going through a bunch of messages, including one from Ollie.

> I was at Tower Bar last night and literally everyone was talking about you.

Oh yeah? I respond. *Good things?*

> You're shaking shit up, that's for sure. Everyone was trying to speculate who you were.

I lean up against the stall. *Got any guesses?*
Nope, he writes. *And I'm not gonna ask.*

> Not even curious?

He sends a shrug emoji. *Idk, you're obviously super smart and funny. I don't really need to know who you are to know that you're pretty amazing.*

I stare at the words and feel my stomach flip, even though he's being corny as hell. Another text comes in.

Maybe that was too forward, he writes. *But . . . it's true.*

> That's certainly a line . . . But I'll take it.

He hearts the message, and I tap out of the conversation, trying to remind myself not to read too deeply into these tiny moments. I don't know this guy. He could be like this with everyone. It doesn't mean *anything*.

I give myself five minutes before I need to go back out there and be a good friend, so I start tapping through stories of celebs the account follows. An overly Botoxed middle-aged model shares kissy photos with her new girlfriend. A Real Housewife posts about her reunion look. A Patriots running back films clips from his yacht vacation in Greece. But then I get to Madison Lee, who, only seconds ago, shared a simple photo, nothing that interesting. It's just a picture of her sitting on the deck of her Malibu home, wearing a bikini and tiny sunglasses.

There's just some plain, unformatted text over the image.

> Huge news, guys: I figured out who runs Deuxmoi. I feel like I should work for the CIA, right??

Suddenly my heart is in my throat and I don't know if I can breathe. It's not possible. There's no way. But what does she think? How did this happen?

I tap and wait with horror for the next slide to load. Is she going to out me—share my photo, my name, the fact that I work for Sasha? But there's nothing. That's it. She didn't post a single other story.

I shove my phone back into my pocket and rush out of the stall, pushing past the put-together moms as they gossip about Teddy Treadwell's brownies and how "that Chase has one hell of a swing." But none of that really registers, because all I can think about is the fact that I have about thirty seconds before Madison Lee drops a massive bomb on my life. Maybe it's karma; maybe I deserve this for outing her shady consignment practices. Maybe . . .

"Are you all right?" Leon asks, taking another sip of Casamigos as I appear back in our row. I'm a little out of breath, and I can feel a bead of sweat roll down my back.

I shake my head and lean down. "Look at Madison Lee's story," I hiss. "Now."

He pulls up her account, and when he sees the screen, he nearly spits out his drink. Leon's eyes are wide, and his hand flutters up to cover his mouth.

"I have to get out of here." I grab my coat from the bleachers and bolt toward the exit, ignoring Victoria and Leon as they call after me. When I finally get to the street, I have no idea what to do.

There's one person who might have advice . . .

I text Ollie a screenshot of her story. *Think this is legit?*

He responds immediately. *Let me look into it. I got you.*

I rest a hand on my chest and lean back against the side of the building, ignoring the kids streaming out onto the street, their squash rackets secured in little backpacks behind them. I squeeze my eyes shut, but as soon as I do, I see images of Sasha throwing a glass vase at my head, her face twisted into some sort of scream or ear-piercing shout. I see her throwing my laptop in the trash, a security guard coming to grab me and throw me into the elevator shaft. In that split second, I see everything I've worked for over the past eight years crumble.

But then a text from Ollie lights up my phone.

> She thinks you're a hostess at Via Carota. Someone named Kate. At least that's what her manager's interior designer just told me.

I exhale, relief flooding my body, my shoulders slumping down from around my ears.

> You know her manager's interior designer?

He sends me a smirking emoji. *Gotta source up somehow.*

Then another one comes in. *You're not Kate, are you?*

I smile as I type out a response. *Nope.*

> Didn't think so.

Suddenly someone grabs my elbow and shakes me. "Crick, what the fuck!" Leon's in front of me now, fear in his eyes. "Does she actually know?"

I shake my head. "She has no clue," I say, a smile spreading on my face. "No fucking clue."

Leon sighs and throws an arm around me, bringing me to him. "Oh my god, thank god." But then he pulls back. "How can you be sure?"

I turn my phone around so he can read the texts from Ollie.

Leon doesn't look convinced. "How can you be sure this guy is for real?"

I shake my head, a flush rising in my cheeks. "I don't know. I just . . . trust him. It's a gut feeling."

"This is not the time to go off gut." Leon's face is flushed, and he throws his hands up. "This is fucking serious, Cricket. One of the biggest stars on the planet says she knows who you are, and you're just going to trust this guy because he says she's wrong?"

"I—"

"You're being so fucking selfish. Do you have any idea how stressful this is for me? For Victoria? Thinking we might be linked to you? Your actions affect us." His eyes are pleading now, but all I feel is frustration that he can't see how this is affecting *me*.

"This has *nothing* to do with you," I say, trying to keep my voice down. "Has anyone said anything to you about it? Has anyone made you think they can trace deuxmoi back to you?"

"Not—"

"Exactly. You both are so concerned about how the account might impact your life, but do you have any idea how much stress and anxiety this shit causes me? Maybe that's why I talk to Ollie about it. Maybe I need someone who might understand how insane this all has been and doesn't make it about them."

I know I'm saying shit I can't take back, but I've had enough of their *what about me?* bullshit.

Leon sighs and presses a hand to his head. "I don't have a safety net, Cricket," he says, a little softer. "Vic's biggest problem would be getting shunned from squash or whatever, but she'll be fine. You know my parents are retired, but there's no trust fund for me. And

Giuseppe is still paying off his law school student loans. I've worked my ass off to be able to support myself, and I just . . . I can't lose my job."

He blinks back tears, and something in my heart loosens.

"Neither can I." My voice cracks.

"Shit," Leon says. "I'm sorry. I know this isn't about me. I'm just . . ."

"Scared," I say. "I am, too. But I'm not going to let this ruin your life. Or mine, for that matter."

Leon props himself up against the building, so our shoulders are touching. "Fuck," he says. "I can't believe how big this has gotten."

I shake my head. "I know."

"Let me see that Ollie guy's texts again."

I hand him my phone and watch as Leon squints at his profile picture. "Shit," he says. "This guy's hot. Now I know why you trust him."

I let out a laugh and roll my eyes. "That's not why! He gives me good advice. Plus he makes me feel smart . . . and special."

"Does he have any idea who you are?" he asks, concern rising in his voice.

I shake my head. "He's in the dark, too. This is through a Google Voice number."

Leon doesn't look convinced. He nods back toward the gym, where Victoria's still inside rooting for Chase. "You should talk to Jake," he says. "He works in tech security."

I furrow my brow. "Isn't he in finance?"

"Yeah, finance *of a tech security company*. He can help you boost security."

"Huh," I say, mulling over the idea. It's not a bad one. Perhaps Victoria's Ken doll husband could be of some use to me. "Victoria hasn't told him about the account, right?"

"Def not. She'll play along with you."

I turn back to my phone, my back up against the wall, and play Madison Lee's story again. She hasn't posted anything else. Just that one slide, with no other explanation. But my DMs are blowing up, dozens coming in at once, all asking me, *Does she know?*

Leon squeezes my hand in a reassuring sort of manner and pulls out his phone. "I'll call us a car."

...

By the time I get home, my inbox is flooded. There must be over five hundred messages in here, all wanting to know how Madison Lee found out—and if she has the right intel. Before I hopped out of the car, Leon handed me half a Xanax, and now that it's finally kicked in, I feel like I can breathe, even though I'm still terrified someone's going to come out of the woodwork and scream my name at any point. I drop my black Balenciaga City bag on the counter and press my hands into the cool marble, trying to ground myself. To feel steady. But then my phone blinks awake.

You okay? Ollie texts.

I grab the phone and make my way over to the corner of my L-shaped couch and start typing. But before I can respond, his name takes over the screen and I see that he's *calling* me on the Google phone line. My stomach lurches, and all my anxiety and stress return. Why the fuck would he be *calling* me? It can only mean trouble.

But, on the other hand, this is *Ollie*, whom I've been texting with nonstop. He hasn't given me a reason to be scared. He hasn't broken my trust. Not yet.

I swipe to answer.

"Hey." His voice is deep and soothing, crystal clear in my ear. The hint of a British accent comes through.

"Hi."

"I didn't know if you'd pick up."

A small smile forms on my mouth. He actually sounds kind of hopeful. Excited.

"Yeah, well, my phone's kind of a shit show right now, so I figured I might as well be distracted for a while."

He lets out a laugh, warm and throaty, and I feel a ball of nerves form in my stomach.

"You doing okay?" There's concern there, too, and I wonder where he is. What he's up to.

"Sedatives help."

He laughs again. "You know she has no idea, right?"

I nod even though he can't see me.

"It's just . . ." I don't even know how to explain what I'm feeling, not to him or to anyone, and suddenly it dawns on me that no one else in the world could ever really grasp what this account can do to me—how it has the power to make me spiral with stress or anxiety. There's no one behind it except *me*. I'm all alone.

"What?" he asks, soft. "Lonely?"

"How'd you know?"

"I mean, unless you have an army of people helping you go through your DMs, verifying every single piece of information and responding to all the followers, I gotta guess it can be a bit . . ."

"Insane," I finish. "It's insane." I tap over to my inbox just to check in and see that the messages won't stop coming. I want to respond to them all, to tell them that that no, Madison Lee has no idea who I am. But instead, I close my eyes and listen to Ollie's voice.

"Where are you now?" he asks.

"Home. You?"

"Same."

We're both quiet, an ocean of silence between us.

"What are you looking at right now?" I ask.

"The Hollywood sign. It's all lit up at night."

"Could you be more of a cliché?"

"Hey, you probably live in like a rent-stabilized West Village apartment or something."

"Guilty," I say, smiling. "Though, I kinda pegged you as a Santa Monica surfer bro."

"Guess we can't assume much about each other, huh?"

"Fair." I tap through Madison Lee's post again, and for whatever reason I start to feel emboldened. "Hey," I start. "Do you think I'd start World War III by responding to Madison Lee? Posting something about how she's full of shit?"

"You'd get buzz, that's for sure."

"You think?"

"Oh yeah. I'd be telling our night editors to write it up ASAP."

"Huh."

"What are you thinking?"

"I have some ideas . . ."

"Coy. I like it."

"Gotta be sometimes."

It's now almost eleven, and I know I gotta hang up if I ever want to get through even half of these DMs. But I don't want to. I want to have him here, in my headphones, as I take this next step, emboldened by his words.

"Can you just . . . talk a bit? About literally anything? I need something to distract me while I do this."

"Do what?" he asks.

"You'll see."

"Devious," he says, "but fun." He then starts describing what his mid-century modern home looks like and I'm lulled into a strange sense of calm as I try not to second-guess myself so I can follow through on my plan. I pull up Instagram and craft a response to Madison Lee, featuring the opening clip of the Britney Spears episode of *Diary*, that old MTV show. Her breathy voice echoes in my apartment: "You think you know but you have no idea." I tag Madison Lee and share the post, holding my breath as it loads.

"So over in the corner, I have a fireplace, which is actually kind of rare in Los Angeles—"

"Okay, you can stop now," I say.

"I was just getting to my great room."

"Go look at Instagram. Tell me what you think."

After a beat he lets out an uproarious laugh, then makes a warm, sweet noise into the phone that sends a tingle to my stomach.

"I know we barely know each other," he says, "but I gotta say, you keep surprising me over and over again."

"Is that a good thing?"

"Definitely."

I lean back into the couch, curling my feet under my butt. "Good."

"And holy shit my phone is already blowing up with people in the biz talking about this." He laughs again. "Like I said, buzz."

I lean back against the couch and go through some messages as we continue to talk, a sense of calm falling over me. I tuck my limbs under me as Ollie starts telling me about growing up in Brixton and how no one in the U.S. makes a proper cup of tea, chiming in when he asks me about my childhood, careful not to reveal any identifying characteristics.

I tell him about Kyle Johns's offer, which he says sounds like an excellent idea. I ask him about working in media and the state of his industry until sleep comes, and with the sound of Ollie still in my ear, I succumb to the night.

■■■

When I blink my eyes open, I see I'm still on my couch in the living room, with all the lights on. It's still dark outside, and my phone says it's 4:00 in the morning and that I've been on the phone with Ollie for five hours.

"Shit," I say, my voice hoarse with sleep. "Are you still there?"

A grumble comes through the receiver. "Oh man," he says. "We must have fallen asleep."

I rub my eyes and stand, making my way to the bathroom. "I'm going to go," I say. "Obviously."

He murmurs something into the phone. "Good night," he says. "Again."

I hang up, a smile forming on my lips as I drag myself through my nighttime routine, even though it seems pointless now. Before hopping back in bed, I check the account one last time to find that since I last looked, basically every news outlet on the planet has picked up my response to Madison Lee. Ollie was right.

The account has sixty thousand new followers. All from today.

Looks like I owe Madison Lee a thank-you note.

Oglenews.com

Who Is Deuxmoi? Madison Lee Says She Knows Who's Behind Anonymous Gossip Instagram Account

If you're at all interested in celebrity spillage, then you are already aware of Deuxmoi and why watching all of her stories is so addicting. If you found yourself here by mistake, take note: Deuxmoi is the anonymous gossip IG account that's been breaking news about surprising celebrity run-ins, blind items, and rumors about the most talented among us.

The best part? No one knows who runs it. The person who curates the account has revealed NOTHING about their identity. Not her age, job, name, or location. Though most ardent followers think she has to be orbiting the entertainment industry based on how good her intel is. (She broke the news about Nate Clyburn and Iris Leonard.)

But now, TikTok pop star Madison Lee has posted on IG, proclaiming she knows who's behind the account. Wild, if true. Madison Lee didn't reveal the potential identity and no one else seems to know who she's referring to. We reached out to Madison Lee's team to try to get them to dish, but no one responded.

After Madison Lee shared her post, Deuxmoi crafted her own response, and posted that classic video of Britney Spears saying, "You think you know, but you have no idea."

Message received, deux!

Madison Lee never responded, but the whole back-and-forth ignited a maelstrom online, as fans and readers began speculating in earnest about who Deuxmoi might really be. A Facebook group called "WHO R U DEUXMOI?" formed overnight and now has more than 20,000 members.

All we can say is that if Madison Lee knows who's behind Deuxmoi, we kind of hope she spills? But if Deuxmoi isn't ready to be known, well, then we get that, too, but . . . all's fair in internet gossip, amirite?

From: kjohns@johnsglobalmedia.com

To: Deuxmoi@gmail.com

Date: September 5, 2022, 7:05 a.m. ET

Subject: Well?????

Haven't heard from you since our last chat. Assume you're still thinking it over. How about this? Based on all the buzz you just got, we'll up the deal to $325k. It's not an exploding offer, but I would like to know within a few weeks. Lmk what you're thinking . . .

Kyle Johns
CEO Johns Global Media

CHAPTER 16

"So, Victoria said you wanted to beef up your . . . security?" Jake is staring at me with a quizzical look as we sit across from each other on the padded benches of their breakfast nook overlooking Central Park.

He's wearing gray joggers and a thin white T-shirt, and when the sun hits his face at the right angle, I can see why Victoria thinks he's hot—in that finance dad bro kind of way—and he does still have that muscular build from playing college lacrosse. Victoria scoots in beside him and refills our mugs from the ceramic French press between us. Both their kids are out at sleepovers from the night before, so Victoria had invited me over under the guise of having a bagel spread from Russ & Daughters, but also to ask Jake for a favor. As the account gains more and more followers—and especially after this Madison Lee debacle—I'm dying to know how to keep all my info secure. I want to make deuxmoi bulletproof.

I poke at the few pieces of fruit salad on my plate and nod. "I'm starting to think I was hacked recently. Like on my Instagram page and email. I want to make sure I'm protecting myself, you know? Victoria said you might have some suggestions?"

Victoria winks at me, and I kick her under the table, trying to remind her to be chill. She's never told him about deuxmoi, and right now I'm more grateful than ever, since I know he'd never agree to help me if he knew what I was up to. Jake plays by the book, no matter what, and would probably think the whole account was beneath him—trashy. He wouldn't want to get mixed up in it and would probably be peeved that Victoria knew this whole time. But since he works at a security tech company, and even though he's in the finance department, she thought he might be able to offer some ideas.

Jake stands and walks over to the fridge in their immaculate white kitchen. He yanks open the door and pulls out a leftover pizza box, flipping the top open.

Victoria clears her throat, motioning to the formally plated spread of lox and whitefish salad, but Jake shakes his head, grabbing a slice of pepperoni from the box. He takes a big bite out of the cold pizza and chews for a while, staring out the window. When he looks back at me, there's a tiny bit of congealed cheese stuck to the corner of his mouth. Victoria shrugs at me like *What can you do?* and continues looking lovingly at her husband.

For a second, my heart tenses. It's been a while since I've been in a relationship like this, one where you don't feel the need to explain the other's strange habits. Where communication is often silent or understood. Doug barely brought me around in public, and when he did, we only had two modes: ignoring each other completely or sneaking off to hook up in the coat closet. There was no in between.

I wonder what it would be like with Ollie. If we would be the type of couple to hold hands at a party or sit on the same side of the table at a restaurant. Would he give me his jacket when I got cold, or would he chide me, saying I should have remembered to bring another layer? Would he want to share dishes at a restaurant, picking things off my plate with his fork, or would he insist we each get our own meal, disinterested in venturing away from one plate? But this is a man who doesn't know my face or my name, who thinks I'm doing something cool, but that's probably about it. Projecting my fantasies onto him isn't going to help anyone.

"You're probably going to want to change all your passwords," Jake says, still chewing.

I nod, even though that's totally obvious advice, and grab a black-and-white cookie from the platter in between us.

"But not to something you'd actually remember," he says. "Or that's guessable."

"So, I guess my mother's maiden name is out, huh?" I say, trying to crack a joke. Though I did use her name the last time I reset the Instagram account.

Jake looks at me deadpan. "Obviously." He shakes his head. "They need to be different for every single account. Then memorize them. Don't use a password reminder or anything like that. Just memorize them."

"Huh."

"And if your phone is compromised, get a few Google phone lines."

"A few?" Victoria asks, concern in her voice. She knows I only have the one.

He nods. "Mix it up when you call people. Makes them harder to trace."

"Got it," I say, tapping out my to-do list in a note on my phone.

"Look," he says, spreading his palms out on the table. "If you've been hacked, there's not much you can do about it except hope that you didn't have any super-sensitive information that could be detrimental if it got out."

My stomach flips. "Sensitive information? Like what?"

"Oh, you know. Bank account info. Evidence of fraud. Nudes." He gives Victoria a smirk, and I want to barf my nova right onto the table. Then he turns back to me. "No offense, Cricket, but I'm sure whatever leaked wasn't that big of a deal. It's not like you're harboring national security secrets."

He's looking at me all smug, and if I were a different kind of person, I'd stand up and point right at him, screaming about how much "super-sensitive information" there really is on my computer, in my cloud, on my phone. The kind of information that would bring down some of the biggest names in Hollywood if they were released. I have the power to destroy lives, make careers, blow up marriages.

But so much of that I would never use—that's why I want to protect it. I don't want it getting out, don't want people getting hurt. Having this much power, this much control, it makes you wary of everyone around you who knows *your* secrets. I'm sure Iris Leonard never thought her co-stars would leak audio of her and Nate Clyburn fucking in a trailer. But sure as hell, the actress who plays her little sister on the show sent it to me and suggested I share it just for fun. I told her I'd never release something like that, which shut her up *real* quick.

I sent the file to an encrypted trash can on my computer, the one full of *actual* celebrity nudes, voice notes from actors shit-talking co-stars, publicists pleading with me to drop dirt on their clients' competition, photos of stars cheating on one another, video footage of threesomes and sex parties and Disney stars doing lines off asses in Malibu mansions. Shit that I would never, *ever* post in a million years. That I'd rather die than see leaked.

But now I'm thinking that encrypted part might not be secure enough.

That's why I'm here, trying to milk every piece of security know-how from Jake. I don't say any of that to him. I smile sweetly and nod agreeably. "Thank you so much."

"Oh, and get some spyware. Pay for the good stuff. It's worth it if you give a shit."

"Noted."

Jake gives Victoria a look that says *How long is this going to take?* and she nods at him like he's dismissed. "If you ladies will excuse me, I have to get some work done before the boys get home." He leans down and kisses the top of Victoria's head before giving her ass a squeeze and heading off to his home office, leaving the pizza box open on the table.

Victoria beams at him.

"So, that was helpful, huh?" Her face is hopeful, all wide eyes and smile, and I feel a sense of gratitude toward her. She just wants to help, to make things easier for me.

"Totally."

...

As soon as I get back to my apartment, I run through Jake's checklist of shit to do and then throw on some *Below Deck* while I dive into the chaos of the deuxmoi DMs. Usually, it's pretty easy to spot trends, like if one celeb had a super busy weekend, there are dozens of sightings, and it looks like today's man-about-town is Max Ryan, a drama writer who became famous after working on some high-brow whodunnit show called *The Museum*. Much to everyone's disappointment, he and his actress bestie are not romantically involved.

There are a slew of messages from people who say they saw him running around New York City:

> Max Ryan on St. Mark's and 3rd

> Max Ryan at Mike's in the LES tonight (Saturday). Maybe his birthday???

> Max Ryan at Mike's with his arm around a girl. Still looked every girl who walked in up and down

> Spotted Max Ryan at Balthazar with a really pretty girl on a date Saturday morning

> Another Max Ryan update: friend of mine had dinner at the table next to his at La Vara in Cobble Hill two nights ago (night after Mike's??). She said it was "very clearly a first date."

> I just saw Max Ryan on a date in Dumbo. "It was a lot because I was just so over yesterday," he said to a short pretty brunette

I compile them into one post and share, since it's so rare that a celeb is seen *this* often in a forty-eight-hour period. All that story does is usher in a whole bunch more Max Ryan tips. Most are mundane—he also popped by a stationery store and a natural wine shop. But then one comes in that nearly makes me spit out my iced coffee.

> That awk moment when I'm one of the girls mentioned in Max Ryan's weekend and not the others. Thx for saving me some heartache. Anon pls.

I throw my head back against my couch and laugh before typing back. *No fucking way. Which one?*

She responds, *Mike's. But def not Balthazar.*

Damn, sorry, I write. *Want me to post anon?*

She gives me the thumbs-up, and the DMs start to explode. Another one comes in:

> I dated Max Ryan for a minute two years ago. After a few dates, I discovered he was DMing my friend's friend. I mean, he was literally DMing her and texting me at the same time. Both of us were 23. He was 35.

> How many late twenty somethings is Max Ryan trying to get with lately? As one of them, I think we should all get drinks (without him) since there are SO many of us. There are so many things I want to talk about with other Maxhoes. Deuxmoi, can you connect us? Let's make some magic and make it happen!

I let out a laugh as I type back to her. *You got it, babe. I'll send people your way if they respond?*

She sends me some kissy emojis. *Just make sure they're legit on IG beforehand.*

I gotchu, I write, before posting her original message.

As my inbox floods with more and more DMs—one of which says that he was staging all of these sightings as promotion for an upcoming rom-com—I say a silent prayer that for all the ridiculous shit I've done, at least I didn't fall for a B-list screenwriter trying to cram as many dates as he can into a forty-eight-hour period in New York City.

Excerpt from Trendreport.com

Anonymous Gossip Account Brings Women Who Dated Max Ryan Together

Felicity Yoon, 22, didn't realize the guy she had been seeing, *The Museum* star Max Ryan, was also dating Olive Parker, 24, until she saw the anonymous gossip account deuxmoi post about Max Ryan's activities one weekend in New York City.

"I was shocked," she tells Trendreport. "We had dinner one night and then I saw online that he had gone on like five other dates that weekend. It's not illegal or anything, but it was just kind of shady."

After she saw deuxmoi's stories, she asked the account to connect her with other women who may have dated Max Ryan so they could compare stories. That's how she got in contact with Parker, as well as a dozen other women who allege they've gone out on dates with Ryan only to realize he was also seeing other women at the same time.

"It's just kind of hilarious that we all connected through deuxmoi," Yoon says. "We got together one Sunday morning and dished about Max and his extremely similar wooing techniques."

Asked for specifics, she politely declined. "The dude's already been put on blast. He got what was coming to him for trying to see us all in the same weekend, but he's not a monster."

CHAPTER 17

"Cricket!" Sasha's voice bellows across the open floor plan, causing dozens of staffers to look up, waiting to see how Sasha Sherman is going to terrorize her poor assistant today.

She's late—again—and I'm holding her English breakfast tea, which is quickly getting cooler by the second. I should have warmed it up before she walked in, but I was too busy texting Ollie, thanking him for saving my ass with the whole Madison Lee thing.

As Sasha stomps down the hallway, I shoot up in my seat, slapping on a fake smile. I hold out the paper cup to Sasha, and she grabs it from me, nearly spilling the lukewarm liquid onto the floor.

She motions for me to follow her into her office. Once inside, she sits down behind the desk and kicks off her Aquazzura pumps.

"Close the door."

I do, widening my eyes at Leon as he passes by in the hallway. He grimaces.

"The Duke Dudley deck was good," Sasha says without emotion.

"Good?" I echo. "Seriously?"

Sasha frowns. "Yes, seriously. What do you want, a fucking trophy for doing your job?"

"Thank you," I say, quiet. But I can't help but feel a bubble of pride swelling in my chest, even though it's been over a week since the presentation and Sasha's had plenty of time to tell me this. But it's the first time Sasha's given me a compliment on my work, and I hate how confident it makes me feel, how she has the power to give me a little boost but often chooses not to.

"I take it you heard the rumors about *The Viscounts* dropping Duke?" She takes a sip of her tea and acts like it's too hot, like I've burned her precious mouth. Liar.

"Just rumors," I say. "Doesn't the studio love him?"

Sasha swivels around and looks out the window, pressing her bare feet into the glass. I try not to gag when I see she's left little toe prints against the surface.

"If he goes down, we go down," she says, though it sounds like she's reminding herself more than she's telling me. "We need to diversify, make sure our other clients know how good we are. We need them to keep referring us. To put it bluntly, we need a backup plan."

I shift my weight from foot to foot. *Well, then maybe you should spend more time courting them*, I want to say, *instead of sleeping in and shutting off your phone for hours at a time while getting your ninety-minute Restorative Detox Wrap at the Mandarin Oriental.*

Sasha swivels around and stands up, shorter now without her heels.

"We're going to L.A.," she says. "Fox is doing a big young Hollywood special and I sweet-talked my old *Collection* boss into letting me style everyone for one of the segments. It's big—Sydney Sweeney, Jenna Ortega, Simone Ashley, Charles Melton. Nate and Iris from *One Percent*, obviously. I'll be taping a fashion breakdown spot with *Access Hollywood* to run as an aftershow."

She smirks, clearly proud of her own networking skills, but it's hard for me to focus on exactly what the job is because I'm still stuck on the first word she said. We. I force myself to be steady. Don't assume shit when it comes to Sasha Sherman.

"When do you want to fly?" I retrieve my notepad from under my arm and press the tip of my pen to the paper, ready to write down her requests.

Sasha smiles, an evil little grin that turns my insides to ice. "*We're flying out Thursday morning*," she says. "You're coming with me."

I swallow my gasp and nod my head like it's no big deal. Like I've definitely been invited on a business trip with Sasha before. Like I know how to travel for *work*.

"Book me a suite at the Beverly Hills Hotel. Get whatever room is cheapest for you. And you know what seat I like on the Delta flight, right?"

"1B," I say. She opens her mouth, but I interrupt. "I'll get whatever's cheapest on the same flight."

"She's learning," Sasha says, her voice light. "I'll send you the final packing list Wednesday night. Alyssa and I still need to finalize some of the looks."

I jot down all that info, making a memo to set an alarm for Wednesday afternoon, so I'll remember to be on the lookout.

Sasha drops down into her chair and spins around a few times, lazily without purpose. "That's all."

I bow my head down and turn for the door, but Sasha clears her throat, stopping me.

"Aren't you going to say something?" she asks. "Express some gratitude?"

A flush creeps up my cheeks. "Of course," I say. "Thank you, Sasha. Thank you so much. I won't let you down."

"You better not," she says. "This is our shot to land new contracts. There's a rumor Iris Leonard is on the hunt for a new long-term stylist. Nate Clyburn, too. If Duke goes down and we don't land someone to replace him . . ." She shakes her head. "It's gonna be tough times around here." Her voice is clipped now, harder than it was a few minutes ago. It's almost like she wants to put me on edge, make me squirm a little bit. Sasha's eyes meet mine, her brow narrowed and on guard. "We might have to let some people go. But if we do well in L.A.—if *you* do well—we can finally talk about that promotion."

In another world I'd tell her to fuck off, that if she wants more and better clients she shouldn't rest on her laurels and just assume that everyone wants to work with her because she once hosted the most popular reality show on the planet. That was almost a decade ago, and based on the DMs I've been getting, most people in the industry know who she is at her core—a cruel asshole.

But I don't say any of that. Because, even despite all that, I know this is my shot to finally reach the next level. My real shot. She's bringing me to Los Angeles, and I'm fucking ready.

‎ **...**

Ollie's texts arrive in rapid succession as I exit the plane, shouldering my bag, which is weighed down by pounds and pounds of lookbooks Sasha had me pack last night at two in the morning, while I was still at the office long after she had gone home. Thank goodness I had the foresight to bring all my stuff to work with me Wednesday morning, knowing I might end up staying there overnight, getting everything ready for the trip.

DEUXMOI GOES WEST!!!!!! he writes, the enthusiasm jumping off the screen. *That's the headline if the Daily Mail knew you were coming out here.*

And yes, obviously I won't tell anyone, he says in a follow-up. *But maybe . . . maybe we can finally meet?*

When I don't respond right away, he writes again. *Too forward? Come on, I'm dying to see you in person . . .*

I try to think of a witty response, something that might redirect the conversation away from me revealing who I actually am. It's tempting, the idea of seeing him, of letting my guard down for real.

But it's risky. I don't know him that well, and I haven't even told him my name or my age. He has no idea what I look like. All he knows is that I work in fashion and live in New York, and even those details seemed like too much to share.

Of course, there are the worries about what he might think about me if we met in person, but that's not why I'm so hesitant. Exposing myself to him, this guy I've only talked to on the phone, would be like giving him all the power to destroy me. What if things went sour between us and he wanted revenge? What if I betrayed him in some way and he wanted to do the same to me? It would be too easy to expose me, to share my info with anyone who cared. Madison Lee even threatening to reveal my identity sent me into a full-on spiral. Knowing there's someone out there who barely knows me—the real me—and has the power to do that, too, is terrifying.

I'll think about it, I write.

Please do, he says.

Then another text comes in.

> You know . . . I had a dream about you last night.

A burst of heat shoots to my core.

How? I ask. *You don't even know what I look like.*

> I can use my imagination.

I smirk, making my way down the terminal. *Were you trying to kill me or something?*

> Not exactly.

> Oh yeah? Do tell . . .

It was hot. That's all I'll say.

Tease.

Actually, that's what I thought
about YOU when I woke up alone . . .

My stomach clenches, heat spreading through my legs, but before
I can respond, I hear a familiar voice.

"Could you be any slower?" Sasha is standing near the far corner
of the gate, and she looks impatient, tapping her Fendi loafer against
the airport carpet. "What, were you sitting in the absolute last row
of the fucking plane?"

Yes, I want to say, *because that was the cheapest ticket available, which
was what you told me to book.* But I just smile and offer for her to go
sit in the hired black car while I wait to pick up the clothing trunks at
baggage claim. She begrudgingly accepts and stomps off, leaving me
with her Louis Vuitton carry-on suitcase and a plastic bag full of trash.

I finally make it to baggage claim ten minutes later, huffing and
puffing my way through LAX, stopping every few feet to rearrange all
the shit Sasha left me with. I rest all our bags on the ground and roll
my shoulders back. Through the revolving doors, I can see the sun is
shining and people in the terminal are already shedding their coats,
hungry to get outside.

My phone buzzes, and I see a new message from Ollie.

Okay, maybe that was too much.

My stomach flips, and I chew on my bottom lip, shifting my weight
from foot to foot.

Def not too much, I say. Then I decide to take a chance. *Was just imagining what our first meeting would be like.*

I mean, it could happen tomorrow . . . he writes in response, and then texts again:

> I'm going to keep the night open for you in case you want this to happen for real. We could even hit up Tower Bar. Do a little sleuthing of your own?

I stare at my phone for a second, not sure how I want to respond. The idea of going on an investigative mission with him to a beloved-by-celebs spot *does* sound exciting, but the *don't be stupid* part of my brain can't help but wonder if he's baiting me . . . if he's luring me somewhere, intending to expose who I really am. These texts. What if they're all a ruse? It's all too confusing and messy to even think about.

Sasha's name pops up on my screen with a text that reads, *Hurry up!!!!* But the bag carousel doesn't look like it's going to move anytime soon. I tell her I'm still waiting for the bags, and she takes a beat before responding.

> I'm leaving for the hotel. Need to nap. Get an uber there.

I want to throw my phone out the revolving door, but instead I back up against the wall and press my spine into it.

I'll think about it, I tell Ollie. *Hard.*

He sends me back a prayer-hand emoji.

I bring my phone close to my chest and peek down, pulling up all the DMs and emails I missed while in the air. Might as well make use of the idle time and take screenshots of messages that seem worthy of posting.

But in the middle of all the spotteds and blind items and tour riders is an email from a Condé Nast email address. Someone named Naomi Rutherford. For a split second I wonder if she's a source, trying to drop some media gossip about Anna Wintour or spill who's going to be on next month's *Vogue* cover. But then I see the subject line.

From: nrutherford@condenast.com

To: Deuxmoi@gmail.com

Date: September 7, 2022, 11:30 am ET

Subject: Press request for whoever runs deuxmoi

> Hello deuxmoi,
> I'm a reporter at *Vivendi* hoping to get in touch with whoever runs this account. We are intrigued by what you've been doing and believe our readers are as well. I want to interview you for our magazine. Thinking a behind-the-scenes piece. What it's like to run this account. Would you be open to speaking with me? I know you're anonymous, but if you want to meet in person, let me know.
>
> Naomi Rutherford
> Senior Reporter, *Vivendi*

I squeeze my eyes shut and let out a slow, long breath. *Fuck. Vivendi* is the real deal. A cross between *New York* magazine and *Vanity Fair*, but if they were both younger, cooler, and a little more tongue-in-cheek. Every year they publish an annual Power Rankings list of young, hot celebs that basically dictates who and what is cool for the upcoming year. Kayla Cole made the cut after she released her debut album. I've already started getting tips about who might be on the cover of this year's issue.

Speaking with them could open me up to a whole new demographic of readers *and* sources—A-listers I haven't been able to make contact with or verify information from. It could legitimize me.

I dial Leon and wait for him to pick up. When he does, it sounds like he's out at a noisy restaurant, silverware clinking behind him.

"Everything good?" he asks. "How's L.A.?"

"*Vivendi* wants to interview me," I say, unable to hold it in.

"Excuse me?" he almost yells.

"About running the account. Behind the scenes. All that."

"Whoa." I hear chair legs scrape against the floor, the sound of Leon leaving wherever he is. "Hold on, I'm going outside."

"Where are you?" I ask.

"American Bar," he says. "And no, there's no one good here." He sighs hard. "But wait, *Vivendi*?"

"Insane, right?"

He hesitates in a way that makes my heart drop.

"I know what you're going to say," I start. "I'd do it anonymously. That's the condition."

"Right, but she's a reporter. She might find out anyway. I don't want to say it, but . . ."

"Flying too close to the sun, I know."

He sighs. "You're going to do what you want but just . . . be careful, okay?"

"Of course."

"And whatever you do, just don't mention me, okay?"

I let out a laugh. "Seriously? How would you even come up?" But when he doesn't laugh, I say, "Obviously, babe."

There's a pause on the other end of the line before Leon speaks again. "All I ask is that you at least come up with a plan in case she goes full detective, okay?"

"You got it."

We hang up and I know there's some risk, like Leon said, but my gut's telling me to do the interview, to see what happens. I head back to my email and compose a response.

There's no way in hell I'm going to meet this woman in person, but we *could* talk over the phone. I've been told that I sound like every basic bitch on the East Coast, so there's no way she'd recognize my voice. Releasing that piece of me out into the world feels . . . okay. That feels safe. Plus, if I talk to a reporter about what I've been up to, then maybe I can drive the narrative, explain what it's like to run the account—that I'm actually checking stuff out, doing my own legwork to explain and report out stories, to check in with celebrities and casting directors.

The loudspeaker crackles overhead, and a distorted voice rings out. "Flight 745 from JFK, your bags are now arriving on carousel eight."

A rush of people pushes past me, but I stay grounded in place, my shoulders pressed against the cold wall. I know what I want to do and how I'm going to do it. I just have to say yes.

I type out an email, my hands shaking slightly with excitement.

Not meeting in person, but we can talk, I write. *7 pm PT tonight?*

I hit send, the message whooshing away into the ether, and then make my way through the crowd. Just as I get to the carousel, I spot the three fifty-pound trunks full of designer clothes that I spent hours packing the night before, going around for another spin, disappearing behind a group of tourists wearing Disneyland shirts.

I try to elbow my way through the crowd to follow them, but I'm thwarted by a bunch of muscley frat bros, too tan and wearing backward flat-brim hats, and a loud-phone-talker screaming. Finally, I give up and root myself in place, the rest of our bags by my side. I crane my neck to keep my eyes on the trunks as I wait for them to circle back around.

Crossing my arms over my chest and ignoring the sweat forming under my bra line, I make a promise to myself that this is the last time I travel to Los Angeles as someone else's assistant.

CHAPTER 18

It takes ninety-eight minutes to get from LAX to our hotel, where the concierge at the front desk tells me Sasha has left me a key to her suite, so I can go up and start organizing the trunks, which are sitting behind me, stacked on a luggage cart. I let out a puff of air and ask the man, "Did she say where she went?"

He looks around before leaning in to whisper something over the counter.

"She's having dinner with Duke Dudley at Mother Wolf." He wiggles his eyebrows, and I get the sense that this man is a hopeful actor, thanks to his severe jawline and impeccable hairline. "She left this message, too."

He hands me a slim envelope, and I open it to find a few lines written on thick cardstock.

> You're on your own for the night. See you at 11 a.m. sharp.

I nod curtly and thank the man before heading up to Sasha's suite. When I arrive, I'm not surprised to see it looks just like the photos on her Instagram feed, classic and cool with views of palm trees and the iconic pink cabanas downstairs.

The bellhop skips away after I hand him a twenty, making a mental note to add that to my Sasha reimbursement tab. It takes all my energy not to flop on her king-size bed and fall asleep right there. Just imagining the look on her face if she found me kind of makes me want to do it, but I resist and instead spend the next hour and a half organizing all the looks, cataloging everything we brought, and making mental notes of where things are so I can be prepared for tomorrow.

By the time I finally get to my own room on one of the bottom floors, I'm so exhausted I want to pass out immediately. I check my phone to find it's only five p.m., and even though I'm horribly jet-lagged, I know I have to stay alert if I want to nail this interview with *Vivendi.*

But not without provisions.

What's your go-to delivery near Beverly Hills? I ask Ollie.

He texts back immediately. *She returns,* he writes, which elicits a snort. *I thought I scared you off.*

> You're gonna have to do a lot more than send some pretty PG texts to scare me.

He sends a laughing emoji, then writes, *Jon & Vinny's. It may be basic but there's a reason why it's always on your feed. That shit's good.*

I nod, pulling up the menu. Just as I'm about to place an order for some spicy fusilli and an antipasto salad, he texts again, this time a photo of a DoorDash receipt consisting of both of those things plus a pizza, some tuna appetizer that sounds incredible, a rainbow cookie, and a couple of chocolate chip cookies.

All my faves, he says. *On me.*

Oh, come on, I respond, not even trying to hide a smile. *You don't have to do that.*

Too late, he writes. *Having it delivered to the BHH under the name Lucille Ball. Just tell the front desk to send it up when it gets there.*

My stomach grumbles in response, and I'm overcome with a sense of gratitude toward this stranger, who all of a sudden doesn't really feel like a stranger at all.

I type out my name—my real name—in the text box, wondering if I have the guts to do this, to reveal my identity, right here, right now. But then I remember the agony that filled my stomach when I thought Madison Lee had cracked it. How nervous Leon was when I said I was doing an interview with a reporter. I'm just not ready.

You're too much, I say.

Just tryna prove I'm worth meeting.

Jesus, this guy is corny. I hate that it's working.

I glance at the clock and see that I still have a little time to go through my DMs and emails before my call with this reporter, Naomi. So, I change into my Free City sweats and hunker down against my pillows, throwing on some background noise on the TV. Pretty soon my feast is here, and I chow down as I share new stories and engage in a back-and-forth with Iris Leonard, who's been recently writing in to dish on her *One Percent* co-stars.

I once asked her why she wanted to give them up, and she sent me a shrugging emoji. *Better them than me, huh?*

I responded as professionally as I could: *You know I'm going to keep posting about you, right? My followers are obsessed with you and Nate.*

You better, she wrote. *But only the RIGHT info. Giving you intel makes me more trustworthy, doesn't it?*

She'd had a point. Tonight, she's spilling about the same woman who leaked audio of Iris fucking Nate on set, though Iris doesn't know that. Apparently, Iris is pretty sure that actress's manager was trying to pimp her out to a few older A-list actors on the hunt for younger stars to screw.

I want to keep her talking, but when I glance at the time, I see it's almost seven. Shit.

Over in my email, Naomi Rutherford followed up: *Still on?*

I squeeze my eyes shut and say a silent prayer even though I haven't prayed since I was thirteen. My AirPods are snug in my ears as I dial Naomi Rutherford.

She picks up on the first ring.

"Deuxmoi," she says, a casual, almost jolly lilt in her voice. "Is it really you?"

"You'd have no way of knowing if it wasn't," I say, feeling more confident than I have all day. "So, let's go with yes."

She laughs. "Touché." I can almost picture her nodding on the other end of the line as she leans back in whatever uncomfortable desk chair she's got inside her home office. I pull my laptop onto my legs and google her. Dozens of photos pop up—author headshots dating back a decade, grainy Facebook photos, a few party pics at book events. Over on her Instagram, which I look at through an incognito browser, she seems tall, with the same shag haircut that all the girls who live in Brooklyn have. She has a hairless cat named Pecan and a boyfriend who runs a music venue I've never heard of. All her friends look like her, posing with potted plants and stacks of paperback books piled high on hardwood floors.

Her LinkedIn says she went to Yale and studied comparative literature. We have no mutual friends on Facebook, no clear connectors tethering our lives together. My stomach settles with relief. She won't find me.

"So," Naomi says. "I bet you know what I'm going to ask you."

"What's that?"

"Well, obviously everyone wants to know who you are." She pauses, waiting for me to out myself, to say anything that might indicate who she's talking to. But I stay silent, knowing she'll have to fill the void. "But you're not going to tell me, are you?"

"Nope," I say.

She sighs. "Worth a shot, huh? My editor would kill me if I didn't ask. And if you do change your mind, you must know that *Vivendi* would be the perfect place to unveil your identity. Obviously, we're so well-respected. It would legitimize you in a million different ways."

I bristle a bit at her notion that I'm not already legitimate, but I try to ignore her offer and move on. "I thought you wanted to talk about behind-the-scenes stuff? How I run the account?"

"Definitely. How you started it, how it works, how you make it all happen. No details are boring. I want to know . . . everything."

"All right," I say, settling into the chair. I breathe in and think for a second, trying to piece together exactly what I want to say and how I want to say it. I could talk about how I get information—how I deduce what's real versus what's bogus—or how certain unnamed celebs like to slide into my DMs, hoping to trade nuggets of information for favorable coverage down the line.

But I know she'll be waiting for me to slip, to reveal a piece of information about how I get to my office or where I live or what it is I do all day that allows me to stay bound to this Instagram account, a little piece of digital real estate so ephemeral it feels like it might float away if I left it untended.

It's a dangerous thing, to be asked about yourself, to be told you're interesting and that you might have some sort of power—something someone else wants. Because if you give away too much, you might just throw away everything you've been building, everything you were hoping to achieve.

I consider my options as she waits patiently on the other end of the line. Through my headphones, I hear obvious sounds of New York in the background—a few sirens, a faint hint of music blasting from a speaker outside her window, the honking of horns, the patience of a reporter waiting to pounce.

Maybe it's being in a hotel room so far from home, or the fact that a hot guy from another city just bought me dinner without even knowing my name or how my face looks when I laugh—or perhaps it's the fact that the account gained another two hundred followers from the time I started this phone call. Whatever the reason may be, I take her questions as an invitation to start talking. I clear my throat and lean back against the fluffy pile of pillows, resting my head against the comforting fabric.

"It all started when I realized . . ."

Reddit
r/Deuxmoi

romp4521: longtime dm fan here. ever since Madison Lee posted she knew who DM is, I can't stop thinking about finding this ish out!!! likeeee who is this person? I've heard she works in fashion. Can anyone confirm???

>**Celebstar1234:** def a fashion person. Maybe in publicity?????

>**Pooooooo___:** no way, my working guess is that she's a back-up dancer for Beyonce. I've got RECEIPTS!

>**ingridgoeseast:** I've heard the rumor that she works for a certain bitchy stylist made famous on Collection. but you didn't hear that from me!!!!!

>**romp4521:** @ingridgoeseast for real? Let's talk . . .

CHAPTER 19

I wake up to the Los Angeles sun streaming into my hotel room, a warm and pleasant feeling taking over my chest, remembering my conversation with Naomi, the reporter, last night. She seemed genuinely interested in what I was doing and *why*, wondering how I'm able to convince people to spill their guts to me—when in reality there's so little convincing. People just *want* to. It helps that I assure them that their secrets are safe with me. As I explained to Naomi, my number one priority is protecting my sources—I would never want anyone to get fired from their job for spilling to an IG account. I actually feel like I could trust her, but then I remember that one of Ollie's first pieces of advice is to never trust reporters and I start second-guessing everything I said to her.

Thanks to being on New York time, I have a few hours to spare before I'm due at the warehouse in Downtown L.A. for the shoot, so I start searching through my DMs and getting a head start on the day's content.

There's a slew of sightings from last night's Lakers game, where Olivia Wilde and Harry Styles were sitting side by side with Drake and his new girlfriend, so naturally *everyone* is freaking out. There's also the start of Adele's Vegas residency, which so many celebs, including John Legend, Andy Cohen, and Sandra Oh, attended. I DM back and forth a bit with a publicist, who wants to get me to start posting about one of her no-name clients, and get another email from Kyle Johns, asking me where my head's at with his offer.

Still thinking, I respond, punting it down the line for another few weeks.

Don't think too long, he writes back. *We could make a splash by summer if we start now.*

I ignore him for now and tap over to the deuxmoi email inbox to read my most recent message.

9/8/22

Sent via form submission from Deuxmoi

Pseudonyms, Please: Betty Frocker
Subject: Fake Cakes

Dunno how deuxmoi worthy this is, but this bakery in LA that is VERY popular among celebrities, influencers, and caterers uses Betty Crocker cake mix for all of their cakes and cupcakes. They try to distinguish themselves as being unique and "luxury" but . . . literally store-bought mixes! They don't even try to hide the boxes.

Signed,

an anonymous former employee fed up with the shitty way they treat their staff.

I stifle a laugh and screenshot the message before sending it to Ollie.

> What bakery do you think this is? Do people care about this shit?

He responds immediately.

Def talking about Poppy Baby. Honestly that would be insane if true. They're vegan and are ALL about using natural, organic ingredients. Or at least so they say. Also, it's Oprah's favorite cake place.

No shit?

Dare you to do a little digging. It's not too far from you.

I pop over to Google Maps and find that he's totally right. Based on the time, I could head over there, grab a coffee, and try to find some intel before getting back in time to get to the photoshoot with time to spare.

Done.

I quickly screenshot the original tip and share it to deuxmoi before brushing my teeth as fast as I can, my eyes glued to the little notification button. The messages come in fast, with dozens of people asking to confirm which bakery might be the culprit. A few even suggest Poppy Baby, too.

I leave them all on read until I see one from Jessie Reagan, the model-turned-cookbook-author known for recipes like Meat Lover's Tater Tot Nachos Supreme.

Babe, I NEED to know what bakery this is! If it's Poppy Baby, I'll lose my shit and never trust a single business again!!!!!! Have I been eating store-bought cake made

> with butter when I thought I was eating all-natural vegan cakes?! I'm losing my shit!!!

I reply, *dw . . . I'm on the case.*

...

Poppy Baby is located on one of the main drags in Silver Lake, where I spy a few of the stars of *Cruel Summer* having coffee and pastries at the outdoor tables.

Poppy's awning is a swatch of pale pink, and the name is scrawled across in bright orange loopy cursive. It's sweet and inviting, with a window full of cakes—beautiful confections of all flavors that kind of make me drool. A chalkboard display out front says in bubble letters: "All vegan! All natural! All SoCal!"

Even though it's only 8:00 a.m., the line is already out the door and I get in the queue behind a tall woman with blond hair, dressed in head-to-toe Alo yoga gear. An oversized Loewe bag hangs off her shoulder. Standing next to her is a smaller woman glued to her phone, loudly snapping gum as she taps her foot with that real nervous assistant energy. And now that I take in the rest of the crowd, I see that lots of the people in line do, too. There are so many young customers, looking up nervously, craning their necks to see how far they've moved up in line over the past few minutes, just trying to get closer to the counter to pick up their cake for whoever ordered it and get the hell outta here before their boss loses their shit.

I've got a while before I should be back at the hotel, so I settle in for a solid amount of eavesdropping, and as I step a few feet up in line, I know the women in front of me won't disappoint.

"You ordered the mocha chip with buttercream frosting, right?" the blond woman asks, her arms crossed over her chest.

"Uh-huh," the smaller one says, nodding without looking up from her phone.

"And you had them write what I asked?"

"'Last penis forever!'" I recognize her voice as fake enthusiastic, the same one I use with Sasha when I want her to think that her idea is genius but it's actually idiotic.

The blond woman shakes her hair out and turns to the side, looking right at her assistant. When I see who she is, I suppress a surprised gasp. Standing in front of me is Lori Powers, the latest runner-up of *The Bachelor*. I've never watched an episode, but people in my DMs are always talking about Lori and the other girls from this past season, in which the contestants were vying for the heart of a hipster DJ from Houston known for loving the Rockets and barbecue ribs. Unclear what his personality is actually like, since the show never really gets into that.

But like most other former contestants, Lori now lives in Los Angeles, working as an influencer and selling advertisements for hair products on Instagram as she tries to launch her own makeup company. Or something like that.

And now, at 8:00 a.m. on a Friday, she's in front of me at this very trendy vegan bakery, picking up a cake for what seems to be a bachelorette party. Why the fuck would she want to be here herself? Unless . . .

I turn around and . . . yep. There are a few paparazzi stationed on the other side of the street and by the bistro tables under the awning, ready to snap photos of people picking up their cakes from Poppy Baby. And right now, they're trained directly at Lori, whose face is all full smiles and well-done contouring.

"Are they getting me?" she whispers to the smaller woman, who looks up from her phone and glances at the cameras.

"Yup. Your good side, too."

Lori nods and glances around. "I kinda thought I'd run into someone here," she muses. "Isn't this Oprah's favorite place?"

The assistant makes affirming noises as we all inch closer to the front door. "Don't worry," she says. "It'll be a good look. Supporting a local business and all. Plus, Stella will love it."

Ah, so the cake is for her co-star Stella James, who got engaged to an L.A. Rams player after a whirlwind romance. The followers went nuts over that one—the former Buffalo Bills cheerleader falling in love with a tight end? Pure gold. She and Lori must actually be close if Lori's here picking up her cake. I make a mental note to send myself an anonymous email and post about this later.

Finally, the line picks up, and when we get inside, I take a look around, searching for . . . I don't know, stray boxes of grocery store cake mix? The whole endeavor feels a little ridiculous, but when I see Lori squeal as she picks up her box and take a selfie with the cashier, an adoring fan, I know I should stick it out.

When it's my turn to order, I tell the barista I'd like a slice of banana bread and a coffee.

"You don't want to try any cake?" she asks. "We're best known for our marble flavor. Peanut butter chocolate, too. All vegan and those ones are gluten free!" Her grin takes up her whole face as she gestures to the glass window full of meticulously decorated cakes, topped with brightly colored confection flowers and fresh fruit, full chocolate chip cookies and macarons. A few seem to be overflowing with chunks of cookie dough and brownie bits, glistening under the overhead lights. My stomach rumbles, and I guess I might as well taste the thing if I'm going to go full reportage over here.

"Sure," I say. "A marble slice."

She nods and slides a silver knife under the cake, slipping my piece inside a cardboard box alongside a hunk of banana bread.

I pay for it all and settle in at a table off to the side, near where Lori and her assistant have set up shop, sipping coffees, turning toward the cameras still outside.

But suddenly, I hear Lori gasp. The color drains from her face, and she angles her screen at her assistant, a look of shock in her eyes.

The assistant looks down and then flits her eyes back up to Lori. "Here?" she asks quietly. "From the *box*?" Her gaze roams the room, fearful and tense, and all of a sudden, it's obvious she's looking at deuxmoi, wondering the same thing I am: Is this place full of shit?

Lori gathers up her stuff and mouths, *Let's go.* Together, she and her assistant try to slip out the door as quietly as possible. I stifle a laugh and take a bite of cake, which, sure, is good. But also definitely sort of tastes like the Funfetti we used to make while stoned in college, though maybe they use milk instead of water, or butter instead of vegetable oil, which would make this *definitely* not vegan.

I wash down the cake with the lukewarm coffee, which kind of reminds me of mud, and hatch a very halfhearted attempt at a plan: If I pretend like I'm going to the bathroom, no one will suspect that I'm actually snooping around for evidence of store-bought cake mixes. I chuck my garbage and walk quickly toward the back of the bakery, where the bathroom and kitchen are situated, keeping my head down and trying my hardest not to look suspicious.

There's no one in the hallway and I can hear the sounds of a few people moving around in the back room. I take a step forward, but just then a large man with a flour-stained white apron appears, his hands on his hips. "You can't come back here," he says, all gruff like he's a cop or something.

I hold up my hands and walk back. "Just looking for the bathroom," I say.

He points behind me, where I know the actual restroom is waiting, and he doesn't move until I smile demurely and step inside the closet-size powder room.

I might as well check Instagram while I'm here, and when I do, I see that the account has been *flooded* by messages of people seemingly obsessed with this news. I swear, it'll always surprise me when people freak out over stuff like this.

> If this is about Poppy Baby, I'm going to lose my SHIT

> They're also assholes to their delivery people.

> Honestly, I saw evidence in the dumpster there once.
> This does not surprise me one bit.

One last stop in the trash, I guess. I wash up and leave through the front door, making a beeline for the side of the storefront. I peek around and make sure no one sees me slip into the small space between Poppy Baby and a juice place, and then I spot the dumpster all the way back, almost behind the bakery.

I creep down there, pulling my shirt up over my nose to try to stop the smell of stinking hot garbage. Thankfully it's an old black tee from Zara. Suddenly, the side door opens and I see someone—a young guy wearing an apron and a backward cap—hauling plastic garbage bags over his shoulder. I press myself up against the side of the building, hoping he doesn't see me, and hold my breath as he tosses the bags up into the trash, landing with a thud. I peek over my shoulder, and for a second it seems like he's going to look right at me, but then he turns and heads back inside, grumbling to himself under his breath.

When I think the coast is clear, I tiptoe over to the trash, still trying to cover my nose and take a peek at what he just threw out. But the lip of the lid is too high for me to see the contents. I grab my phone from my pocket and reach it up as high as I can, angling the camera toward the dumpster. I take a few photos, my arm outstretched, trying to get as many shots as I can. But then I hear the side door swing open again, the squeaking of hinges, and know I've got to get out of there if I don't want to get caught.

I let out a puff of air and make a run for it, sprinting toward the back alley that exits out the other side, where I know there aren't any paparazzi.

"Hey!" someone calls behind me. "What are you doing?!"

But I don't stop until I get halfway down the next block and don't dare pull out my phone until I'm safely inside the hotel elevator alone, little beads of sweat sliding down my back. But when I open my camera roll and see what's there, I cover my mouth and laugh: an enormous clear garbage bag stuffed with rectangular cardboard boxes proclaiming the name *Betty Crocker* across the front—and butter wrappers that say Costco's brand, Kirkland.

The tipsters were right.

Hungry LA

Poppy Baby Accused of Making Cakes with Store-Bought Mix

One of Oprah's most recent "favorite things" may not be so favorite anymore. Famed Los Angeles vegan bakery Poppy Baby has been a go-to stop for celebrities to purchase must-have cakes in recent years (they famously made a custom three-tier chocolate chiffon version for Katy Perry's last birthday party). But according to tips posted on the anonymous Instagram account deuxmoi, they may actually use store-bought Betty Crocker cake mix—and animal products like butter, eggs, and milk—to create those showstopping confections that they market as vegan.

Deuxmoi didn't name the bakery when she posted the tip, but eagle-eyed L.A. residents were quick to jump on the tip and head over to Poppy Baby's Instagram account, where they left hundreds of comments, saying they know they're the bakery in question.

"I saw betty crocker boxes in your dumpster!" one user wrote.

"So did i!" another said. "And you're charging $75 for a miniature cake that feeds only four people! I call bullshit."

When reached for comment, Andrew Jenkins, the longtime owner of Poppy Baby, hung up the phone. We'll update this story as we learn more.

CHAPTER 20

I make it back to the hotel just in time to meet the four production assistants tasked with helping me get the trunks out of Sasha's suite, into a van, and over to the photoshoot, which is only a few blocks away from the hotel. But the whole process takes over an hour, and by the time we have all the clothing hung up on metal racks, ready to be prepped, I'm sweating through my black T-shirt and praying Sasha doesn't notice when she arrives.

The PAs are fresh-faced in that sun-drenched Los Angeles way— all dewy and smiley—and are delightfully professional, dressed all in black, too, just like Sasha asked. They've clearly worked for Fox for a while and are focused on making sure we get the clothes hung, steamed, and sorted so we can get the shoot going as fast as possible.

"Time is money!" one of their supervisors shouts as we hustle around the space in not-so-graceful choreography.

I snort and cover my mouth, trying to hide my amusement. But one of the PAs, Lucia, turns to me and rolls her eyes. "It's like he watched a *How to Do Hollywood* video," she whispers before rushing off to straighten a fallen clothing rack. I decide I like her immediately.

The other PAs huddle around the craft services table, filled with platters of fresh fruit and pastries. I reach for a bunch of grapes when another PA, named Ben, leans over, nodding toward a stack of biscuits. "Those are from Poppy Baby," he says, arching an eyebrow.

"Oh yeah?" I ask, genuinely surprised. "They're vegan, right?"

Ben looks at me all serious. "Well, they're *supposed* to be." He glances around like he's about to tell a secret. "But I just read on deuxmoi they use store-bought cake mix *and* butter. Can you believe it?"

I nearly choke on a grape. It's the first time I've heard someone drop "deuxmoi" in casual conversation, and I can't help but admit that it feels *insane* to know that this guy assumes everyone would know what he's talking about.

"No way," I say. "That's wild."

He crosses his arms and grabs a banana. "Seriously. I heard Eater's doing a whole big investigation now."

"Damn," I say, making a mental note to do a sweep of coverage later and see how far this tip traveled. But that'll have to wait.

We have about twenty minutes before Sasha is due to get here. Looking around, I feel like we've got the place in order, ready for her to make some styling magic happen.

I run my hands over the pieces of clothes, admiring Lucia's steaming skills, and hang up a stray belt that's fallen onto the floor. The place looks good, organized. Like an actual stylist put this together and not some helpless assistant. Over by the wall, dozens of heels, pumps, and boots are lined up, organized by style then designer, in alphabetical order. I try not to gush over a pair of bright purple Roger Vivier satin mules with a crystal cube in each heel. Next to the shoes, Lucia's finishing up the jewelry table, where velvet-lined trays are filled with necklaces, earrings, and rings, sparkling as they catch the light. Jennifer Meyer sent over some items from her new collection, but I can't help but eye the diamond chokers from Anita Ko, sitting in their own Lucite boxes in front of a security guard watching them with a close eye.

Over on the far wall, pictures of all of Sasha's planned looks are pinned to a V-flat, and I grab the iPad on the table to make sure each look is loaded there, too, for easy access as Sasha walks around the room from set to set as we shoot.

But with every step, I'm hyperaware of my phone in my back pocket, beckoning me to look at the account, to see what's happened—if there are any Poppy Baby updates, any emails from Naomi, any DMs that need replies, tips that *have* to go up now. Any texts from Ollie . . .

I clear my throat and tell Lucia and the other PAs that I'm running to the bathroom, but when I get there, I lower the toilet seat and sit on top, thumbing through my DMs. There are a bunch of hilarious reactions to the Poppy Baby news, including one from a beloved vegan celebrity chef who is genuinely devastated—*I've been ordering their cakes for years!!*—and lowkey furious—*I'm going to sue for false advertising!* Food writers are hitting me up, too, asking for details. I tell a reporter from the *Los Angeles Times* that yes, I definitely saw a Betty Crocker box and a butter wrapper in the dumpster, before checking in on some of the non-bakery drama tips of the day.

There's a message from one of my usual sources, Iris Leonard's publicist, Mary Jo Ehrlich, who's a pseudo-celebrity in her own right since she recently left one of the big agencies after suing them for discrimination and launched her own firm. Now she's considered to be one of the biggest power players in publicity.

> Babe, just sharing some news that Iris and Nate are going to be featured in a big Young Hollywood spot with Fox, alongside the likes of Sydney Sweeney and Charles Melton. They were the ONLY stars from One Percent asked to be part of it. Shoot happening soon and will probably release in a few weeks. HUGE deal for Iris, obv. Hoping this launches her into leading lady parts.

"Bitch, I'm here!" I want to scream through the phone, but instead I just respond: *Love it. Can I post??*

She sends me a thumbs-up and writes *anon pls.* I share the screenshot, blocking out her name just as the door swings open and bangs against the wall. Footsteps get louder, squeaking against the linoleum, and I look up, alert.

"Cricket?" someone calls. "Sasha just got here."

Shit. "One second!" I flush the toilet and hurry out of the stall, washing my hands at a record pace.

Lucia looks at me, wide-eyed but a little more on edge than she was twenty minutes ago. "Everything okay?" I ask as she opens the door for me. I try to keep my voice light, as if that might quell whatever's going on.

"We should probably run," Lucia says. Her voice is bubbly but a little strained as she glances at me sideways. "Sasha doesn't seem . . . enthused."

Uh-oh. "Has she thrown anything yet?"

Lucia's eyes go wide, and she stops short in the middle of the hall. Her mouth hangs open just a bit. "Is that something we should expect?"

I shrug. Best not freak to her out right away. Sasha will show her true colors in a sec anyway. "Not if we do our jobs well."

Lucia now looks frightened, but as soon as we get back to the set, I know she should be. We all should be. Sasha's face is bright red as she unleashes a verbal tirade on a balding white man with a headset and a clipboard. She swings her head around and I want to hide, but I know it's no use as she spots me turning the corner, her eyes narrowing. "There you are," she says, loud enough to make half the people in the room turn.

"I was in the bathroom," I mumble.

"What? Were you vomiting up your breakfast?" she says in an equally loud tone that makes my insides shrivel. One of the photographers shakes his head, clearly mortified on my behalf. "I've been waiting for you for ten minutes. Where the hell is my tea?"

"I thought you went out for breakfast with—"

She puts on a whiny voice and imitates my words, an even bigger embarrassment, and right now I want to disappear into the wall.

"There's no time. Iris Leonard's car is arriving any second. I need you to just make sure everything is in order for her looks," she snaps. "Got it?"

I nod and wait a beat to see if she needs anything else.

"What are you waiting for? Go!"

She shoos me away and then spins on her heel, retreating to the other side of the room, where Iris's publicist, Mary Jo, has just shown up. For a moment, I'm amazed by the fact that she has no idea who I really am—that she doesn't know I'm the person she literally *just* spoke to on Instagram. She probably sent those DMs when she was walking in from the parking lot, only feet away from where I'm standing now.

She looks at me, but she barely registers my presence. In her eyes, in real life, I'm a nobody. A nonentity. No one with power or influence, just a background player who can get her a green juice.

Someone touches my shoulder lightly, and I spin around on my heel.

"Are you okay?" Lucia asks. She motions behind her to where Sasha is still fuming, fists clenched by her side.

When I see the look of concern on Lucia's face, I can tell she's worried about me, maybe even embarrassed. That realization turns my throat scratchy. My palms sweaty. I don't want pity. I don't want her to feel bad for me, a grown woman who was just berated in front of a room full of strangers. All I have to do is act normal, like that wasn't totally humiliating. "Absolutely." I nod my head hard before leaning in and cupping my hand around my mouth, lowering my voice. "She gets like this, you know. Best to just stay out of her way and not give her anything to criticize." I scrunch up my nose and shrug in a *what can you do?* way, but Lucia doesn't seem to buy it. "How about we get Iris's first look prepared, yeah?"

Together we set out the outfit—a Jil Sander high-waisted, wide-legged sailor pant paired with chunky platforms and a Saint Laurent color-block tweed jacket, no undershirt—and I sneak a peek at Sasha, laughing it up far away from me. My heart rate settles, knowing she's calmed down. I see she even has a large English breakfast tea, which means she may even be . . . happy. Good. That means I might have a few minutes to spare.

"I'm just gonna get some water," I tell Lucia, who barely registers me as she moves over to help the photographer with the lighting.

I duck into the hallway near the craft services buffet and back up against the wall before pulling out my phone, tapping over to Instagram. As predicted, there are dozens of replies, asking about the young Hollywood shoot.

Nate Clyburn himself even responded: *Whoops, guess I should get outta bed and get my ass to the shoot then! Heh.*

A few other publicists slide into my DMs, wondering who else is on the shoot—likely trying to get intel for their bosses or cover their own asses for not getting their clients booked. I respond to a bunch with some shrugging emojis and post a few screenshots of sightings: Jerry Seinfeld at Barney Greengrass with his daughter, Jordan Peele browsing at the Barnes & Noble at the Grove, Reese Witherspoon spotted at a home goods store in Nashville, Priyanka Chopra eating lunch at Nobu in Malibu, Lil Nas X tipping really well at a midwestern Italian joint while on tour. Classic content that will elicit the usual kind of enthusiasm.

It's a risky move, posting so out in the open, but no one's walked by in minutes. Priyanka just followed the account, replying to her sighting with a kissy face, and Reese Witherspoon's daughter asked me to tag the store, noting that they're a small women-owned business. I oblige, then post a few more screenshots about BakeryGate, and message back and forth with the folks from Hungry LA, who are looking into the cake box situation, too.

I know I should call it quits now, but more replies come in the more I post, and I go through them as fast as I can, trying to read at hyper-speed.

"Cricket!" Sasha yells, her voice shrill and high.

Fuck.

I stuff my phone into my pocket and grab a hot tea from the table, rushing it over to where Sasha is standing.

"Thought you might want a refill." I hold it out to her, and she looks at it like I may be trying to poison her. "English breakfast tea," I say. "Unsweetened."

"I know what it is. I didn't ask for it. Jesus. You're more brain dead than usual today."

I lower my hands and set the tea back down on the table next to me, wishing I could chuck it at her face.

"Iris is just about here. I need you to go make sure her driver knows where to park."

"Got it," I say, turning toward the door.

"You need the car info, idiot."

I pause and swivel on my heel so I'm facing her annoyed, frustrated face.

"A black Jeep with tinted windows."

"On it."

"Tell them to pull around the back," Sasha says. "And don't you *dare* make small talk. You sound like a dying frog when you're nervous."

Someone titters with laughter as they walk by, and I try to hide my reddening face behind my curtain of hair. As I make my way toward the back entrance, I wonder why the hell *she* isn't going out there to greet Iris Leonard. Shouldn't Sasha's face be the first one Iris sees if Sasha wants to make a good impression? Win this woman over as an actual client? Instead, Sasha turns back to her phone, tapping her heel against the concrete floor at a rapid pace.

Stepping outside, I'm at least grateful for the L.A. sun shining down on me, and I feel a sense of relief that at least I'm out of Sasha's sight line. For now.

I don't see any signs of Iris and realize there's no one around. So, I pull out my phone and post a few more stories. But then suddenly my phone rings and Sasha's name pops up. My stomach sinks as I answer.

"I told you to have them pull around the *back*," she screams.

I whip my head around, hoping to see the Jeep but the parking lot is still empty. "They're not here."

"Obviously," she says. "They're in the front. I told *you* to go that way and tell them to come around the back. For fuck's sake. How many times do I have to tell you what to do? Run around and show them where to park."

She hangs up, and I sprint around to the front of the building, clutching my phone in my hand. Shame builds in my chest, and for the first time, I realize that I'm half-assing my job more than I ever have before, putting more effort into deuxmoi than the job I've spent eight years trying to protect. I shake my head, blinking back tears.

You got this, Cricket. You're not an idiot, no matter what Sasha says. Just pay attention. That's all. Pay attention.

I pick up the pace when I see the Jeep, double-parked on the street, causing cars to pile up behind it. Shit. I rush up to the driver's side and wave sillily until the man at the wheel rolls down his window just so I can see his eyes and nothing else.

"I'm with Styling by Sasha," I say, trying my best to be friendly and professional. "You're here for the young Hollywood shoot?"

He grunts.

"Great. You can pull up right around the back and park in the reserved spot."

The driver turns around and says something to the person sitting in the back seat, who must be Iris. I can't hear what she's saying, but the driver's neck is thick as it bobs up and down while she speaks. After a few seconds, he turns back to me. "They want to get out here."

"In the middle of the street? There are paparazzi everywhere."

The man says nothing, but I can see in his eyes that there's not much up for conversation. I move aside and he opens the door, stepping down onto the street. He's thick and muscular, but shorter than I would have thought, with a black baseball cap pulled tight over his face. He walks around to the back and opens the door.

Suddenly, I realize Iris isn't alone in the car. A toned white man steps out with a shock of thick dark hair and a fitted white tee. It's Nate Clyburn, relaxed and happy as he stretches out his limbs. Then he turns back to the car, extending a hand to Iris, who takes it with her delicate manicured fingers. She steps down and they're here, together, on the street. He places a hand on the small of her back. An intimate gesture. One that he hasn't done publicly before. I glance behind the car as a handful of paparazzi swarm them, snapping photos as they walk hand in hand toward the studio. That's when I realize this was all planned. They *want* to be photographed together, heading into this shoot. They probably called Backgrid themselves.

Evil geniuses.

Iris doesn't look my way, but Nate glances in my direction and for a second, my stomach spasms. Does he recognize me from that night at the Bowery Hotel, the night I saw them with Leon? Or that random time we went to Mike's and Victoria tried to get him to flirt with her? Is it possible he could put together the pieces—that *I'm* deuxmoi? But as soon as we make eye contact, his eyes flit down, then back to Iris, who's looking at him like he hung the moon. He nips at her ear, causing her to yelp out flirtatiously and lean in toward his chest. The buzzing of cameras flashing, lenses clicking fills the air.

The door to the warehouse bursts open, and Sasha appears, with steam nearly pouring out of her ears. She doesn't even look at me, and I can feel her wrath from here. But she fixes her face in a flash, putting on a smile.

"Iris! Nate! It is so incredible to meet you two—at the same time, no less." She extends her arms to hug them both. "We had no idea you'd be arriving together." Her voice has an edge to it, and I'm wondering if they notice. "I'm Sasha Sherman, your stylist for today."

Iris leans in and air-kisses Sasha on both cheeks. "Of course we know who you are," she says, her British accent more pronounced than in the videos I've seen of her. "I'm a die-hard *Collection* fan."

Nate looks at Sasha, and it's obvious he has no idea who the fuck she is but he accepts her hug, which is a little too familiar, and backs off before following Iris through the door Sasha's holding open. He throws the cameras behind us one last look and a wave, ducking inside.

I run up behind them, but before I can get through the door, Sasha slams it so I'm left out on the street. I clench my fists and tense up, knowing that was on purpose. But I need to keep my cool. Especially if I want this day to turn around, if I want Sasha to even consider a promotion.

I yank at the door handle, but it doesn't budge. I pull again. Nothing. I shake my head, realizing Sasha just locked me out. Shit.

Sasha's going to scream at me if I'm not back to help out so I run around the side of the building where the service door is still propped open and duck back inside, rushing to the set. My phone vibrates, and I see a text from Leon.

> Um, why the fuck is this reporter from Vivendi emailing me asking if I know you???

I stop short, confused as hell, until I get a text from Victoria, too.

> A VIVENDI REPORTER IS EMAILING ME ASKING IF YOU RUN DEUXMOI! WHAT THE HELL IS GOING ON!!!!

My head spins like crazy as I try to make sense of these texts. How the hell did she find them? Is it possible that she . . .

And then I check my email, where a message from Naomi Rutherford is staring right back at me.

I press my back against the cool wall and read it, my heart beating fast.

From: nrutherford@gmail.com

To: Deuxmoi@gmail.com

Date: September 9, 2022, 3 pm ET

Subject: Re: Press request for whoever runs deuxmoi

> So great chatting with you last night. Loved hearing all about how you started the account. So interesting! I wanted to ask a few additional questions.
>
> You said you wanted to stay anonymous and I can see why. But while doing my research, I was able to find some identifying information about you: According to my reporting, your name is Cricket Lopez. Can you confirm?

In an instant it feels like the floor is falling out beneath me. I open my mouth, trying to swallow air, but nothing comes in and I can't breathe. I clutch my phone and feel its sides dig into my palms. I already dodged Madison Lee's assumptions, but Leon was right. A real-life reporter with a whole editorial team behind her may have had different tactics—databases to look into, or ways to dodge my tech security. We had no connections in common on social, but that only means so much. But she clearly found me—and, by extension, Leon and Victoria, who explicitly told me over and over again that they did *not* want to get involved or be associated with any of this.

I press the back of my palm to my forehead, all hot and sweaty, and rack my brain for what kind of information she could have found.

But then it dawns on me.

The S-Corp Giuseppe made for me. We went ahead and added my real address to it, assuming no one would actually go and look it up since no one even knows that I have a business entity for the account.

But she must have found it. Because she's an actual fucking reporter. Shit shit shit.

She must have been able to trace my information to the address somehow—maybe through my utility or phone bill, or by stalking my fucking landlord, a lovely Italian man named Frank who sometimes leaves boxes of cannoli at my door during the San Gennaro Feast.

I need Ollie. He'll know how to deal with this situation. I need to respond to Victoria and Leon. I need to tell them to do nothing; I need to apologize for putting them at risk.

But before I can do any of that, a voice rings out, causing a shiver to shoot down my spine.

"Cricket!" Sasha screams. "Where is the navy skirt? The custom patchwork mini from Miu Miu?"

I stop dead in my tracks, phone in my hand, and look up, blinking. I rack my brain, trying to remember. I can't even picture what item she's talking about. There were no navy skirts on the packing list. Only one item from Miu Miu. Patent leather pumps we were saving for Sydney Sweeney. But now Sasha wants something we definitely do not have in Los Angeles, so I'm royally fucked.

Sasha stomps over to me, fists clenched by her sides. "Where is it?" she hisses.

I glance around the room—at that sweet PA Lucia; the director, who's clearly getting impatient with this whole day; Iris Goddamn Leonard, who's sitting in a makeup chair scrolling on her phone while someone slathers foundation on her blemish-free face—and suddenly I want to be anywhere but here. At home in Manhattan, on my couch, poring over my DMs. At the squash tournament with Victoria, scoping out the celebrity dads, or hiding in Bemelmans with Leon, gossiping about the new assistant class over at the labels.

I want to be walking through Central Park, where I'm totally anonymous, where no one knows that in about three seconds Sasha Sherman is going to scream at me in a nondescript warehouse full of one hundred beautiful people and even more beautiful clothes.

But first, I need to say something. Anything. "It's at the office," I say in a hushed voice. "It wasn't on the packing list."

Sasha's eyes go wide. "Yes, it was."

I shake my head. "Sasha, I'm so sorry but—"

Sasha stuffs her hand in her back pocket and pulls out a folded-up piece of paper. She nearly rips it in half as she flattens it out, her eyes scanning the page. They stop midway down. "Right here," she says, spinning the paper around so I can see it. "*Miu Miu navy skirt in custom patchwork.*"

I glance down and see the timestamp of when she printed it. Seven a.m. yesterday morning. She must have changed it right when I finished everything up the night before we left. I missed the updated list.

My stomach drops, and a bubble of shame forms in my chest. For the millionth time since this whole shoot started, I want to melt right into the floor. I've never fucked up like this, not in the eight years I've been with Sasha. Sure, I've forgotten the occasional lunch order and double-booked her schedule once or twice when I was still green. But I've never packed wrong. Not once.

I open my mouth to speak, to apologize, to say *anything*, but Sasha holds up her hand, and I snap it shut.

"Get out," Sasha says, her voice hard and sturdy. "You're not needed here anymore."

"But—"

The music in the warehouse has stopped, and I can feel all eyes on us, heads turning, people whispering, wondering how the fuck Sasha Sherman's assistant could be this dumb.

"You forgot one of the most important items for the shoot and you've been on your phone all day." Her eyebrows shoot up when my mouth drops open. "Yes, I've noticed. You're not that stealth." She shakes her head and wiggles her fingers toward me. "You are clearly of no value to me here." Her blue eyes stare at me, all ice. "Get. Out."

I blink back tears, willing myself not to cry here, in front of Sasha, in front of everyone. I keep my shit together and nod briefly, spinning on my heel and speed-walking toward the back door. When I push it open, I gasp for air and try to catch my breath.

I walk without thinking, to get away as quickly as I can. I only get a few blocks on the busy street before I burst into tears and sink onto a bus stop bench, cradling my head in my hands.

When I look up, I see a billboard of Duke Dudley's face smiling back at me, inviting me to consider him for an Oscar for his latest World War II blockbuster.

"Fuck you," I say out loud, wishing I could say it to Sasha, to Madison Lee, to that prying *Vivendi* reporter I never should have agreed to speak with. To literally anyone other than the person I should be furious with—the person who has thrown herself into creating something that has grown into a beast, something she can't control all on her own, something that has actual *power*. The person who can't take credit for it, who can't come right out and admit to what she's done. The person who got herself into this impossible situation in the first place.

The person . . . the person is me.

CHAPTER 21

As soon as I get back to my hotel room, I flop down on the bed and bury my face in the pillows, trying to block out everything around me. The sounds of traffic and cars honking down below, the memory of Sasha's face, spittle forming at the corners of her lips, the silence that filled the room as I walked away, and that fucking email from Naomi Rutherford threatening to ruin everything I've built, everything I've tried to keep so separate.

I let myself wallow for minutes, my face pressed against the plush pillows, until my heart rate slows to a normal pace, until my breathing returns to something resembling steady. Then I push myself to sit and force myself to text my group chat with Leon and Victoria.

Do nothing, I write. *I'm trying to figure out what's going on. I'm so fucking sorry.*

They both reply immediately, and I can't bring myself to look at their messages, knowing how badly I let them down, how furious they must be.

But then my phone buzzes with a message from Ollie.

So, what do you say? On for tonight?

I drop the phone into the sheets and push myself to stand, pacing around the room. Everything in my body wants to see him, to see if this chemistry we've created on the screen might actually translate to something palpable in real life. But after the day I've had—the shit I have to deal with right now—I don't want to see anyone, let alone someone who knows me only as the person who runs deuxmoi.

There's absolutely no way to know if I can trust him. I thought this reporter would respect my privacy, the fact that I didn't want anyone to know who I am. But that was totally naïve. Bullshit. Of course she would go digging. Of course she would play detective. *Of course* she would try to find out who my real friends are and invade their privacy, too.

And let's be real: It wouldn't be surprising to find out that Ollie, as the editor of *Elaborate*, is doing the same thing. Using all of his Hollywood savvy to get the scoop on who everyone in Hollywood has been messaging through Instagram. Who's to say that once he sees me, knows my name, he won't go telling everyone in this town? Get me fired? It's not like I'm anyone interesting, even. I'm just . . . me. No one famous. No one worth outing. But I can't risk it. I just don't trust him. Not yet. Even though I wish I could.

I start typing.

> Had the worst day, don't think I'm up for it.

He starts to respond immediately, but then those three bubbles disappear. I bite my lip and watch them reappear, then vanish. Finally, he answers.

> I get it. You're in a tough spot.

> Yup.

> Is it because you don't know if you can trust me yet?

I sigh, deciding to be honest. *It would give you so much power. Too much.*

> Fair.

But then he sends another text. *Just know, though, I have no interest in outing you. I don't give a shit who you are in a professional sense. All I want to do is actually meet the person who keeps making me laugh at all hours of the day, who impresses me with her intelligence even through a fucking text message.*

Damn, I say. *You continue to be a huge corn ball but I'll take it.*

I'm serious, he writes. *That dream I told you about? It was fucking good.*

As I wonder how to respond, I tap out of our conversation and see my phone is full of other texts, emails, and DMs that need answering. Fires that need to be put out. Stories that need to be looked into. But all I want to do is zero in on Ollie's words and forget about everything for just a moment.

A bold feeling courses through my veins.

> Sounds hot.

> It was pretty x-rated.

Really? I'm intrigued. I open the top button of my jeans and slide them down my hips, just a little, resting a palm on my stomach.

Do you want me to describe it to you? he asks.

> Yes.

> All the details?

> Yes.

> Tell me you want it.

I want it, I write, my fingers tracing my stomach.

I'm waiting, letting the anticipation build inside of me as the sides of the phone dig into my palm. But then a block of text comes in and I feel a hitch in my breath as I read what he says.

> I'll skip the part where we went to dinner and start with the part where I took you back to my hotel room. We hadn't kissed until we got to my room and I had locked the door. We had a few seconds of looking at each other, like "what now?"

Ok, I write. *I'm on the edge of my seat. Then what?*

> I walked toward you but before kissing you, I ran my hand through your hair, reaching for the back of your head. I pulled your head back so I could softly kiss and bite your neck.

I nod to no one but feel my own hand warm on my skin as I press into my stomach.

He sends another text.

> With my other hand, I pulled your body to me, grabbing you by the ass. I could hear you breathing. Hard. I bit your lips before finally kissing you.

I reach my hand lower, until I reach between my legs as the heat builds, waiting for more from him.

> As I grabbed your hair, I put my hand inside your jeans, squeezing your butt, pulling you to me even closer.

He starts typing but then stops, and everything in my body lurches forward wanting more from him.

Is that too much? he asks. *You can tell me to stop.*

I type back with one hand, *No, I don't want you to stop. Can I be honest?*

> You better be.

> This is making me wet.

Good, he writes. *Can't say I'm not having fun myself.*

Keep going, I write, feeling my insides on fire, clenching and waiting for whatever he's about to unleash.

> You stopped kissing me then and said, do you have any idea how into this I am right now? so I asked you if I could check for myself. You said yes and I unbuttoned your pants and slid my hand inside, on top of your underwear to see if you were right.

I work at myself, my fingers reaching, grasping. I crane my neck and close my eyes, imagining him here.

Did you put your fingers inside me? I type.

Getting there, he writes. *After rubbing your pussy, I put my hand inside your underwear and kissed you, sliding my fingers deep inside of you, and you reached into my pants for my dick.*

I wish you could feel how hard it is, he says.

My breathing picks up, and I know I'm close. So fucking close.

> Now?

> Now.

> Fuck.

I mirror his movements, wishing, even for this moment, I had let my guard down enough to invite him here, to make this a reality.

> It didn't take you long before I brought you so close to the edge.

I squeeze my eyes shut, rubbing myself harder, imagining his weight on top of me, his breath in my ear, the way his skin would feel, bare against mine. I move my fingers in a circular motion, feeling the warmth pulsing hard, deep.

Can I cum? I ask, needing his permission, wanting it desperately.

You better, he types, and I release, bucking up against my hand, dropping my phone into the sheets.

A wave of relief passes over me, and I kick my pants off to the side before grabbing my cell again.

Well, shit, I say. *That was . . . wow.*

> Honestly? For me, too.

Really? I write.

Yes.

He follows up with another message: *If we ever meet in person, I don't know what I'd do.*

I lean back against the pillows. *All of this, I hope.*

> And more.

I bite my lip, feeling every bit enamored of this stranger.

Thanks, I say. *I needed that.*

> Not more than I did.

I drag myself into the bathroom and take my time showering and moisturizing before wrapping myself in a fuzzy robe. All I want to do is sleep, dreaming about whoever the hell Ollie really is, and forget about the shit show waiting for me on my phone. But after this bizarre, horrifying day, I give into my body, my cravings, and let go of my phone, letting my exhaustion take over and guide me into sleep.

CHAPTER 22

"Fuck!" I wake up with a start to the sound of my alarm blaring on its loudest volume. I groan and roll over, checking the time. I'm already late, and I have two texts from Sasha, telling me I better have a black car ready for us in the lobby in thirty minutes. Bleary-eyed, I schedule an Uber and send her the confirmation. She reads it and doesn't respond.

I drag myself out of bed and try to take the fastest shower of my life, ignoring the desire to jump back into bed and read the texts Ollie sent me the night before. Instead, I throw everything in the room into my suitcase and shoot him a message.

> I'd say thanks for last night but that feels weird.

> Honestly, it's me who should be thanking you. Let's make this a regular thing . . .

I send him a smirking emoji and grab the last of my crap before heading out the door. My hair's still wet and my phone's half-charged, but somehow I make it downstairs with five minutes to spare, just enough time to get a bone-dry cap for me and an English breakfast tea for Sasha. Maybe it can be an olive branch.

I back up against the wall near the front desk and crane my neck, keeping one eye trained on the elevator bank. No Sasha. Not yet. I pull out my phone and hold it close to my chest as I tap over to the deuxmoi inbox, knowing I'll see the email from Naomi Rutherford, which weighs heavy on my chest. I still have no idea how I'm going to deal with that mess.

I peek up from my phone right in time to see Sasha exit the elevator. I put a smile on my face, smoothing down my black leather jacket. Her tea is still warm in my hand, and I hold it out as I hustle over to where she's walking. I recite my apology over and over in my head and let the words tumble out of my mouth when I meet her.

"Sasha, I'm—"

"Let's go." Sasha grabs the cup from my hand and stomps out to the curb, dragging her luggage behind her.

Our Uber is waiting, and I help the driver load all Sasha's bags into the back as she settles into the front row of the Suburban. I climb into the back and prepare for the longest car ride of my life, knowing that Sasha will give me the silent treatment all the way to JFK.

At least that gives me more time to think about how to deal with *Vivendi* threatening to ruin my life.

■■■

Sitting, once again, in the last row of coach, I'm grateful that Sasha is so far away up in first class. I'm in the window seat, and by some stroke of good luck, there's no one in the middle. Carefully, I take my phone out and hold it so close to my chest I can barely read it. Scouting out the people around me, I deem the whole operation safe and relax my shoulders as I start going through DMs in the account, screenshotting ones I can use in stories. I toggle on and off between email and trying not to think about Naomi's message.

My phone buzzes with a text message from Leon, interrupting my train of thought.

> I'm pretty pissed at you about this whole Vivendi thing but . . . you need to see this.

He follows it up with a link to an Instagram post from someone I don't recognize. Someone named Hilary Mitchell. She may be a no-name actress. Or potentially a model. Looks like she appeared in a country music video a few years ago.

Watch her stories, Leon says. *They're about Duke . . .*

Dudley? I type. *So???*

Leon sends me an exasperated face. *Just watch. Then check your DMs. My guess is shit's about to blow up . . . he's already trending on Twitter.*

The captain starts making announcements over the loudspeaker and I pop in my earbuds, drowning him out. The woman has about fifteen thousand followers and I definitely don't recognize her, even when I'm greeted by her face, taking up the whole screen, as I hit play on her stories. Her voice fills my headphones, and all of a sudden, I'm filled with a sense of dread. Her tone is dour and her voice warbles as if she's nervous—no, terrified. Whatever she's about to say cannot be good.

I'm finally ready to speak out about Duke Dudley . . .

We met when I was seventeen . . .

He told me he wanted to drain my blood, that he had a quote vampire fetish . . .

I can't even believe I'm saying this . . .

I loved him . . .

He took advantage of my love . . .

I lived in fear. He had access to my phone, my keys . . . he cut me off from everyone I knew . . .

I watch the stories one more time, her voice punctuating each word, fear and adrenaline obvious. I cover my mouth with my hand, feel my heart beating hard within my chest. I wonder if Sasha has seen these yet—if she knows these allegations are flying around out there. I wonder . . . I wonder if *this* is why Duke was rumored to be dropped from that Regency series. Maybe the studio knew these kinds of stories were circulating. Maybe . . . maybe there are more allegations out there.

Maybe they're true.

When I refresh her profile, I see she's added more stories. Suddenly, my throat is sandy and I'm having trouble swallowing. But then I see they're screenshots of text messages, Duke Dudley's name labeled at the top.

I'm 100 percent a vampire, he writes. *I want to suck your blood and drain you dry, then fuck the shit outta you. HA!!!!!!*

Her response: *I don't know about that.*

Come on, he wrote. *It can be like last time. In Barbados?*

> My neck was bruised for a week.
> My friends were asking questions.

Leon sends another text. *What are your DMs saying???*

Looking, I respond. My phone is still close to my chest as I hear the captain say we have another few minutes of taxiing on the ground, and I tap over to my messages.

There are hundreds. Way more than a usual weekend morning, and I can tell based on the little snippets I can see on the screen that most of them are about Duke.

Holy fucking shit, I text Leon. *It's a minefield.* He texts back a shocked face and a few more question marks, but I can't answer him now. I need to read.

Over in the DMs, it is pure chaos.

I scroll quickly, seeing that a lot of my regular sources have just sent me the same link that Leon did with shocked faces. Lots of "not sure if you saw this but . . ." type messages.

But then I see one woman, echoing what Hilary said. I scan her message fast and see the words "vampire fetish" and "love bombing" jump out at me. But then I see who sent it: Eleanor Cauley Rhodes. Sasha's old assistant.

My heart leaps into my throat as I read her message more clearly.

> I hope you saw Hilary Mitchell's posts about Duke Dudley. What she's saying is all true. Every word. I know because it happened to me. It's time he gets outed.

If these women are telling the truth, then there have got to be more people out there who have similar stories to these—more people who Duke, that seemingly sweet doofus who let us dress him in ridiculous designer suits for his wedding and always remembers birthdays, has hurt. And based on the messages, these rumors have been swirling for years within certain circles in Hollywood. If he got his hooks in Eleanor, does that mean Sasha and Alyssa know, too?

Then I remember what Eleanor wrote to deuxmoi all those months ago.

Too bad she also has a habit of pimping out her underlings to that same big client.

She must have been talking about Duke. Sasha must have known. Sasha must have handed Eleanor to Duke on a fucking silver platter.

I'm so sorry for whatever's happened to you, I write back to Eleanor with shaking fingers. *Thanks for bringing this to light.*

She sends me a heart.

> Feel free to post this but keep me anon. Maybe my voice can back up Hilary's.

I twirl a strand of hair around my finger. I pause only briefly, trying to understand the weight of these allegations. Obviously, they could do some damage to Duke, not to mention bring Styling by Sasha down with him. But I believe Eleanor and Hilary. Who the hell would lie about this shit? Especially Eleanor. She's been through the same kind of hell I have with Sasha.

I draft a text to Ollie, sending him the link to Hilary's profile.

> These stories about Duke Dudley. Have you heard them before?

He responds fast, the typing bubble barely appearing.

> Oh yeah. I've heard shady rumors about him for years. Especially the vampire thing. Very well known within the scene.

For real? I write.

> Yup. That's why I never put him on the cover of Elaborate.

I shake my head and lean back against the airline chair, feeling the rough fabric scratch against my scalp. I rack my brain, trying to think of what to do, when it dawns on me that I should probably touch base with Hilary if I want to re-share on deuxmoi. Perhaps there's a world in which she wasn't prepared to receive the kind of attention being reposted on my account would bring.

I dash off a message to her, sending it as fast as I can. Based on the captain speaking overhead, I only have a few minutes before takeoff, and you never know what can happen with airline Wi-Fi.

She responds immediately.

You can share, she says. *The people need to know.*

I let out a shaky breath and screenshot her stories, tagging her and telling readers to watch her stories for more information. But as I'm about to hit post, I hear a commotion coming from the front of the plane, behind the curtain to first class.

I stick my head up over the seats, craning to see what's going on. Even from here, I can see Sasha, stomping her foot up and down, screaming at the flight attendant, who probably did nothing but serve her still instead of sparkling water. I slither down in my seat, embarrassed for her and the way she treats people. But then I realize that she must have known about Duke's reputation. And if she sent Eleanor to him so he would stay happy with Styling by Sasha, then she's pure evil.

Emboldened, I head back to Instagram and hit post before sharing a screenshot of Eleanor's messages with her name blocked out. I watch the little upload circle fill all the way in as the story makes its way into hundreds of thousands of people's feeds.

The pilot's voice crackles again over the loudspeaker. "Prepare for takeoff," he says.

I spy the flight attendant basically pushing Sasha down and I shake my head. What an asshole.

Just as Sasha's butt hits the seat, the plane starts speeding ahead and I keep my eyes glued to my DMs, watching the number tick up and up as more people respond. But as Los Angeles gets smaller and smaller below me, and my cell service drops out, I notice that the Wi-Fi signal is still dark on my phone.

I keep refreshing, stress and terror coursing through my veins. If the internet is down, I'm about to be stuck on this plane, having posted the most consequential story I ever have to my feed without any way of telling how it will go . . . without any way to update it.

Sheer panic grips me, and I wait minutes for the pilot to tell us we can unfasten our seat belts and unlock our tray tables. But there's no mention of the internet. I reach up to the buttons above me and punch the call signal, saying silent prayers as I watch the flight attendant walk down the aisle toward me. His name tag reads *Spencer*, and he's gelled his hair into a shellacked shell, complementing his *very* white teeth.

"What can I help you with, miss?" he asks in a calm and steady voice.

"What's up with the Wi-Fi?" I ask, strained. "I can't seem to connect."

He must sense my desperation because his mouth turns into a pout and he pats my hand. "It's out for the whole trip. Something about the signal box." He stands and straightens out his vest. "We can offer you a complimentary snack tray?" His face is all eager smiles and arched eyebrows, but all I can do is shake my head.

Spencer wanders back into the flight attendant area near the restrooms and starts chatting away with his co-workers, totally oblivious to the fact that the next five hours will be complete and utter torture for the passenger sitting in 32F.

DGAF Daily

Breaking Down the Duke Dudley Allegations: Why One Woman Calls the Oscar Winner a "Vampire"

This morning, a number of disturbing screenshots showing text messages between actress-model Hilary Mitchell and Oscar winner Duke Dudley began circulating on Instagram. The texts show Hilary, who says she dated Duke on and off for three years (even though he's been linked to country star Celine for the past decade), texting with someone in her contacts labeled "Duke Dudley" as he tells her he wants to "drain her blood" and that he is "100 percent vampire."

In videos posted to her account, Hilary also says that Dudley was "abusive" toward her and that he isolated her from friends and family while they were together. "He told me no one could touch me aside from him and that if he found out I was dating other men, even though he was married, he would come to my house and kill me, before turning me into a vampire."

Hilary posted the stories last night, and her sentiments soon went viral, especially after anonymous Instagram account deuxmoi reposted the information. Since then, more women have come forward, saying similar things about Dudley, who was recently fired from the big-budget Regency series *The Viscounts*, news that deuxmoi also broke last month. While the streamer has yet to make a statement, Dudley announced that he was stepping back from the project one week ago. At the time he said he was leaving it to "spend more time with his children and family, and take some much-needed relaxation."

An Austin, TX, model, Ursula Lin, wrote on her own account:

"Hilary Mitchell's stories mirror my own. I'm a victim of Duke Dudley's, too." She then shared screenshots of text messages that she claims are from the Oscar winner. In one, he says, "I'm so hard thinking about sinking my fangs into your neck." In another he says, "You haven't sent me nudes in two hours. Where are they? If I don't receive an ass pic in five, I'm leaking the other ones. You know I'll do it."

In another story, Lin wrote, "Hilary had the courage to come forward about this predator and now I do, too. I'm not afraid of Hollywood's so-called nice guy Duke Dudley anymore."

Harold Temper, a longtime attorney for Dudley, said in a statement, "These assertions about Mr. Dudley are false. Full stop. Any interactions described were fully consensual. This is a misguided attempt to tarnish Mr. Dudley's reputation. That's all I'll say on this matter."

CHAPTER 23

As soon as the plane begins its descent into New York, I try refreshing Instagram, pulling down the feed over and over again until finally I see my phone get one bar, two bars, three full bars of signal. Relief washes over me until I see there are hundreds of replies in my DMs asking for details, berating me for posting something like this, and, more concerningly, sharing even more stories similar to Hilary's. I glance over all of them until I feel a nudge in my side from the older man who was sleeping in the aisle seat throughout the entire flight.

"Miss?" he asks with a gentle voice. "I think it's our turn."

I look up and find the plane empty save for a few flight attendants sweeping between seats.

"I'm so sorry," I tell him with a sheepish smile, and practically fall over my feet scrambling over the armrest to get out.

I grab my carry-on bag from the overheard compartment and drag it behind me as I rush out of the plane, knowing that Sasha will already be waiting for me, pissed it took me so long. But when I get into the terminal, she's nowhere to be seen.

I pull up her number and hit call, but not before dozens of texts finally come through, all from Ollie, Victoria, and Leon. They say the same exact thing:

> You've gone completely viral.

My phone speaker crackles, and I shove it against my face. "I left already," Sasha says, her voice hard and frantic. "Grab whatever luggage you checked at baggage claim. I couldn't wait for you."

"Is everything all right?" I know it's a dumb question as soon as it comes out of my mouth. Of course things aren't all right. She screamed at me in front of a room full of people yesterday, and now her biggest client is front-page news for abuse allegations, saying he's a fucking *vampire*.

"You're clearly dumber than I thought," Sasha says, clipped and mean. "Honestly, Cricket, after the past twenty-four hours, you're lucky you still have a job. Drop my luggage with my doorman tonight and then show up on time on Monday, ready to go, or I really might throw you out on your ass for good. Understood?"

I swallow the lump in my throat and nod, even though she can't see me. "Understood."

■■■

It takes an hour before I'm in the back seat of an Uber heading straight to Sasha's Upper East Side apartment with all of her crap. Only when my back is pressed up against the leather seat of the car do I finally get the courage to start going through messages about Duke. I screenshot and post until my fingers hurt, and as I do, I take in stories more harrowing and brutal than the next. One message reads:

> This Duke stuff is bad and true. My friend is really close with him and tried to force him to get help since his drinking and drug habits have gotten out of control. I always knew he was into kink, but had no idea he was hurting girls until I saw Hilary at his house once, her

neck covered in bruises in the bathroom. People close to him have been trying to help but he's icing us all out. Substance isn't the root cause but clearly isn't helping. Dude needs a clear mind to deal with all of this and doesn't have one. It's all really sad. I should have told someone sooner. Anon pls.

Another one says:

Blind item: Saw the movie star who's been under fire for vampire (wtf?) allegations sitting poolside at the Parker in Palm Springs drinking a piña colada. Seemed totally unphased by rumors going around. Maybe unaware??? Either way, he was hitting on girls left and right, even though he's married. I want to tell these girls to run. Anon obviously

One of my regular sources who works on the studio side of things writes:

Lionsgate actively looking to replace Duke in Gillian Flynn's new thriller that was supposed to start shooting next week. These allegations are too big and too real to ignore. Anon, babe.

I swallow hard as they all go into my feed and finally make my way to see what people in the mainstream are writing about Duke. When I go to my Apple News app, I'm greeted by Duke's face, smiling out from an article linking to People.com.

Pretty soon, I see everyone's covered it: E!, the *Daily Mail*, *Cosmopolitan*, *Elle*, *Glamour*, *Page Six*, *HuffPost*, and *Us Weekly*. There are dozens of YouTube clips of news anchors talking about Duke, hot takes flying around Twitter, long threads about similar allegations that have gone unexamined for years. And the unimaginable thing that ties them all together is that most of these pieces of media mention . . . me.

> Deuxmoi broke the news . . .

> First reported by deuxmoi . . .

> The account was amplified by deuxmoi . . .

> Deuxmoi reposted the story . . .

A low-simmering anger starts churning in my stomach, mostly at the outlets that are claiming I "broke" this news. It's ridiculous. All I did was re-share these women's stories from their own Instagram accounts in a few posts and help their voices be heard. And besides, this story was already trending on Twitter before I even posted about it. Why even mention me when these stories are about him and his actions?

I debate sharing a comment about this on my account, but before I can compose anything, I see another email from that sleuthing snake, Naomi Rutherford. But this time, to my horror, it's coming through my Styling by Sasha work email.

From: nrutherford@condenast.com

To: clopez@stylingbysasha.com

Date: September 10, 2022, 4:08 pm ET

Subject: Are you Deuxmoi?

Dear Cricket,
I'm a reporter with *Vivendi* working on a story about the anonymous Instagram account deuxmoi. Apologies for

DEUXMOI.

writing out of the blue, but my reporting leads me to believe that you run this account. Care to comment?

Best, Naomi

My insides freeze as I tap out of the app. Then I see she left me a voicemail. When I listen to it, it's all I can do to not burst into tears.

"Heeeey! Following up again. Hate to keep doing this, but my editor wants to rush publishing our profile now that this Duke Dudley story has gone completely viral. So . . . call me back? I'm going to need your response to my emails by 10:00 p.m. tonight."

The clock on the Uber's dashboard says it's 6:07 p.m. Four hours. I only have four hours to figure out how I'm going to outsmart this woman who found out my identity.

CHAPTER 24

I've only been home for ten minutes when the banging starts against my door. My heart stops for a second and my brain jumps to the worst-case scenario. What if that's Naomi tracing me like a stalker back to the address on my corporation filing forms?

I tiptoe over to the door and peek through the keyhole.

"I have you on Find My Friends, I know you're in there," Leon says, his voice a mixture of worry and frustration.

"Same!" Victoria says. I spy her rifling through her purse for something. She pulls out a slim bottle of Ketel One. "I left dinner at Sant Ambroeus and brought supplies, so I think I win the best friend award—even though you seem to have sent an unhinged reporter after us!"

I groan, but my chest loosens and I swing open the door, letting them in.

"You weren't picking up," Leon says, shutting the door behind him. He sheds his coat and shoes and grabs the bottle of vodka from Victoria. He sets it on the table and yanks open my cabinets, pulling down three tumblers and filling them with ice. Then he looks right at me. "I'm so fucking mad at you."

I press my fingers against my temple. "I do *not* need this right now."

Leon shakes his head. "Siccing a reporter on us? We told you this was going to happen. We begged you to leave us out of your messy bullshit."

Victoria winces like she's in pain and rests a hand on Leon's biceps. Then she turns to me and says, "I hate to say it, but Leon's right. You need to get her to kill this thing."

"Don't you think I'm trying?"

Leon softens. "Yes, babe."

Victoria butts in. "You know how she found us?"

I shake my head.

"An old Facebook photo taken at Brother Effing Jimmy's six years ago!" She's basically yelling now, which she never does, so I know she's really pissed.

"The one time I let you guys drag me to that hellhole," Leon says. "Fucking four-dollar happy hour." Then he waves his hands all around. "But you know we have jobs and lives and shit, too. If people find out I'm connected to deuxmoi, I could get fucked at work."

"Don't you think I know that?" I say. "You've only said it one hundred times."

Leon crosses his arms over his chest. "I could get taken off the list for notifications about the VIP sales at Bergdorf's." He pauses. "Don't you dare laugh!"

Victoria throws up her hands. "Chase could get kicked out of the squash league. No one wants deuxmoi's best friend around, sharing inside stories about them."

A flush creeps up my skin. "You've got to be joking right now." But their faces are still like stone.

"We're not even going to talk about what happened in L.A.," Leon says.

"You heard about the shoot?"

He scrunches up his face. "Alyssa."

I rest my forehead on my kitchen island. "How the hell do I still have a job?" Leon starts to say something, but I cut him off. "Forget it. That's the least of my problems right now."

Victoria tips hefty pours of vodka into each glass, and I nod at her to pour an extra finger.

She splashes pineapple into my drink before sliding one in front of each of us.

I take a long swig of it, feeling the alcohol burn as it goes down my throat. "I know the *Vivendi* thing is top priority right now." Victoria opens her mouth, and I put a hand up to quiet her. "And yes, I'm going to take care of it so you can keep your weird WASP club membership or whatever." She pouts, but I keep talking. "But we haven't even talked about Duke. Leon, this fuckface tricked us all. Have you seen these allegations?"

Leon's face pales, and he shakes his head, looking down. "Harrowing doesn't even begin to describe."

"Have you talked to Alyssa about it?" I ask.

He grimaces but then glances up. "She knew," he says quietly. "She told me she'd heard stories over the years—how some young women didn't want to work with him. Producers, too." Leon leans in. "She even mentioned that one of Sasha's old assistants got involved with him."

"Holy shit," Victoria says, shaking her head. "I'm so glad I don't work in this industry anymore." She glances at us both. "No offense."

I drain my drink in two slugs, ice knocking against the side of the glass. Everything is fuzzy, and it's so hard to think straight. I know it's not from the booze—it's from everything hitting me all at once: Duke's survivors, the *Vivendi* story, the possibility of getting fired—of fucking over my friends. Maybe I should just take Kyle Johns up on his offer to buy deuxmoi. That would make this mess someone else's problem for once. I wish I could call Ollie right now. He'd know what to do.

Victoria and Leon duck their heads close together and start yammering away, running down every single allegation against Duke.

Hearing the stories again, I want to throw up. But then I see it's 8:00 p.m. Only two hours before I need to give Naomi an answer—before I seal my fate in one of the most iconic magazines on the planet.

I exhale, trying to calm my nerves, but all I feel is shaky breath.

Suddenly the room is quiet. "Are you gonna puke?" Victoria asks in a quiet voice. "You look like that time in high school when we had a dozen cherry-flavored Jell-O shots at the lax pregame."

I shake my head. "I don't know." A lump forms in my throat, and before I can stop my body from reacting, I feel sobs coming up, choking me as tears start to fall. Victoria springs up from her seat and wraps an arm around my shoulder, pulling me to her. Even though her life is all squash matches and private-school fundraisers, stationed in a penthouse so far from where we grew up, she still smells like she always has since we were kids—like fresh laundry and Giorgio Beverly Hills perfume, though back then she used to steal it from her mom. Safe and inviting, during a sleepover or tennis practice. Victoria, always safe. I wish I could stay in her embrace forever and forget that only inches away, my phone is waiting for me, with so many landmines I don't know how to traverse.

Leon gets to work making another round of drinks and softens his voice. "I know you're in full crisis mode, but you need to figure out what you're going to tell the *Vivendi* reporter. And it better not involve anything about us."

I sigh and press my fingers into my temples. "I want to tell her to fuck all the way off."

"Okay, well, that's not going to help."

Victoria looks at me intently. "How should we respond? What should we say? She's been hitting us up nonstop."

"Stay quiet. Pretend like you didn't even get an email."

"You don't think that's even more sus?" Leon asks.

I shake my head. "Give her nothing."

Victoria's face turns to one of worry. "I can't have Jake finding out about this," she says. "You know how private he is."

I sigh and clench my fists. "I love you, but this isn't about you or Jake. It's about *me*. My life."

Victoria crosses her arms. "I'm sorry, but somehow we're roped into this, too, now, so no, it's not just about *you*. I've been pretty nice about this, but do you know what could happen if people at Charles Day School find out I'm associated with deuxmoi?"

"You've made it perfectly clear that you won't get into whatever bullshit country club you're applying for." I take another sip of my drink.

Victoria's face hardens. "That was rude."

Leon extends his hands. "Can you just acknowledge that your actions affect those around you?" He lets out an uneven sigh. "I get you need help, but please try to understand how stressful this is for *us*."

I look down at the watery contents of my glass and realize they're right. Deuxmoi has become so much bigger than I thought it could ever be, but right now . . . I need my friends.

Victoria sighs. "Maybe it's time to consider the Kyle Johns offer."

I wave at her. "Not the point right now."

Victoria slams her hand down on my kitchen island. "Oh my god, Cricket. There's someone out there who wants to *pay* you for what you're doing and has a legal team that could shut this shit down."

I don't want to admit that I thought about that myself only moments earlier.

"Plus, this guy would offer you way more than what Sasha does," she says, her voice clipped and frustrated. "You've been working for that monster for eight effing years. Eight years with no promotion, no raise, no nothing! You literally started an anonymous Instagram account that's all you can talk about—all you think about!—because she was making you so miserable. Why are you not acting like getting handed an exit strategy is the biggest gift on the planet?"

She's nearly yelling now, speaking so fast that the words are falling out of her mouth, faster than she can control them, until suddenly she has said what she has been wanting to say all these months—that deuxmoi has turned me into a monster.

The weight of her words lands on me hard, and I sit up straight, my spine erect. "Is that what you really think?" I ask. "That deuxmoi is the only thing I care about?"

Victoria touches her forehead with her hands and purses her lips. She sighs, exasperated, as Leon leans over the kitchen island so I can't see his face.

"I love you. More than anyone. Sorry, that includes you, Leon."

Leon keeps looking down, away from us both.

"But you haven't asked me about my life once in the past four months." Victoria's pretty mouth turns into a pout and her bottom lip trembles, her telltale sign that she's trying to hold back tears. "The one time you showed up for me at Chase's match, you stormed out in the middle."

"That was because Madison Lee—"

"Yes, yes, I know all about Madison GD Lee."

"That could have been—"

"What?" Victoria asks. "Detrimental to your career? Well, it kind of seems like *you* are detrimental to your career. So maybe you *should* just quit and work with this Kyle Johns guy. Cash out, fulfill your destiny, and have some support on this. Because you sure seem happier working on this account than you ever have at Sasha's. And to be honest, I don't know how much longer I can listen to you bitch about that evil woman—or have your mess jeopardize my family's reputation."

My face flushes, and I search for a response. But I have none. All I can do is open and close my mouth in shock, in sheer awe that for once Victoria has laid it all bare on the table.

"Look, we've all had a little bit to drink—" Leon starts.

But I shake my head. "No," I say. "She's being honest for once."

Victoria crosses her arms over her chest and bites her lip to stop the tears. But then her phone breaks the silence, ringing from inside her pocket. When she looks at the screen, her eyes narrow. "That's the babysitter. I told her to only call if it was important."

She picks up the phone and turns her back to us. Leon chugs the rest of his drink as Victoria starts talking.

"Is everything okay?" Victoria says. After a beat, "You gave him *what*? Dax is allergic!"

Victoria turns around, her eyes frantic, and starts mouthing things at us. I don't make anything out, but she pulls on her coat and gives me an apologetic, desperate look before running out the door. She lowers her phone and then looks me right in the eyes.

"Something has to change. You can't keep going like this. All I ask is that you leave us out of it."

Then she slams the door behind her and the silence in the apartment is deafening. I look at the clock again and see it's almost nine.

"Do you think she's right?" I ask Leon, blinking back tears.

Leon sighs and slides into the stool next to me, placing a warm hand on my shoulder. "Ever since you started working on this account, it's the most motivated and excited I've seen you in years."

I try to take in this information, wondering how everyone else perceives me. How is it that these people in my life may know me better than I know myself?

"The last thing I want for you *or* me is for Sasha to find out that you're running deuxmoi, but maybe this whole Kyle Johns thing is actually the answer. Maybe you can follow Victoria's advice. Put out this *Vivendi* fire and then work with this guy to monetize deuxmoi and make sure it never happens again. You know how amazing I think you are, but maybe . . ." Leon pauses and winces a bit. "Maybe trying to keep up your old life while starting this new one is impossible."

I finish the rest of my drink in one long slug before wiping the back of my hand on my mouth.

Leon smacks his hand against the counter. "Now's the time to stop feeling sorry for yourself." He grabs for my phone. "Let's deal with this fucking *Vivendi* bullshit right now."

"Excuse me?" I say, reaching for my phone, which he's now holding out of reach.

"I'm going to help you draft a response to this bitch." He sees me smile and then purses his lips. "This is more for me than it is for you. I'm not about to be exposed as being best friends with the woman fucking up Hollywood."

"Aaand that's your cue to get the fuck out of here," I say, shoving a fist into his shoulder playfully. I try to get my phone, but Leon pulls it away.

"Nuh-uh," he says. I can see him tapping into my email and my heart starts pounding.

"At least go to the Notes app," I say, desperate.

He rolls his eyes and starts typing. "'Dear motherfucking cunt-face.'" He looks up. "Too much?"

I pour myself another drink, feeling the vodka going straight to my head with every sip. "Tell her she has the wrong girl."

"'Your sources must be full of shit,'" Leon says. "'Who the fuck is Cricket Lopez?'"

I snort and add my own line. "'Hasn't that idiot been Sasha Sherman's assistant for eight years? What loser would do that?'"

"Hey," Leon says. "That's my best friend you're talking about." But then he peers at the phone. "Actually, that's good."

I swallow the rest of my drink. "How about something like, 'Maybe you should have learned better reporting skills at Yale and not just relied on outdated S-Corp filings and creepy stalking tactics to find out my name and address. Don't you have anything better to do? Get a life.'"

Leon's mouth drops open. "That's what she did?"

"Pretty sure."

"Fucked-up snake!"

Leon slides the phone over to me. "Here's your perfect response. Dare you to send it."

I squint at the screen and see a short typo-laden piece of gibberish with a whole bunch of "fucking cunts" in it. "Great call, babe," I tell Leon, discarding the draft before a slipped finger sends it the wrong way. "I'm so fucked, aren't I?" I ask.

Leon comes around the island and pulls me in for a big hug. He kisses the top of my head. "Nope," he says gently. "You can't be. Because if you are, then we are, and that's just not happening. You'll figure out a way to fix this." He pauses, holding his breath. "Right?"

I look up at him and see fear in his eyes, the worry lines on his face deepening. Even though part of me is pissed that he and Victoria are making this whole thing about them, I get it. Really, I do. Because if the tables were turned, I'd be mad as hell, too. I have to find a way to tell Naomi she's got the wrong girl. For me, but also for them.

"Of course, I'll figure it out," I say, leaning my head against his chest. "Why don't you go home. Get some sleep. I'll keep you posted on how this goes, okay?"

Leon agrees, leaving me with the bottle of Ketel One and a few lemon wedges, and I fix myself another drink. The clock's counting down, and I'm in desperate need of a plan.

I move to the couch, and as soon as I sit down, my phone vibrates in my hand. Panic courses through me as I glance at the screen, expecting to see Naomi's name pop up. But then I see it's Ollie and my heart rate slows to a normal pace.

"I just wanted to check in to see how you're doing," he says, calming and assured.

I press the phone harder to my cheek and grasp the sides so tight it starts to hurt. "Not great, to be honest."

"You should be proud of getting that Duke Dudley news out there, you know. I just saw Hilary thanking you on Instagram. She says people believe her more than they did the day before."

"Huh."

But when I don't say anything else, he lowers his voice. "Is something going on?"

I debate whether to share everything with Ollie, this man who has never seen me and doesn't know my name or anything else about me. But . . . maybe that's why I feel like I can say anything to him. The fact that he *doesn't* know that I've been an assistant for eight years, or that I wore braces for all of middle school and still sleep with my retainers, or that I collect *Betty and Veronica* vintage comic books, or any of the other countless tiny details about my life. And so, I unload and tell him everything that's transpired over the past day, about Naomi and *Vivendi* and Kyle Johns and everything in between.

"And now I need to respond to this reporter in the next seventeen minutes if I want to have any control over my life at all."

I pause to catch my breath.

"Are you asking me for advice?" His voice is calm and kind, soothing even.

"I have no fucking clue what to do so, yes, please."

He takes a big inhale like he's preparing for battle, and then he starts talking fast in a way that tells me he's dealt with crises like this before. "I've been in this reporter's shoes before," he starts. "She wants to break this story because, as we both know, finding out the identity behind deuxmoi would be big. Clicks, views, ad dollars, whatever. But also, major cred to whatever outlet figures out the mystery."

"Boo," I say, which makes him laugh. It's deep, nice and gravelly, matching the face I've seen in photos, the ones that populate Getty Images and his Instagram feed, where he's seen wearing a well-fitting suit and a collared shirt with the top button open.

"So maybe she *did* find some sort of information that links your real name to the account."

"Boo again."

"But *Vivendi* is a legit publication. They have to dot all their i's and cross all their t's. My guess is that they don't have as much proof as you think they do."

"Really? Even if they emailed my *friends*?" My heart starts beating fast. This means I might have an out.

"Yup. I bet they're hoping you'll respond and confirm your name so they can run with it."

"Huh."

"So, if you really want to stay anonymous—"

"I do."

"Deny, deny, deny."

"Seriously? That's your advice? Deny?"

"Yup."

"Will that actually work?"

"You said that you think she knows it's you because she may have found an address associated with deuxmoi, right? Well, there's nothing else tying you to the account besides that. And who's to say that you even live there? All you have to do is say that she got some faulty information and that she's got the wrong person."

"But—"

"But nothing," he says. "It doesn't matter. Trust me. If you deny it, she can't print it because the fact-checkers can't confirm it. Just play dumb and you'll be fine."

"How do you know this?"

"Because that's what I'd do if one of my reporters was on the case."

"I'm a case."

"You are one hundred percent a case."

I rest my head on my knees and press the phone closer to my cheek. "I should have seen you in L.A."

He doesn't say anything for a sec, and I wonder what he's thinking. But then he sighs. "I get it. You don't know if you can trust me yet."

"Well, now I think . . ."

"Yeah, but now it's different."

We're both quiet, and I look up at the clock on my oven and see it's five to ten. "Shit," I say. "I gotta do this."

"Well, maybe call me later," he says, his voice dropping to a low, heated tone. "If you need some cheering up, I know what I can make you do to feel better . . ."

"Oh yeah?" I ask, a small smile forming on my lips.

"Oh yeah."

"Don't get me all hot right now," I joke, feeling warmth spread through me. "Not before I have to make one of the biggest judgment calls of my life."

He laughs a little but then clears his throat. "Oh, and one more thing."

"Yeah?"

"You should think about the offer."

"What offer?"

"Kyle Johns."

"Oh."

"You could stay anonymous if you really want," he said. "Might even up the cool factor. But he's not as bad as he seems," Ollie says. "He's turned some brands around. Could be huge for you—a way to change your life in a real, tangible way."

"Maybe," I say.

"Good," Ollie says. Then after a beat, "You got this. I'll be around to make you feel better."

Finally, we both hang up and I can still feel the warmth of where my phone was pressed against my skin. I stand up and stretch out my limbs. I could call her—open myself up to a whole conversation. But I could also just . . . shoot her an email. Nip this whole thing in the bud as fast as I can. I pull up my email, finding the message from Naomi.

I hold my breath as I type the words, so fast I can barely process them as they appear on the screen.

> Sorry to say you got the wrong girl. That's not me.
> Never heard of her.

I hit send and let the email disappear into the ether, slamming my computer closed and saying goodbye to this god-awful day for good.

Slack conversation between Naomi Rutherford and *Vivendi* editor in chief Ramsey Gates

Naomi: no dice on deuxmoi

Ramsey: wtf does that mean?

Naomi: she won't confirm. Says we got the wrong girl

Ramsey: bullshit

Ramsey: there's no fucking way

Ramsey: you have her ADDRESS

Naomi: I'm aware. What do you want me to do?

Ramsey: Did you talk to legal?

Naomi: They said we can't say it's her if she denied it

Naomi: I mean . . . we could publish the name associated with the address? Just explain my whole detective legwork, say I found it on the S-Corp filings?

Ramsey: Idk Naomi. That's gonna fuck us if it's not her. Did you reach out to the woman? The real woman?

Naomi: I sent her an email to a work email but she never responded

Naomi: Obv it's her

Ramsey: Sorry to say but you're shit outta luck. Gonna have to do a write-around

Naomi: fuuuuckkkkk

CHAPTER 25

"So, you did it?" Ollie asks, his voice a little lighter than it had been an hour earlier.

"Deny, deny, deny." I'm under the covers now, wearing a Skims tank and sleep briefs, and have Ollie on speakerphone while I cruise through the last of the DMs in my inbox. I'm still sort of drunk, but I can tell that the relief running through me is *real*, that Ollie's advice was gold.

"That's my girl," he says.

"Now I'm your girl?"

He laughs. "Do you want to be?"

"It's going to take a lot more than the occasional extremely hot text message to make me someone's 'girl.'"

Ollie pauses, and I can hear his breathing grow a bit louder. "Like what?" he asks, his tone shifting.

I tap out of my DMs and pull up Ollie's account, studying a photo of his face. His sharp jawline. His high cheekbones. The way the left side of his mouth curves to one side when he smiles. A surge courses through me as I press one hand to my stomach, under the soft cotton, my fingers stretching out over my bare skin.

"Tell me what you'd do to me if we were together," I say, emboldened.

He clears his throat. "You set the scene."

"My apartment. You're here for the first time," I say, looking around.

I can hear him lie down, the groaning of a couch or perhaps a bed under him. "This will be good," he says.

I press my palm into my tummy, moving it down, a few fingers inching under the band of my underwear. "Well, it's a little awkward at first—"

"Awkward?!"

"Hold on, I'm getting there," I say, letting out a little laugh. "Mostly because we're both nervous. We . . . want each other."

"True, true," he says.

"So, I fix you a drink, all coy and cute, leaning down into my freezer, sticking my ass up." I pause. "And what are you doing right now?"

"Watching you. Wanting you. What next?"

I squeeze my eyes shut for a second, feeling my hand move lower down my body. "Fuck the drink," I say. "You're sitting at the stool behind my counter and I walk over to you slowly and stand in between your legs. I place your hands on my waist, move closer to you. I lower my face to yours and finally, we kiss—"

"Uh-huh," he says.

"A little tongue and lips and warm and wet."

He laughs, but then his voice lowers. "Come on," he says. "Make it good for me." His voice sends a shiver through me.

"Okay," I say, steeling myself for what's next. "I press myself to you and can feel you getting hard through your jeans. I want to make you wait for it."

"Tease me," he says, his voice catching.

"I step back from you and peel off my shirt."

"Good," he says, and I can almost feel him straining through the phone.

"I walk back toward you, and you pull one breast out of my bra, leaning down to take it in your mouth."

"I'd put your nipple between my teeth and pull, just a little," he says, his voice turning into almost a growl, and I'm surprised by the desire pulsing through me, the frenetic tension coursing through my legs, my arms, my chest.

"Then what?"

"You step back and take off your pants, so you can touch yourself. So you can slip a finger inside," he says. Then he stops. "Can you do that for me? Now."

I let out a sound I don't recognize, one that I haven't made in months, and I exhale, following his directions.

"Are you doing that?" he asks.

"Yes."

"I want you to let me lick that finger."

"You can," I say, breathing heavily, working another finger inside myself.

But this isn't enough. I want more.

"I want to see you," I say.

"Really?" he asks, surprised.

"Yes," I say. "I'll show you everything. Except my face."

He laughs then. "Well, shit. Staying anonymous even while I'm trying to fuck you." But then the camera pops up and a wave of excitement hits. Am I really going to do this?

I whip off my shirt and wriggle out of my underwear, angling the phone so it shows what's below. Without thinking too hard, I swipe to answer.

Ollie inhales sharply as I watch him enter the frame. His chest is bare and muscular, dotted with a few swoops of dark curls. His hair is mussed and tousled, flopping to one side in an adorable manner, and his handsome face stares at my body in concentration, a little flushed. I follow his eyes to where he's focused on my chest, my nipples hard and pink, extending to the screen.

"What do you think?" I ask, raising a hand to squeeze my left breast, pinch it between two fingers.

"You're beautiful," he says, reaching a hand down his belly.

"Can I see?" I ask, moving my phone so he can see my lower half, too, my hand cupping my sex, a finger curling inside.

His mouth drops open, and he moves his camera down so I can watch him pull at his dick, thick and hard between his legs.

I lick my lips. We're both breathing hard, but I want him to keep talking.

"I've never done this before, not with someone I don't know," I say.

"Me neither," he says, his eyes not leaving me, watching my fingers move inside me. He's got a hungry look on his face, one that makes me want to stretch out in front of him, give him all of me. When he speaks, it's with a voice I haven't heard yet, one that's fierce and direct and so fucking hot. "I want to taste you while I touch you," he says. "I want to lick every drop that comes out of you."

I throw my head back and close my eyes. I'm slick now, and I move the phone so he can see. "Like this?"

I watch his eyes nearly bulge out of his head as he nods. "I wanna fuck you so bad," he says.

"How?"

"I'd kiss my way up your stomach and slowly slide inside you, filling you all the way up," he says, his voice catching. "Then I'd move in and out, teasing you until you beg for more."

I pretend like my fingers are him and follow his movements, bucking my hips up as he talks. "You're driving me crazy." He grunts in agreement. "How long does it take me to cum?"

"Not long."

"How long?" I ask again, more urgently now, wanting him to release me, to send me over the edge.

"Not until I kiss you, not until I hear you moan inside my mouth."

"Now," I say. "Now."

"Now," he agrees.

I let out a groan, feeling a rush of energy, of liquid heat, of tension release all inside me, and I hear similar sounds escape Ollie through the phone, a strain and then a sigh.

"Shit," he says, softer, tired.

I drop the phone into my sheets and lean back against my pillows, my skin damp with sweat and, all of a sudden, exhaustion.

I pull on my tank top and pull my duvet tight up around my stomach, angling the phone so he can see my mouth, my neck, a few more identifiers.

"That was fucked-up," I say, trying not to laugh.

"Damn, I get a half-face shot now?" he asks, leaning into the camera, smiling with those pink, full lips.

"You earned it." The clock on my phone says it's past 1:00 a.m., and even though I have nowhere to be tomorrow, the enormity of the day washes over me and suddenly I'm desperate for sleep. "Good night, Ollie."

He presses two fingers to his lips and then to the screen, sending a pitter-patter through my chest. "Good night, whoever the fuck you are."

CHAPTER 26

The last thing I want to do after yesterday's roller coaster is see Victoria, but as I wake up to the sun shining through the curtains in my bedroom, I realize I have seven missed calls and thirty-five text messages from her saying that she wants to talk.

I leave her on read for an hour, while I get myself together, looking for a response from Naomi that isn't coming, and going through my ever-expanding box of DMs, reposting and sharing new information about Duke Dudley and other alleged victims who were brave enough to come forward.

But finally, when my phone erupts for the millionth time and Victoria's name flashes across my screen, I answer.

"Forgive me for not exactly rushing to respond," I say, putting the call on speaker so I can keep DMing with the hostess at Lucien about which members of the *Gossip Girl* cast will be dining there tonight. "You basically told me I'm a selfish asshole. Maybe I deserved it, but I'm still kinda mad."

Victoria sighs. "I know," she says, and I can hear traffic zooming by behind her. "But how mad are we talking? Mad like when I spilled aioli on your Chanel purse a week after you got it on the RealReal? Or mad like when Doug invited you to his family's beach house in Mantoloking but then told you not to show up once he realized his parents were going to be there and he didn't want you to meet them?"

That's the thing about staying this close with your oldest friend.

They know everything about you—how to press down on a bruise only they can see, how to make you laugh even when you want to push them away, and what words to say to remind you that there's no one in the world who knows you in the way that they do.

I lean my head back against my sofa and close my eyes, forgetting about all the DMs and horrible stories piling up in my inbox.

"I guess not as mad than when the orthodontist humiliated me, but madder than when you almost ruined a fucking *Chanel*."

I can almost hear Victoria nod on the other end. "I can live with that."

"Ha," I say, but I'm not laughing. Not yet. "You really hurt me," I say.

She sighs. "I hate to say it, babe, but you hurt me, too."

I open my mouth to protest, but she keeps talking.

"Come downstairs."

"What?"

"I'm outside. Come on, let's go for a walk."

"But—"

"But nothing. I don't care if you have to post four hundred spotteds. I came all the way from the Upper East Side. Get your ass down here. We need to talk." The line goes dead, and I do as she says.

Victoria's always been this way. Even when we were in ninth grade and she thought she deserved an A from a teacher who gave her a B-. She wouldn't take no for an answer, wouldn't back down until the teacher caved and had her do two hours of extra credit homework in order to bump up the grade.

She always came prepared and determined, ready to explain herself and be heard. She was never passive-aggressive, a trait I deeply admired and loved about her. Victoria was the reason I got the Sasha job all those years ago, too. The person who told me to lead with confidence and act like I knew exactly how to interact with the famous and beautiful, even if I had never stepped foot on a photoshoot.

That was back when she lived in the converted studio in the West Village, when she insisted I come over before the interview so she could dress me in her Stella McCartney black silk blouse, a pleated skirt, and square-toe Saint Laurent boots. The same woman who bought me a lapis-blue Smythson leather notebook when I landed the job, who celebrated every birthday and milestone with a homemade, from-the-box yellow sheet cake, even though now she can afford a thousand of those bland fancy cakes where sprinkles spill out the middle.

So, because of all that, I do as she says and shove my feet into a pair of Vejas, throw on a sweatshirt, and head to the first floor, where I see she's waiting for me on the street.

She spins around, and when she sees me, she holds out her hand, a small paper cup of coffee extended toward me. Under a Nili Lotan trench coat, she's got on a full Lululemon athleisure uniform, Vince slip-ons on her feet.

"It's not a peace offering," Victoria says as I take the coffee. "It's an intervention."

"What the fuck is that supposed to mean?" I sip from the lid, pleased to find it's a bone-dry cap just the way I like it.

"Come on." Victoria grabs me by the elbow and starts walking, pulling me with her onto the side streets over toward a courtyard.

We walk a few blocks in silence, listening to the sounds of cars passing and subways rattling underneath, a busker on the street corner playing the trumpet. When we get to a red light, Victoria leans her head up against my shoulder and hugs me tight on my side.

"I'm worried you're losing yourself in deuxmoi," she says, and for a second, I think her voice might break.

"Shh," I whisper. "Don't say the name too loud." I glance around, seeing who might be here.

Victoria laughs and lets me go. "This is what I'm talking about.

You need some *balance*. I'm sorry if what I said last night hurt your feelings, but no one else is going to tell you this because no one but Leon and I know what you're actually doing."

"So?"

"So, I think you need to hear some cold hard truths."

I sigh and sip my cappuccino. "Like what?"

"Like the fact that this is literally all you do and you don't get paid for it. Or the fact that it *is* impacting the way you do your job. And, to be honest, your relationships."

She pauses there, pursing her lips, and I want to butt in, to make an excuse, but I know she's right. I *haven't* been there for her as much as I have in the past. I can't even remember the last time we went out and *didn't* spend the whole night talking about the account—who was DMing me, who I was trying to get info on, who wrote about my stories. Maybe if I were her, I'd be upset with me, too. And maybe I'd have good reason.

Victoria stops and looks at me straight on. "Be honest: Do you think your obsession with the account affected your job performance in L.A.?"

I rack my brain for a response. Forgetting the skirt was *bad*, but it was an honest mistake. Anyone could have done that. But maybe if I had been more on my game, I would have checked the server early that morning for any updates. And if I wasn't so obsessed with my phone, rushing off to check it every second, then Sasha wouldn't have been as pissed as she was from the get-go. I've learned over the years that I can't control her actions, but I can mitigate them or at least manipulate her moods with *my* actions. But . . . thinking about all this now, I just don't want to do that anymore. It's not like she's performing open-heart surgery and I'm handing her dirty scalpels. It's *styling*. Why am I killing myself?

Victoria squeezes my hand. "Do you?"

"No," I say. "It didn't. But all I know is that running deuxmoi is making me think about things differently, about my *life* differently. I can't be Sasha's shit-eating assistant forever."

Victoria throws up her hands, spilling coffee all over the concrete. "That's what I'm saying!" She loops her arm in mine. "I just want you to start thinking about finding a way to make this your *thing*, Crick. Your job or your future or whatever. Clearly, you're good at it, whatever *it* really is. You have power. You enjoy it. And honestly, it's *fun*. People like it."

"So, you're saying you think I should take the Kyle Johns offer?"

"Yes."

I think back to what Ollie said, that Kyle really might be able to help me. "I'll think about it."

"Good. Because even if I don't want to be outed as a friend-of-deuxmoi, I know that you deserve better. You deserve more than what Sasha's giving you."

I let her words sink in, let them buoy me as she leads me back toward my apartment. We pass open-air bistros where couples sit close behind tables, staring at their phones. Queues of teenagers waiting in line for the latest streetwear drop outside a nondescript loft, their heads ducked down toward their screens.

I wonder, as we pass them all, if some of them, with their eyes glued to the moving images in front of them, are looking for more information, more content, more stories . . . from me.

Text conversation between Cricket and Ollie

Ollie

I can't stop thinking about you, about the other night.

Cricket

Me too.

Maybe we make FaceTime a regular thing??

I'm counting on it.

Fuck yeah.

Wait, side note, what happened with Vivendi??

I haven't heard from her since I denied it . . . maybe she's gone MIA?

Toldya it'd work

Cocky much?

Hey, who's the one that helped you ninja your way out of an extremely sticky situation?

Fair.

Ollie

Just glad you're feeling better about it all.

Cricket

I feel like I have to change my number. All my passwords, too. No more leaks. My fragile emotional state can't handle it

I'm no tech guru. Gonna have to go elsewhere.

Right

I bet that Kyle Johns guy has good security . . . did you make your decision yet?

This week. I'm nervous

Why??

IDK

I like the idea of getting out of my day job but trusting someone else with the account is . . . a lot. It's all mine now. I don't know if I want to give that up

Ollie

But think how much you could do with backup from a company like that. Worth thinking about.

Cricket

For sure

But, more importantly, I'm coming to New York next week . . .

Oh yeah?

Planting the seed now in case I can change your mind from last time

Maybe. . .

That's not a no!

Nope. Definitely not a no . . .

Excerpt from *Vivendi*

Behind the Scenes with @deuxmoi, Instagram's Accidental, Anonymous Shit-Stirrer Who We Can't Get Enough Of

. . . Just who is the person behind deuxmoi? This intrepid reporter tried her hardest to find out, employing a sort-of-sketchy hacker-adjacent expert and her best friend, who has become obsessed with this particular mystery. And even though the reporting revealed a name of someone likely to be the owner of the account, *Vivendi* couldn't quite prove without a doubt that she is the person actually pressing share.

After all, there could be a shadow network of deuxmoi posters. Or perhaps I spoke with someone who deuxmoi asked to step in on her behalf for the interview. Whatever the case may be, if our search turned up accurate results, then one thing is for certain: Whoever deuxmoi is doesn't really matter. This woman is of no interest to anyone, celebrity-wise. She is a no-name. A no one. And perhaps that's why her allure is so strong.

But after she exposed Duke Dudley for his alleged assault and harassment, she was catapulted to another level of scrutiny. (Dudley's team, in a statement, said that the allegations against him are completely false and that deuxmoi is likely someone with an axe to grind who is knowingly posting incorrect information. "Whoever she is, her information is baseless," Dudley's lawyer said.) Keep in mind, Dudley is now being investigated by the police; has been dropped by his agent, publicist, and manager; and has been cut from the massive Netflix series *The Viscounts*. Recent sightings show him hiding in a villa off the coast of Belize. His lawyer says they could sue deuxmoi for defamation and slander.

All we know is that we'll keep following deuxmoi with the hopes of one day figuring out who exactly has been wreaking havoc in Hollywood.

CHAPTER 27

I'm standing in line at Maman with Leon, waiting for our morning coffee, when my phone starts buzzing like crazy.

"Order for Leon!" the barista says, holding out our drinks. Leon grabs the cardboard carrying tray, but I'm stuck in place, trying to find the source of the notifications.

"Come on," he says, tugging on my elbow. "We gotta go." He's right, too. Sasha's coming in early today and demanded everyone else do so as well. But I have a text from Ollie.

> Vivendi is live.

He sends the link, and my heart nearly beats right out of my chest. I hold my breath as it loads, trying to keep up with Leon, who's a few steps ahead of me, walking fast back to work.

Holy fucking shit, I reply. *Good or bad? IDK if I can read.*

Ollie responds. *It could be worse.*

My chest begins to settle, but then I walk right into Leon's back, not realizing he's stopped as we wait for an ambulance to cross the street.

"What's wrong with you?" Leon asks, turning around. "You look like you're going to be sick."

I shake my head, my mouth dropped open, and turn my phone

around so he can see the story. The headline screams out to us, with an illustration of a phone and a bunch of celebrities taking over the entire screen.

"What does it say?" I ask him. "I don't know if I can handle it."

I watch Leon's eyes move over my phone, his brows furrowed and his lips pursed.

He clears his throat and looks up, clearly relieved. "I'm not named."

I smack his chest.

"Neither are you."

"Really?"

"Really. Now hurry up, Sasha's going to kill you if you're not back in five."

I make a plan to read the article as soon as I'm safely hidden in the single-stall bathroom at work, but for now, for a moment, all I feel is enormous relief.

...

It takes until 3:00 p.m. before I finally have a free moment to hit the bathroom and read Naomi's piece. At first, I'm thrilled that Ollie's plan worked—she didn't out me. And sure, I'm pleased that the account has gotten five thousand new followers since the story published. But I'm slowly starting to realize that it started a domino effect where now, other news outlets are suggesting that I'm the person to blame for blowing up Duke Dudley's career—that I'm the reason this news got out and that the end of his career is somehow *my* fault. Everyone's quoting that bullshit line from his lawyer, and now I'm getting tagged in stories by Duke Dudley stans, asking me why I fucked up his career.

A ball of rage begins to build in my stomach. They think *I'm* to blame for this? What absolute garbage. I press the heel of my palm into my forehead as I type "deuxmoi" into Twitter, seeing what pops up.

> The fact that Vivendi allows Duke's people to say the allegations are a lie and to blame deuxmoi is frankly disgusting.

9:48 AM October 10,2022 Twitter for Android

> This is a weird thing to feel passionate about, but deuxmoi is 100% not to blame for the Duke Dudley thing. She didn't even "break" the news. Just shared stories from women already out there.

1:49 PM October 10, 2022 Twitter for iPhone

> What the fucky fuck. He needs to have his rich white male privilege card revoked. To shame another woman. The audacity. And shame on Vivendi for letting him do that in their pages.

2:39 PM October 10, 2022 Twitter for Android

Then I see a tweet from @Naomirutherford, one that nearly has my jaw on the floor.

> Spoke to deuxmoi about being deuxmoi. I think I know who she is . . . but she'll never confirm ☺ Peep my latest for Vivendi to see how she played a part in the Duke Dudley story, too.

1:58 PM October 10, 2022 Twitter for iPhone

My face feels like it's on fire as I realize what she's done. Naomi has tried to get back at me—to punish me—for not confirming my identity. Now, she's coming for me in the shadiest kind of way.

I press my head back against the bathroom door and think hard about my next move. If I make a statement, that will just draw more attention to the situation. But I can't let her do this. I can't say *nothing*. Based on my inbox, the most engaged followers are already up in arms over this.

Which kind of makes me think . . .

I screenshot a bunch of those tweets and a few of the messages in my inbox. Then I share them all, one after the other, until there are twenty-five in total. Enough to get the point across, clearly.

Then I take a deep breath and drop down to sit on the top of the toilet as I compose my response.

I type then retype, and then type again, until finally I know what I want to say:

> I'm not down with any publication who's trying to blame me for an actor's scandal. I never knowingly share false info and was just trying to help these women get their messages out.

■■■

I head back to my workspace and place my phone in the secure spot in between my knees, under my desk, so no one can see that I'm parsing through my DMs, trying to figure out where to go from here.

Leon drops by with a worried look on his face. "Okay, I just read. Are you okay?" he asks.

"Somehow," I say, sipping my now-cold cappuccino from earlier.

The door opens, and I glance toward it, anticipating Sasha's return from some lunch she scurried out to. But it's just Alyssa, hustling down the hallway with her head ducked down.

"Alyssa thinks Sasha's out meeting with one of her lawyers right now," Leon whispers. "And not for a good reason."

I set down my drink and look at him with wide eyes. "Seriously?"

He nods. "Yep. She thinks we're going under."

I shake my head. "And somehow that's not the worst thing I've heard today."

"That whole blaming you for Duke thing?" Leon rolls his eyes. "That's ludicrous and everyone knows it." But then his mouth turns into a smile. "But . . . how many followers did you get?"

I swat at his arm. "That is so not the point."

He gives me that *bullshit* face, and my shoulders slump.

"Five thousand."

Leon's eyes go wide. "That's not bad."

"I'd just rather it be for something . . . better."

"Honestly, though, this might help you up the offer with Kyle Johns. Have you countered yet?"

I shrug. "I don't know."

"Well, based on the way this shit show is going, you might need to be hiring me to work at Johns Global Media in a month."

I drop my forehead in my hands. "He'd be my boss, though. What if I'm stepping into a whole different, more awful Sasha Sherman situation? It would just be another . . ." I wave around at the near-empty room.

Leon nods. "Go back with the biggest number you can think of. See what he says."

"I'll think about it. Still might not be worth it."

Leon crosses his arms over his chest. "You know . . . since this whole thing started, I feel like I've seen a new side of you. Someone who . . ."

"Won't take shit?"

"Kind of. No offense."

I roll my eyes. It's no secret I let Sasha walk all over me.

"No, it's just . . . you seem lighter. Freer. It's good not to put all your eggs in Sasha's fucked-up basket. Lord knows it's easier to get into Harvard than to get a promotion around here."

"Ahem, look who's talking, Mr. Promoted at Twenty-Five."

Leon waves at Alyssa and mouths something to her as she passes down the hall. "I got lucky," he says. "But you . . . you've made your own luck, wherever this whole tornado takes you. Proud of you, babe." He squeezes my shoulder and pauses. "And mostly thrilled that my name's not out there associated with you right now."

Before I can say anything, he hops off my desk and runs after Alyssa. When he gets to her, she links her arm in his and the two walk off down the hallway, making a left into her office, their heads ducked toward each other. A pang of jealousy stings my chest, but maybe Leon's right. I have paved my own path recently. It's bumpy and fucked-up, but at least it's mine. That's more than I can say for half the projects I've worked on over the past eight years, where Sasha just slaps her name on it at the end and tells me to find my own way home.

The office is dead, so I take advantage of the moment and look down at my phone under the desk. But when I see the message at the top of my Instagram inbox, I have to catch my breath.

It's from Alyssa. The *real* Alyssa. The same account where she often posts photos of her cat stretching in good lighting, chic outfit rundowns outside her Brooklyn brownstone, posed shots of her with celebs like Issa Rae and Hari Nef—people who aren't even our clients.

She's *never* messaged me before, not on deuxmoi, even though she's been following for months.

I bite my lip as I open her message, and when I see what she's written, I have to read it twice to understand what she's trying to say—what she wants to do.

> Anon pls: No one's talking about all the people who enabled Duke Dudley to get where he is today—the studio execs, his co-stars, the people who turned him into a hero. If you want someone to blame, think about people like his longterm stylist. No one will come out and say it because they're so scared of her. But she's enabled him for years. He pulled these same tricks on one of her assistants years ago and she knew about it—did nothing. Ignored bruises. Helped him find new girlfriends. Behind closed doors she blames her silence on signing an iron-clad NDA but . . . come on. Complicity isn't cute. Not anyone. Not ever.

I check the timestamp and see she sent it moments ago, right when Leon was over here. From my desk, I can see her dark hair peeking through the window of her office, shoulders hunched up around her neck as she looks down.

Instagram says she's still online.

> Do you want me to post this as is?

She may not say "Sasha Sherman," but it's pretty fucking obvious who she's talking about. For some reason, I feel protective over Alyssa. I don't want her doing something I think she might regret—especially when we all know how this might go over when Sasha sees it. If Sasha finds out Alyssa wrote this.

Alyssa writes back immediately.

> Yes. I used to love this guy but I found out the truth months ago when his wife came to me in confidence after finding texts on his phone (don't post this). I reached out to one of our former assistants and heard

even more. It makes me sick. Now, I'm rethinking every interaction we ever had—things I thought were normal were not. And I just want the world to know there were people, even people like me, who covered for him. I'm so ashamed of my loyalty to him. I just want to make things right.

My heart pounds in my chest, and I think about the assistants who came before me—the ones who've spoken out about Sasha's nasty dealings, ones like Eleanor, who fled the industry to get away from people like Sasha, people like Duke.

I send Alyssa a heart and do as she says, blocking out her information as I upload a screenshot of her original post. I slap on some "Duke Dudley update" text and send the story out into the ether, knowing that as soon as followers see it, the floodgates will open once again and I'll get more and more messages about Duke and the people who kept him at the top, including Sasha Sherman.

■■■

I haven't been doing actual, real, legit work for more than thirty seconds when I hear the elevator ding near the entrance. I swivel my head to see Sasha clomping out onto the floor, a petite woman dressed in a St. John knit suit by her side.

Sasha's wearing a flowy Zimmermann dress and she still has her Celine sunglasses strapped to her head. Her face is ducked low while the woman next to her talks quietly, using her hands to punctuate certain words. My stomach flips, and I stand, not knowing what to do with my hands.

I grab a folder full of looks for Sasha's approval and hold it out to her as she passes, but she doesn't take it. Instead, she walks directly into her office with the woman and closes the door, not making eye contact with anyone.

Who the fuck is that? I text Leon.

> Let me ask Alyssa.

A beat later: *She says that's her private publicist.*

Yikes, I respond.

> Maybe because of what you just posted??? Playing with fire . . .

I look up and see Leon wincing in the corner of the floor. Alyssa's usually rosy cheeks are a dull gray, and it looks like all the life has been sucked out of her face. She retreats back to her office and yanks on Leon's elbow, pulling him inside.

While Sasha and the mystery woman meet in her office, I scroll through my DMs, my phone under my desk on my lap. Sure enough, there are loads of replies to Alyssa's tip. Even one from Eleanor Cauley Rhodes:

Can confirm, she wrote. *A certain stylist tried to serve me up as bait during a shoot once, which led to the worst year of my life. I'm glad to see this garbage is finally coming out. No wonder I left New York . . .*

I keep looking up, stealing glances at Sasha's office, wondering if she knows that only feet away from her, the people who once feared her are slowly chipping away at the once-perfect image she wanted to project. But the next time I look around, I realize the room is empty. I sit up straight in my chair and swivel around.

"Looking for me?" Sasha's standing behind me like a fucked-up ghost, and my heart nearly pounds right out of my chest.

"Yes," I say. "Sorry, I—"

"Was on your phone, yes, I see."

Fear churns in my stomach. I stand up and try to meet her at eye level even though I'm three inches shorter than her and she's wearing four-inch platforms.

"Can I get you anything?"

Sasha taps her foot impatiently. "Cut the shit. You know we're in free fall right now."

I try to swallow, but my throat is dry as sand. "I heard."

"Yeah, well, so did everyone on the planet."

She rips her sunglasses from her face and drops her head in her hands, and for a second, I wonder if this is what it looks like to see Sasha be vulnerable.

But as quickly as she softened, her hard edges reappear. "The trades have been hounding me all morning," she says, her voice clipped. "If they call for comment, hang up."

"Hang up?"

"Are you dumb? What did I just say?"

I look down and make a fist, my nails digging into my skin hard enough to feel something.

Sasha turns on her heel and heads back to her office. But not before muttering something to herself. "Fucking deuxmoi . . ."

That's what makes me lose it.

"You know, it's not really deuxmoi's fault," I say, the words tumbling out. "If what Duke did is true . . . he's to blame, not the people talking about it."

Sasha turns back around, so slowly it terrifies me. Then she looks at me hard, her eyes narrowed as they run up and down my frame. "That top makes you look poor. Don't you ever wear it in my presence again."

She slams her office door behind her, and I sink back into my chair, wondering why the hell I had to say something.

With shaking hands, I pick my phone back up and start to scroll mindlessly, until I hear an uproarious noise coming from Sasha's office. At first there's a scream, then the sound of glass shattering, anger rising.

I spin around and see that Sasha's chucked her phone straight at a Murano vase full of tulips. The concrete floor is covered in petals, wilted stems, and glass, Sasha's broken phone floating in a little pool of water.

Her fists are curled by her side, flexing and unflexing, and she's breathing so hard I think she might throw up. But then she yells my name.

"Clean this shit up," she says.

I stand, unwilling to meet her eyes, and rummage around my desk for paper towels, trying to blink back tears.

I drop down to crawl on the floor in her office and carefully gather her mess, her destruction. But then she hinges forward, her hands on her knees, and lowers her voice into a whisper.

"If you hear anything about who the little fucker is that runs that account, you better tell me, okay? That bitch is going to get what's coming to her."

Sasha stands up and walks out of the office, stepping over my curled-up body. I swipe at shards of glass, piles of dirt, and stomped-on flowers, and retrieve her phone from its near-busted state.

But when I see what's on it, glitching over and over from water damage, I realize what she was looking at that caused her to finally hit her breaking point.

There, on the screen, is deuxmoi, Alyssa's betrayal right there for everybody to see.

CHAPTER 28

By the time I get home from work, I feel like a deflated balloon—all the air sucked right out of me. When I used to feel this way, I'd book a barre class or head to get drinks with Leon. I'd take a long walk and people watch, feel the energy of the city and let it bring me back up.

But now . . . now, all I want to do is bury myself in deuxmoi, the one place where I feel safe right now. I order sushi takeout and plop down on the couch before checking my DMs and emails. A calm settles over me as my thumbs get to work, screenshotting and replying, sleuthing for more stories.

But then I see a message from the official Styling by Sasha account, which only one person has access to: Sasha Sherman.

> All the rumors about Duke's longterm stylist are fucking FALSE. She had no idea what was going on . . . PERIOD. That's all there is to the story. Oh, and she's also an extremely kind boss. The people who say otherwise just don't know what it takes to succeed in this business. Kids these days do not understand the value of hard work.

I can't help but let out a laugh. Sasha has gone full-on delusional if she thinks anyone would post this message masquerading as a tip.

I don't even do her the honor of responding before my phone lights up with a call from Ollie.

"Is it bad I was hoping to hear from you tonight?" I say, not even trying to play it cool.

He laughs on the other end. "No," he says. I can practically hear him smile. "But that's good because I just landed in New York."

My body tenses. I totally forgot he was coming here. The last time we spoke, he said the ball was in my court, and that if I wanted him to come over all I had to do was say so. I bite my lip and dig my toe deeper into the couch. What would it *mean*, meeting him? Here, at my home? For one, it would completely blow my cover; it would let him in completely. The first person in the world besides my best friends who would know.

But this is the guy who's already seen the most intimate parts of me. Inviting him here might mean we could try to see what the past few months have meant, if anything at all. If I never do that—if I never even *try*—then what the hell am I doing? I think of Leon with Giuseppe and Victoria with Jake. It's not that I *need* a partner, but I haven't had this great of a spark, a connection, with anyone, *ever*— and he hasn't even met me or seen my face.

If it's all going to hell, which it sure seems like it might, then . . . *fuck it.*

Before I can think better, I blurt out what I've been wanting to say for weeks.

"We should meet."

There's a pause, a weighty one, and I hear him inhale, let that breath out slowly. "No fucking way."

"What are you doing tonight?"

"Depends what you're about to say."

I curl my knees in toward me and close my eyes. "Come over."

"Are you sure? I don't—"

"Come. Over."

He laughs. "Well, shit. All right. I have a work dinner, but . . . after?"

"Yep."

"Send me the address."

I hang up and type in my apartment information before I can think better—before I can stop myself from playing it safe and cool and letting my fear of risks get the better of me.

> I'll be there by ten.

...

The next three hours are excruciating, and I try to pace myself, sipping on a glass of wine, but pretty soon it's 9:45 and I have to force myself to look at deuxmoi in order to not freak out completely.

One from a regular source, a waiter at Pastis, catches my attention. It's a photo of a big round table, full of men and women laughing over plates of steak and chilled oysters and bowls of fries.

> Michael B. Jordan having dinner with his agents and some media people rn. Ordered the usuals, including a few rounds of martinis. Tipping like crazy and taking photos with fans. All around great time.

I make moves to post the photo, but then I look a little more intently, zooming in on the shot. I cover my mouth. No shit. It's Ollie, sitting right between Michael and his agent, lifting a martini glass, laughing with his head thrown back.

Copying the photo, I move over to my texts and shoot him the image. *Look what someone just sent me.*

He responds immediately. *Am I about to be deuxmoi legit now?!*

I send him back a shrug emoji. *Depends how long it takes you to get here . . .*

I'll be on time, he writes. *Promise.*

I start pacing around my apartment, wondering if it's a bad idea to have another glass of wine or if I should change out of my leggings and T-shirt into something more stereotypically sexy. But what the fuck am I going to do? Put on a black lace teddy to meet this guy? Not when we've been sexting for weeks. It's almost too cliché. Too loaded.

So instead of doing anything, I keep posting to deuxmoi and try not to stare at my front door.

But suddenly, the buzzer rings and I nearly jump out of my skin. With butterflies in my stomach, I press my thumb to the call button and clear my throat. "Hello?"

"It's me." He sounds like he does on the phone. Strong and confident. British. But he also sounds different . . . loose, maybe. Or a little nervous. That thought relaxes me—that we're both in the same boat, wondering how the hell this is about to go down.

"Are you ready?" I say through the intercom.

He laughs. "Do you have to ask?" I buzz him in. I know it only takes about ninety seconds for most people to get from the front door to my apartment, and every single one is a challenge in patience. But finally, after what feels like a lifetime, I hear a knock on the door and his voice on the other side.

"Special delivery."

My fingers shake as I unlatch the lock and twist the knob. My heart pounds as I take my first look at Ollie standing in front of me. He's taller than I pictured. Broader, too, with big forearms that are crossed in front of his chest. But his build isn't what surprises me. Not really. It's the shit-eating grin on his perfectly symmetrical face and the careful, hungry look in his eye as his gaze travels down my frame, seeing me in real life for the first time. I watch as he takes in my face, his cheeks flushed, his jaw tight. His dark hair is thick and shiny, falling in soft waves to one side. It's all I can do not to reach out and run a few strands through my fingers to make sure he's real.

Finally, I say something.

"Hi."

"Hi."

I back up, not wanting to turn around, to *not* look at him. "Do you want to come in?"

He takes a step inside, almost sheepish, and shrugs out of his gray Sandro wool jacket, revealing strong shoulders that look bigger in person than they did in photos.

All of a sudden there's a thick energy in the room, one that's heavy, full of anticipation, of hope. I try to think of what to do next and take a page from past me. "Do you . . . want a drink?" I ask.

He smiles, all straight teeth and pink lips, and nods. "I think that would be good."

"Wine or vodka?"

"Vodka," he says.

I walk to the kitchen and can feel his eyes on my butt, watching my hips as they move side to side. I drop ice cubes into tumblers and pour some Ketel One over them. When I spin around, he's sitting on a stool at my kitchen island, his elbows propped up on the marble.

"You're shorter than I thought you might be," he says, taking a sip.

"You're taller."

"This is wild, isn't it?" he asks, running a hand through his dark, wavy hair. "I can't remember the last time I was nervous before a date."

"A *date*?" I laugh. "I don't know if this qualifies."

He stands then, leaving his glass behind him, and walks around the island so there's nothing between us, just still air, full of possibilities and potential. "What would make this a date, then?"

I shrug. "I don't know. Dinner. Flowers. Drinks made from ingredients that didn't come from my freezer."

He nods, as if he's mulling over what I'm saying. "That's it, huh?"

"Pretty much."

"Dream bigger."

Then, finally, against all the odds that brought us together, Ollie reaches forward and presses two warm fingers to my chin, sending a shock to my core, heat between my legs. He brings his face close to mine, so close that I can smell his breath, all lemon and mint and promise. His mouth is only millimeters away and I wait a beat, until finally I can't let another second go by without feeling his lips against mine.

I wrap my arms around him, touch the baby hairs on the back of his neck, his muscled shoulders tensing. His mouth is warm and wanting as his tongue darts toward mine. His hands run the length of my back, resting on my ass, firm in his grip.

He pulls back suddenly, and there's a look of surprise on his face, all flushed and curious. "Well," he says. A smile tugs at the corner of his lips. "This is way better than a phone."

"Come here." I pull him to me. His kissing is urgent now, ferocious, and our hands are moving fast, forceful, pulling at fabric and grasping at flesh. He pulls my T-shirt up over my head and dives into my chest, pulling one breast out of my bra and taking my hard nipple in his mouth, thrusting one knee between my legs.

Heat builds inside me, and it's enough to make me explode, to make me realize there has never been a man who has coaxed this kind of desire, who has made me so desperate for release.

His teeth press into the soft skin on my chest, and I gasp, knees buckling beneath me. I sink to the floor and pull Ollie down with me, on top of me, feeling him hard through his jeans, against my hips. I reach for his belt buckle, but he shakes his head, kissing up my chest, my neck, the tender spot behind my ear.

"You first," he whispers.

Keeping his mouth close to my face, Ollie extends his palm over my stomach, sliding it up under my breasts, cupping each one, and then back down to my core. "Is this okay?" he asks.

I nod and watch him smile as he pulls down my leggings, his finger pads soft over my underwear, before pushing them aside and setting his fingers right at my entrance. I gasp, pulling him close, and he groans, harder now against my leg. He slides his hand down over me completely, before extending his fingers, pointing and flexing, as they move in all the right ways that make my hips tilt, moans escaping my throat. I grab his hand with mine to help push his fingers deeper inside me.

I reach for him, press his mouth to mine yet again. His tongue flicks across my teeth before he moves back to my chest, tugging me there. His hand keeps in time as he rubs me, circling the most tender part of me until, finally, all at once, I give in to him, to whatever it is that we've built. My body caves, tensing and wanting and—finally—releasing as his warm hand stays gripped on me, holding me, coaxing me to come for him—for me.

I exhale with a guttural noise, and finally, finally, my whole body relaxes, melting into the kitchen floor, as this man plants slow, tender kisses on my bare stomach, my hips, the insides of my thighs.

After a moment, Ollie rolls over, onto the floor beside me, his body heavy and languid, completely relaxed. His chest rises and falls softly, as if he's catching his breath, and he props himself up on one elbow, so he faces me, still tangled in the heap of discarded clothing,

I look up at him, taking him in, his smile and pensive eyes, roaming my body, as he drags his finger up and down my curves.

"So," he says. "Are you finally going to tell me your name?"

I let out a laugh and cover my mouth, rolling over so I'm on top of him, my bare chest close over his, ready for whatever comes next. I lean down, my hair fanning out around his face, until my mouth is pressed against his ear, where I whisper my name softly, revealing the last secret between us.

CHAPTER 29

I open my eyes gingerly, one at a time, stretching my limbs out from the deep sleep, until I feel the warmth and weight of someone next to me. Everything that happened last night comes rushing back, and all at once I feel the heat between my legs reignite, the memory of Ollie here, with me, for the first time.

Ollie rolls over and spoons me from behind, wrapping an arm around my middle, pulling me to him. He rests his chin on my shoulder and drags a thumb across my bare breast. I press my butt back to find him solid, ready behind me. I wait for him to stir further, to make a move, but he mumbles something into my neck and I remember he's still on West Coast time.

It's 8:00 a.m. and it only takes me a minute to decide I deserve to take a sick day, not that Styling by Sasha *has* sick days. But for this? Fuck it. I reach for my phone, careful not to move too much, and dash out an email to Sasha and Nelly, who coordinates the temp desk.

> I've been vomiting all night. I think this thing's food poisoning. I'm taking the day off. I'll be in tomorrow.

Sasha will probably throw a fit, but I've only called out sick twice in my entire time with Sasha, and both of those times were for viruses that sent me straight to the ER. Using this kind of power is electric. Magnetic. It makes me feel like maybe I can be the type of woman who quits her job and sells her own company to some media tycoon, who spends the morning in bed with a hot man she barely knows, running back the greatest hits from the night before.

My comforter looks so cozy snuggled up around his stomach. I think about climbing on top of him, planting small kisses on his face, which seems to have sprouted the beginnings of a beard overnight. But he looks so peaceful and I should use my day off as a way to get caught up on deuxmoi happenings, so I decide to let him sleep.

I step into a pair of Cotton Citizen sweatpants and a tank top and stuff my feet into my Ariana Bohling slippers, then pad quietly into the kitchen, preparing to make coffee for us both. I know from our bajillion conversations that he likes his light, with lots of oat milk, which I always keep stocked in the fridge.

I set up the coffee maker as quietly as I can, careful not to wake him, and as soon as it starts brewing, I stretch my arms above me, feeling the early-morning breeze cool against my midriff. Smiling, I make a plan to bring him coffee in bed. Maybe I'll run to the bakery downstairs and grab us croissants. Maybe . . .

Shit.

In my bliss, I've knocked over his bag, a Shinola brown leather satchel, and the contents spill out, making a loud crashing sound as pens start rolling on the hardwood floor. I crane my neck to see into the bedroom. Still conked out.

I kneel down and start stuffing things into the bag—a few notebooks, a silver business card holder, a well-worn paperback on economic trends, a pair of sunglasses, and some ziplock baggies full of nuts and dried fruit, which is actually kind of adorable.

I pull the bag up onto the chair and move it off to the side, but then I hear something buzzing down below. I bend over and see a stray phone all the way under the table. Its screen lights up with notifications. I swore I saw his phone in the bedroom, on the nightstand. In fact, I know I did. It buzzed last night, while I was sitting on his face, and he swiped at it, knocking it under the bed before getting back to business.

Ollie's probably just one of those workaholic types who has two phones—Leon got a work phone when Alyssa promoted him, and hell, Sasha has, like, four. Though *that* never made sense to me.

I lean over and grab it, plunking it down on the table, just as the coffee machine goes off. It smells like heaven, and I pour myself a cup before sliding back into my seat at my kitchen table. I start going through my DMs, trying to figure out if there's a theme or celeb I want to focus on today, but almost as soon as I open Instagram, his phone starts buzzing again with an incoming call.

The screen lights up, and it's impossible not to look at it, to see what's going on. But when I see whose name is on the screen, my heart leaps into my throat.

Kyle Johns.

I wait in confusion until the call ends and then I see the notifications pop up on his phone. Three missed calls from Kyle, all within the last hour. A few seconds later, there's a notification for a voicemail, also from Kyle, and then a text comes through. Ollie may be smart, but apparently he's one of those guys who keeps his messages right there out in the open, so anyone looking at his screen can see what they're saying, and when I see Kyle's words, my heart stops.

> Dude, call me.

Ollie mentioned that he was familiar with Kyle, but why didn't he tell me they were on a "dude" texting basis?

But then Kyle texts again.

> Just imagine: you taking the reins of deuxmoi and elevating it to massive heights. It'd be fucking epic. She's close to saying yes. I can feel it!

My heart sinks into my stomach as the reality of what's happening slowly sets in. There's only one reasonable explanation for all of this: Ollie is the former editor in chief Kyle has in mind to run deuxmoi. That Kyle Johns has been courting Ollie to ditch *Elaborate* and take over deuxmoi once he buys it. And Ollie must have known about this all along. He must have . . .

He fucking tricked me.

It's all starting to make sense—why he continued to bring up the deal with Johns Global Media, why he kept talking about how great it would be if I struck out on my own, if I quit my terrible, horrible job, if deuxmoi had additional support.

All because *he* would get to reap the rewards while he and Kyle sidelined me completely.

There's an enormous lump in my throat, one that I can't swallow, and I feel like I can't breathe. But then suddenly I hear footsteps coming from the bedroom and Ollie's groggy voice ring out. "Do I smell coffee? You're my angel."

But when he comes closer, he stops abruptly right in front of me.

"What are you doing with my phone?"

I look up to see Ollie staring at me quizzically, only wearing boxer briefs, looking adorable in a way that makes me want to punch him in the throat.

I toss the phone toward him, and it clatters on the table before bouncing on the floor. Ollie lunges for it, and I stand so I'm looking down at him on the floor, arms crossed over my chest, fury boiling up inside me. He looks at his screen, then up at me, with a face full of recognition, of shame.

"That's all this was, huh?" I say, trying to hide the tears, the breakage in my voice. "You screwed me so I'd sign a deal with Kyle fucking Johns? So you could run deuxmoi? Has this been your plan all along?"

Ollie scrambles to stand and holds out his hands, like he's going to plead with me. "You don't understand. It's not like that. Kyle's an old friend. He—"

"He what? Tried to get you to come work for him by dangling deuxmoi like a carrot in front of your face? Let me guess. He told you that if he bought my whole business that you'd get a piece of it," I spit.

Ollie stares at me, slack-jawed, his hair sticking up in all the right places. He looks like he's about to try to defend himself, dig himself out of whatever grave he's already lying in.

"I never should have trusted you." As I say the words, the reality of what's happening crushes me like a tidal wave. He *knows* who I am. *He* has the power now. He can ruin my life in an instant. All he has to do is call Naomi Rutherford over at *Vivendi*, or send a simple email to Sasha Sherman, or text Kyle Johns my real name. He could run my info as an exposé in *Elaborate*, for all I know. I gave him ammo without thinking twice.

Ollie looks at me, his mouth a big wide O, and his eyes wide and worried. "This is all a big misunderstanding," he says, pleading. "It's not like that. It's not what you think."

I let out a laugh. "Are you fucking kidding me right now? *It's not what I think?* Bullshit." I shake my head furiously and stand, widening my stance, summoning all the rage inside me. "You need to go."

We both stand there, the silence loud and pulsing between us. He makes no move to get his clothes or his bag, so I say it again, louder and with more conviction.

"Leave."

His neck hinges forward, and his head drops. He slowly gathers his things, and I can't bear to watch him pull on his pants or his shirt. I wish there was something he could say that would make this all right, that would make this all a bad dream. But there's no use in wishing. He showed me who he really is and became a lesson, a reminder of what I have to do to protect myself.

Trust no one.

He walks to the door, his fingers wrapped around that goddamn phone. He puts his hand on the doorknob and turns back around.

"I won't tell anyone who you really are," he says before shutting the door behind him.

And as he leaves, his footsteps echoing in the hall, I finally burst into tears, wishing with every bone in my body that I could believe him.

Page Six

Kyle Johns Rumored to Be in Talks to Buy Deuxmoi, Adding to His Media Empire

Media mogul Kyle Johns has his eyes set on acquiring anonymous celebrity gossip Instagram account deuxmoi. Sources say his goal is to turn the account into a full brand, with an editorial website, additional social media accounts, events, and more. When asked about the rumors, Johns's publicist Deirdre Gerson said, "Deuxmoi is a hot property with potential. It's ripe for acquisition. Whoever lands it is lucky."

Grabbing a slice of the deuxmoi pie would actually be a smart move for Johns—or any media executive. The account went from thirty thousand followers to over a million in just six months and has helped break dozens of celebrity news stories—including weddings and baby announcements. Notably, it also shed more light on the allegations against Duke Dudley, who has been all but blacklisted from Hollywood after multiple women came forward, accusing him of having an abusive streak and vampire fetish tendencies.

The person behind the account has yet to reveal herself and didn't return *Page Six*'s requests for comment.

CHAPTER 30

"You sounded so freaked out on the phone, I came as soon as I could," Victoria says, barreling into Cafeteria up in Chelsea. She's wearing tennis whites and carrying a bag that has a racket handle sticking out the back. She slides into the seat across the table from me and looks at me with big, watery eyes.

"You were at a tennis lesson?" I ask.

She waves her hand. "Who cares?" She flags down the waiter and orders a latte, an omelet, and a platter of table pancakes, which she's done since we frequented late-night diners in high school. She smooths her hair down and leans in. "What the hell happened?"

The story spills out of me, how Ollie cracked me right open, got me to be vulnerable, and then lied straight to my face. I tell her how I ditched work and invited him over, full of pride and gumption, and how, this morning, I felt like the biggest fool on the planet when I learned he was in talks with Kyle Johns to take over deuxmoi all along.

Victoria nods emphatically, a concerned look on her face, as she listens attentively, gasping at all the right moments.

The whole time I'm talking, my phone keeps buzzing incessantly, causing me to look at it, until finally, Victoria picks it up and stashes it in her purse.

"Give me that!" I say.

"It's him," she says, cramming a forkful of pancakes into her mouth. "No."

I slump back in the booth and take a big glug of coffee. "I wish I never started this account. I should just deactivate it. Go dark and not say anything at all."

Victoria jolts up. "Hey," she says, her voice soft. "You've made it this far. You beat that reporter. You can beat this."

"Not worried about your Racquet Club membership?" I ask half-heartedly.

"Where do you think my tennis lesson was?" she says, laughing. "We got accepted two days ago."

I roll my eyes. "Classic."

Vic reaches across the table and grabs my hand. "What's the worst-case scenario here, huh? Let's game it out."

I bite the inside of my cheek and close my eyes, mulling over everything that's happened. "Well, I guess, it would be Sasha finding out and firing me."

Victoria laughs. "Okay, getting out of there would be a blessing. That woman's a tyrant."

"But I've worked there for eight years. It would be like blowing it all up."

She shakes her head. "If I hear you say the phrase 'eight years' one more time, I don't know if we can be friends anymore. You'd be better off without that job. What else?"

"The world finds out who I am and starts harassing me, putting my shit on blast. Like, what if they dox you or Leon? Or my grandma?"

"Nana would be *fine*. Doesn't she live in a gated community in Boca? No one's getting in there." She pauses. "Leon and I will figure it out."

I sigh. "If people find out it's me, I'll never get another job. My whole reputation will be shot."

Victoria chews and nods her head like she's taking in what I just said, really thinking it over. "Okay," she says. "I get that. But do you even want another styling job after this?" she asks. "You haven't talked about your ambitions as a stylist in *months*. Now it's all about the account, how you can grow it and change it and make it into an even bigger *thing*. Don't you ever think about making *that* your full-time job? Think of what you could *do* if you had more time and resources."

She's out of breath now, like she's been wanting to say what she just said so many times over the past few months and finally it just all came tumbling out.

"Sorry," she says. "It's just . . . you're my best friend and I hate to see you wasting your time working for someone who throws food at your head and calls you an idiot."

I wince. "It's not—"

"And don't you defend her. It's like you've got Stockholm syndrome."

I push a bite of pancake around on my plate, knowing she's right.

"Maybe partnering with Kyle and that British himbo isn't the move. But you should seriously start thinking about a way out. You could write a book, get sponsorships, do branded events. There's *so* much opportunity out there, and I worry you're missing out on it because you're so tethered to this woman who hates you."

We're both quiet for a second, and then I hear my phone buzzing deep within her bag. I extend my hand and give her a look, asking for it. She rolls her eyes and digs it out, slapping it in my palm. "Fine."

I glance at the screen and see a text from Sasha.

> Sick or not, come in tomorrow at 9 a.m. We need to talk. Don't be late.

My stomach drops all the way down to my shoes, and I turn the phone around so Victoria can see it. She frowns and nods her head slowly, up and down.

"Well, all right, then."

From: kjohns@johnsglobalmedia.com

To: Deuxmoi@gmail.com

Date: October 7, 2022, 3:28 p.m. ET

Subject: I'm still waiting . . .

Haven't heard from you in a while. What do you think? I already have ideas for who could be an excellent partner for you to take this shit WIDE with. Would love to know your answer ASAP . . .

Kyle Johns
CEO Johns Global Media

CHAPTER 31

I'm totally fired.

That's the first thing I think when I jolt awake at 6:54 a.m. the next morning, my brain all fuzzy from a night of restless sleep. I woke up twice in the middle of the night after having nightmares that Ollie told the world—and Sasha—who I was. One consisted of Duke Dudley chasing after me down a crowded Midtown street with vampire fangs, while the other featured Sasha trying to run me over with a black town car. My subconscious is not subtle.

I check my phone and among the dozens of notifications, I see a Venmo deposit from Leon: "$5 for a dry cap. You need one."

I send him a heart emoji, before going about my morning routine with the seriousness of a monk, applying moisturizer and serums and blow-drying my hair until it looks presentable enough for my last day as an employee at Styling by Sasha.

It's a crisp day, warm for fall. The kind where you only need a leather jacket and the leaves are falling, crunchy on the sidewalk. I exit my apartment and decide to forgo my usual Uber and walk to work, giving myself a half hour to clear my head.

I pass by an all-glass building facade, one of those chrome monstrosities, and get a glimpse of myself in the mirror. I look so unlike how I feel inside. In my chunky Stuart Weitzman block-heeled booties and black Frame jeans, I look polished and put-together, confident and nonplussed. If I saw me on the street, I would assume this person knows exactly what she wants in life and how to get it. I would have no idea she has been an assistant for the better part of a decade, that she lets her morally corrupt boss walk all over her. I might even believe that she has a million followers interested in whatever morsels of news she might drop, that she could build a digital empire, that she might actually know how to turn it into a business—all on her own.

The light changes and I keep walking, one foot in front of the other until I reach our office in SoHo with its red bricks and adoring tourists, apparently undeterred by Sasha's entanglement with Duke Dudley. I look up toward the Styling by Sasha floor, where I know I'll meet with her in just a few minutes, where she has already decided my fate.

And for the first time in a long time, I realize I'm finally ready to determine my own future.

...

I walk through the office, knowing it will be the last time, with my head held high and my gait more strident than usual. I don't stop at my desk to set my bag down, and I don't head into the kitchen to make Sasha her English breakfast tea. Instead, I walk straight to her office, where I see her sitting behind her desk, her glasses low on her nose, as she scrolls on her phone, a frustrated look on her face.

Keep your fucking cool.

I knock on the door as authoritatively as I can, and when she looks up, unsurprised, I sweep through the door.

"Food poison girl returns. Did you at least lose any weight?" She smirks, looking me up and down. "Guess not." She motions for me to sit, but I know if I do, I'll lose all my nerve. I'll revert to who I was a few months ago. And I'm not that person anymore. I plant my feet more firmly into the floor and grasp the strap of my bag a little tighter.

"What, not gonna sit?" Sasha shrugs and kicks her feet up on the desk. "Fine. Look—"

But before she can say another word, I blurt out what I've been going over and over in my head since I first stepped outside this morning.

"I quit."

The words drop like a bomb, and Sasha plants her feet back down on the ground before rising to her feet, her hands planted on her hips.

"Excuse me?"

"I've been your assistant for too long, and it's clear that I've outgrown this place. There's no future here for me."

"Oh please. You've *outgrown* this place? You sound like an entitled millennial."

My stomach lurches forward, and I know I'm only a few steps away from flying off the handle and ditching my whole *keep calm* schtick. *Breathe*, I tell myself. *Just breathe.*

But then Sasha starts walking toward me with a finger outstretched.

"You ungrateful piece of shit," she hisses. "I gave you *everything*. I let you pitch in meetings—"

One meeting.

"I brought you to Los Angeles for a photoshoot—"

Which you then kicked me out of.

"I gave you access to my life—"

So I could hide your disordered eating habits and get screamed at every day.

"I treated you like a little *sister* and this is how you betray me? You're just like all the other assistants—headed for some suburb in North Carolina where no one knows the difference between Gucci and Pucci. Good luck landing another fashion job without my recommendation, which you're obviously never going to get. You're just as worthless as I always thought you were."

That's what causes me to start laughing. "Worthless?" I throw my head back, amused. "Well at least I'm not a monster like you are. At least I don't terrorize my staff to make myself feel better. At least . . ." I take a big breath before twisting the knife even deeper. "At least I didn't send an assistant over to Duke Dudley like she was a room-service sandwich and cover for him all these years, knowing full well what he was capable of."

Sasha reels back as if I've slapped her, and for once, I wonder if I've gone too far.

But before she can say anything, I summon the words I've been wanting to say for weeks.

"I've put up with a lot of shit over the years, but based on the stories I've heard, I barely got the worst of it. You're lucky more people don't know the real you. So, no, I'm not quitting because I'm ungrateful or because I'm sad I didn't get to go to a few more photoshoots or meet a few more celebrities. I'm quitting because I finally realized I don't deserve to be treated this way. I'm not your doormat or your punching bag. I used to idolize you on *Collection*. How you were so confident and smart and knew exactly what to say. I wanted to work here because I wanted to be like you." I sigh, the weight of my decision suddenly light on my shoulders. "But now? The thought of being like you is so repulsive that I'd rather be an assistant for the rest of my life than spend one more minute in your presence. You are a nar-cissistic, delusional, washed-up has-been, and just like your styling, you are irrelevant. Good luck finding someone who will work for you half as hard as I ever did."

I reach inside my bag and grab my badge, the one I've carried around day after day that gets me into this building, and finally, I slam it down on her glass desk.

"Like I said before, I quit."

CHAPTER 32

It only takes a few blocks for the weight of my actions to sink in. I fucking quit. I wonder if I should feel elated, untouchable. Because right now all I feel is sheer terror.

I grab my phone with shaking hands and make the call that's been hanging over my head. Kyle Johns picks up on the first ring.

"I was waiting for you to respond," he says, the thump-thump of a tennis ball hitting a wall behind him. "So, what do you say?"

I take a deep breath and pick up my pace, walking fast through the busy streets of SoHo, not really caring where they lead me.

"It's a good offer and I'm very flattered," I say.

"So, you're in. Fantastic. We'll get—"

"But I can't accept."

I hear him cough on the other end of the line, surprised. "Excuse me?"

"I'm not interested in selling. Not right now."

"Well, what do you want? We can negotiate, you know. I can probably go up to—"

"Nope." I don't want to hear numbers. I don't want to be persuaded to give up something that I know, deep in my gut, is mine. "I appreciate you reaching out, but I'm going to try things my way for a while."

Kyle groans. "You've got balls," he says. "But if you live to regret this, you know where to find me."

He hangs up without much fanfare, and I immediately feel a release deep within my chest. For the first time in a long time, I finally feel . . . free.

I walk a few more blocks and fight the urge to call Ollie to share the news. I have to remind myself that he's not someone I *do* that with anymore. We don't share the minutiae of our lives, what we had for breakfast or where I want his tongue on my skin. He has yet to tell the world who I really am, but that doesn't mean he won't someday. His silence doesn't mean I forgive him—that I can trust him.

I debate calling Leon or Victoria. No doubt, Leon has already heard from people in the office, and maybe he even told Victoria. But for some reason, I want to keep this little moment to myself, to hold it close until I get home and get back on deuxmoi before figuring out where I go from here.

I'm now at the entrance to Washington Square Park, which is full of NYU students sitting on blankets, half-empty bottles of wine in front of them. Buskers strum their guitars in front of top hats, and artists kneel down, chalking the street. Plans swirl in my head and I know the possibilities are really endless, just like Leon and Victoria said. But I know I need to act fast, since I quite literally don't know where my next paycheck is coming from.

Shit.

Maybe I am screwed. Maybe this was all a mistake. Maybe I just made the worst decision of my entire life and I'm going to be totally fucked. Maybe . . .

But then, a young woman walks by me wearing a hoodie emblazoned with the logo for Mike's, the West Village bar that Nate Clyburn co-owns. It's maroon and simple, oversized but noticeable. She looks like she's part of the East Village crowd, with chunky platform sneakers and biker shorts barely visible below her sweatshirt. Her nails are painted different shades of blue.

Without thinking, I stop her in her tracks. "Question," I say. She pulls out an earbud. "How much did you pay for that sweatshirt?"

"Huh? Why do you care?"

"Market research." I cross my arms over my chest and try to look authoritative.

She rolls his eyes but answers. "Sixty-five bucks."

"Do you go to Mike's often?"

She shrugs.

"How'd you hear about it?"

"Deuxmoi," she says. "It's this anonymous Instagram account."

I nod, trying to hide my surprise. "Oh yeah. I think I know it."

"All right, bye." The girl gives me a weirded-out look as she walks past me. "Freak."

My heart starts pounding and my brain is moving so fast, I have to slow my steps in order to make sense of the idea forming in my head. But once it clicks, the answer is so obvious I can't believe I haven't thought of it yet.

All I need to get started is the belief that followers will support the account in the real world, too. I whip out my phone and send a text to Leon and Victoria.

> I know how to make deuxmoi my real job.

CHAPTER 33

By the time I round the corner onto my block, Victoria has already found me a vendor in the tristate area who she swears will provide the best quality and most affordable sweatshirts in two weeks' time, as long as we get the design to them by Thursday.

Thankfully, Leon has already mocked up a version of the logo he created months ago, slapping it down the arm of a black hoodie and updating an insignia to go on the front.

Chic, he says. *Though I wouldn't be caught dead repping DM.*

Same, Victoria says. *No offense.*

I mean . . . also same, I write. *Way too risky.*

If all of this goes well, if I make good on this bet, I might be able to make quitting worth it. And that's *without* all of the other ideas buzzing around in my brain.

I'm staring at my phone, typing out bullet points in my Notes app—additional clothing we could sell, ideas for a podcast I could start, brands to work with—when someone says my name in a British accent that sounds so familiar, it makes me stop in my tracks.

I look up, and though I've only met Ollie once, seeing him in front of my building, leaning up against the brick wall, feels like the most natural thing in the world. But then I remember the reality of what he's done—how he betrayed me, what he might reveal about me—and suddenly, I'm overcome with rage.

"Can we talk?" he asks in a soft voice.

Anger curdles in my chest, and I want to rush right past him and head up the stairs, reclaiming the independent excitement I found just moments ago. But I know he has control. He knows who I am. It's not so simple anymore.

"What do you want?" I ask, hating the desperation in my voice. "Are you going to blackmail me or something so you won't reveal my identity?"

Ollie looks legitimately offended and steps back as if I've slapped him. "Who do you think I am?"

I shrug. "Someone who was trying to convince me to take a job so it would benefit *him*."

His shoulders tense up around his neck.

"Someone who *slept* with me and kept me on speed dial so I would trust him. It's pretty fucking shitty—"

"I told Kyle no," Ollie says, cutting me off. "Weeks ago. Way before we met in person." He steps toward me, extending his hands. "He had offered me the VP of Editorial role and told me we'd turn deuxmoi into a gold mine. He really did. Said he was making you an offer you couldn't refuse. But once I got to know you, I knew I couldn't take it."

"Did he hit you up about this before or after you reached out to me for the first time?"

"Before." Ollie drops his head and rubs the back of his neck with one hand. I hate that I now know what that part of him feels like, how the fine hairs there are fuzzy against my skin.

"So, you *did* get in touch with me under false pretenses. You just wanted to get to know what was up with deuxmoi before considering this job."

"It was so fucking stupid. But yeah. And then once we began . . . talking," he says, blushing, "I realized there was no way I could take that job, no way I could be your *boss* if the deal went through. Plus, hearing you go off about the account, I knew you could make magic all on your own. You don't need Kyle Johns. You don't need *me*." He pauses, like he's gathering courage. "That's what I like about you. You're fearless."

"So, why was he texting you?"

"The editor he found fell through. He wanted to talk again."

"And?"

He steps toward me. "I said no, obviously."

"Well, I just turned him down."

A smile forms on Ollie's lips, tugging at the corners of his mouth. "Damn."

"And I quit my job."

His eyebrows shoot up. "No shit?"

We're both quiet as the sound of taxis and buses and loud phone-talkers clamber on around us.

"I'm going to do this thing on my own," I say. "See what happens."

"Good. If anyone can . . ." He clasps his hands in front of him, flexing his fingers like he's nervous. "I just want you to know, I meant what I said. I'm not going to tell anyone who you are."

I open my mouth, but he stops me.

"I know you don't believe me, but I have no interest in outing you. Really. Here, I'll tell you a secret as collateral."

"Oh yeah?"

He throws his head back as if he's thinking hard. "Here's one that makes me look bad. When I was fifteen, I fucked my best friend's girlfriend. Terrible thing to do. But I did it. I also cheated on a test at uni. A big one. One that would have got me expelled. Oh, and I also lied in order to—"

But I hold up my hand. "Enough," I say, holding back a laugh, against my better judgment. "I don't need your rap sheet."

"I want you to trust me again."

I glance up at the sky, a bunch of pigeons flying overhead. "I don't know if I ever will," I say. "But . . . we can try. Maybe."

"Maybe?"

I nod. "Maybe."

He smiles that stupid fucking smile that causes my stomach to spasm, desire to inch its way back into my body. But I compose myself, standing up straight and lengthening my spine.

"And besides, if you do out me, I'll just take a play from your book," I say.

"What was that again?" He steps toward me, almost close enough that I can feel the warmth from his hand extending toward mine.

"Deny, deny, deny."

Elle.com

How an Anonymous Gossip Account Came Out with One of the Season's Hottest Drops

You can't go anywhere in Downtown Manhattan without seeing a reminder that normies like us are always on the lookout for celeb sightings. That's because the name of the anonymous gossip account deuxmoi is basically everywhere these days thanks to a new line of merch.

One of our editors saw *One Percent* star Nate Clyburn wearing a deuxmoi sweatshirt at his bar, Mike's, while another of our designers spotted Madison Lee, who famously beefed with deuxmoi in the early days of the account, rocking a dad hat with the DM logo on it. Even pop icon Kayla Cole was spotted wearing an oversized deuxmoi tee during rehearsals for her latest tour.

Deuxmoi released its first line of merch during a feverish twenty-four-hour window last month and it sold out within minutes. Alongside the hoodies and hats, there were also sweatpants, bike shorts, and stickers up for sale. If you weren't one of the few who copped pieces, have no fear, deuxmoi said in an interview that she plans to release new exclusive lines every season. They'll reflect inside jokes she has with her followers, celebs of the moment, and locales made iconic on her page.

Deuxmoi was tight-lipped about how much she made in sales, but our style analyst, Gertrude Kirby, says that based on the available figures, it's likely that the account could have netted $300,000 in profits.

"It's clear deuxmoi has tapped into something here," Kirby says. "People want to rep the things that interest them. I guess that's deuxmoi."

When asked what's next for everyone's favorite anonymous gossip, deuxmoi said, "The possibilities are endless. Guess you'll have to keep following to find out."

ACKNOWLEDGMENTS

Thank you to my super-talented cowriter (and part-time therapist), Jessica Goodman, who was able to capture my voice and vibe by just gabbing for hours like two longtime friends. Thank you, Jess, for shaping anecdotal and pivotal moments from the past two years into a fun and captivating story and being an amazing collaborator in the process.

The biggest thank-you to my agent, Eve Attermann, and editor, Asanté Simons. Thank you, Eve, for your guidance, faith, and support, and for your experience and expertise, which helped me find the perfect home for this story at William Morrow. Thank you, Asanté, for your gracious counsel and for completely understanding this novel from day one.

Thank you to my team, Bari, Chelsea, Sanjana, Amanda, Jenni, and Abe, for all your continued support and encouragement.

There would not be a novel without the fans and followers of Deuxmoi. To all the friends, fans, peers, collaborators, contributors, and even the haters I have met along the way, THANK YOU!!! This wild ride would not have existed without all of you!

I have the best parents in the world! Thank you for your love and unwavering support. Thank you to Ferris for simply being the best and to all my friends who have been incredibly supportive, patient, and understanding.

Lastly, thank you to the celebrities.